DIL

By
Raymond Warrillow

They would not assassinate the most famous and the most loved woman in the world…or would they?

ISBN 978-1-909435-06-3

Was Princess Diana assassinated, or was her death a tragic accident? If she had died in an ordinary traffic accident, why was there a cover-up? The motive to kill Princess Diana was very powerful. If she had married Dodi Al-Fayed, a Muslim, and had given birth to his children, it would have brought down the British monarchy. The people of the UK would never accept a king with a Muslim stepfather and Muslim half-brothers and sisters.

DIE LADY DI

It is 1997

Chapter One

Timothy Freeman stared at the small white tablet lying in the palm of his hand. He could take most things on the chin and regarded himself as a hard man. It disturbed him to think that depression could render him helpless and suicidal. Until three years ago, he had always been an optimistic, happy-go-lucky chap. It was a bit of a mystery why he should suddenly get depressed. One minute, he was normal, and then the next minute, while thinking about the future and old age, he was shattered by feelings of helplessness and futility, and within a few seconds, he had lost the will to live. His thoughts had become confused, and his body felt as if it had been turned into cardboard. It had been terrifying. His sangfroid had been given a death blow, and his thoughts were now permanently tainted by pessimism.

He sighed and blew out his cheeks. Without his little white tablets, he would be unable to cope with even the most mundane things. At times like this, when his problems crowded his thoughts, he could feel his depression fighting with his medication. He popped the tablet into his mouth and swilled it down with a drink of water. It was soul-destroying and embarrassing to be forced to rely on drugs to survive. He was forty-eight, slim and handsome.

His main problem in life, apart from depression, walked into the kitchen. He sat watching his girlfriend, Jane Bremner, strut about. His relationship with Jane was deteriorating at an alarming rate. Living with a raving mad woman was enough to push anyone over the edge. He had stopped loving her some months ago and was now at the point of hating her. There was no way he could continue living with a woman who was an angel for three weeks of the month and a devil when she was having her period.

Even though he thrived on excitement (or at least he used to), he now needed some form of stability in his life. Jane, his live-in girlfriend of three years, had, at first, seemed like the answer to his dreams. She was thirty-six and was a tall, slim, pretty blonde with a decent figure, and even though sex with her was still enjoyable, he now wished he had never set eyes on her.

It was Sunday morning. Jane had moaned almost non-stop on Saturday and, about an hour ago, had picked up where she had left off. He watched her walk back and forth across the kitchen as if in a hurry. He had moved into the kitchen to escape from her tantrums and find a short period of solace, but she had followed him and was now washing up.

He lit a cigarette and pondered on her extremely aggravating and frustrating antics. Did she really suffer from premenstrual tension, or was it just an excuse so that she could take her frustrations out on him? Her moods had been getting progressively worse. They had started as just a day or two of moodiness, but now lasted a full week. If, while she was in one of her moods, he tried to talk to her about her problems, she would go screaming mad and throw things about. He had a nasty suspicion that she enjoyed hurting him.

"It would help if you did some decorating," she said. "This place is a dump."

"I don't like decorating, and it's not a dump." He looked about the kitchen. It did need decorating, and the units needed replacing. He spread his hands. "I'll admit the house does need decorating, but even if I renovated the entire house and made it into a palace, it would not make the slightest difference. You would still be depressed."

"I would not," she insisted. "And I am not depressed; I'm unhappy."

"You are depressed, and there's nothing I can do to help you." He moved his chair back so that he could run out of the kitchen if she began to throw things at him. He was reluctant to try to reason with her, but things had to be said. "You need help."

She turned and glared at him with wide, staring eyes. "What do you mean I need help?"

"You need counselling or antidepressant tablets."

"I do not," she shouted. "I do not need tablets. I'm not suffering from depression. I'm just cheesed off and fed up."

"Why are you cheesed off and fed up? And I don't believe it has anything to do with the state of the house."

"The state of the house is only a part of the problem."

He waited for her to tell him what the other part of the problem was. She continued washing up. He rolled his eyes. She was beginning to aggravate him. "And what's the other part of the problem?"

"You."

He frowned. "What do you mean, me? What have I done?"

"It's the way we live that depresses me."

He spread his hands. "What's wrong with the way we live?"

"Everything."

"What do you mean, everything?" He resisted the temptation to tell her she was talking like an idiot. "How can you say everything? We have a good life. We don't have any money worries, and we go out for a meal several times a week. Could you be a tad more specific? Everything covers, sort of … everything."

"For a start, you should get a proper job."

"What do you mean? I have a proper job."

She stared at him and placed her hands on her hips. "You do not have a proper job."

"I do." He glanced at her figure without making it obvious. She was putting on weight and now had love handles.

"You do not. A proper job is when you go out in the morning and come home in the afternoon. You don't go out to work for months and spend your days playing golf, painting your pictures and working out. You then suddenly rush off somewhere, and I don't see you for weeks, sometimes months. What sort of life is that?"

"I don't want a nine-to-five job."

"And why haven't you got any mates? All the men I know have mates."

"I do have mates. I don't have any close friends, I must admit, but what difference does that make?"

"If you had friends, we could go out with them. We always go out on our own. I have several friends, but you don't like any of them, and you hate the sight of my mother."

He stood up and walked towards the door. Her voice was now almost a scream. It was time to get out of the house before she hit boiling point, and cups and saucers began to fly about the kitchen.

"Where are you going?"

He stopped and turned around. It was about time he told her how he felt. It was neither the time nor the place, and she would probably go berserk, but it had to be done. No cups were within her reach, although a frying pan was within grabbing distance of her left hand. He decided to take a chance that he would be out of the front door before the frying pan hit him on the back of the head. "I'm going down the pub to get away from you. You're driving me mad. Every month, it's the same. I can't take much more of this."

"Oh, so it's all my fault," she screamed. "It's always my fault. It's never your fault, is it?"

"How can your depression be my fault? You need to see a doctor."

"I do not. If you made an effort, things would be different."

"I'm not going to argue," he said. "It's pointless arguing with you when you're like this. We'll talk when you're back to normal." He put on his coat and walked out of the kitchen and along the hall.

She followed him. "That's it, just walk away. Isn't it about time you became a responsible adult and stopped acting like a child?"

He resisted the temptation to tell her to piss off in case she was ill. He opened the front door, stepped outside and closed it behind him. If he stayed with her, he would end up either going mad or hitting her. As he walked down the path, he heard her scream and the sound of breaking glass.

He climbed into his Range Rover and drove away from his house in Blossomfield, Solihull, to his sanctuary, the lounge of his golf club in Knowle, Solihull. As much as he hated being alone, he would have to move on and find pastures new. What he needed was a woman without kids, who was attractive, good company, did not moan and was good in bed. It was a tall order for a man approaching fifty.

There was no one he knew in the golf club lounge, so he sat down on his own with a drink. He was bursting with frustration and anger, and it took two pints of lager in quick succession to dilute his troubles to a bearable level. Jane was turning him into an alcoholic.

"I hope you're not driving home, sir?" a voice behind him said.

Timothy smiled. Even though the voice was being disguised, he knew without turning around that it was Roger Tweed. "Hello, Major. You can get the drinks in." He turned around, and the smile dropped from his lips. Roger was wearing an eye patch. "What happened to your eye?"

Roger was carrying two pints of lager. He placed the drinks on the table and sat down. "I had cancer in the eye. It's been sorted."

"What a bastard," Timothy said. "It's a good job; it's only the one eye."

Roger nodded and leaned back in his seat. "I thought I'd see if you were here before phoning you."

"Is it business?" Timothy asked.

"Yes." Roger took out a cigar and lit it with his fancy gold lighter. He was fifty-three and had the charms and good looks of a film star, although he was now at least a stone overweight. He was, as always, dressed immaculately in a suit and tie, and his black shoes shone like mirrors. "We need to leave when we've had this drink."

"How long will I be away?" Timothy asked.

"Just one night. You'll be back home by tomorrow."

Timothy took out his mobile phone, intending to tell Jane he had to work and would not be seeing her until tomorrow, but thought better of it. He did not feel up to talking to her, and so he put his phone back into his pocket. He would like to know why the job was so urgent, but would have to wait until the briefing. Roger was a stickler for the rules. "How's Bev? Has she divorced you for running after young women?"

"She knows all about the young women. She's a pain in the neck. She's even fatter and more disagreeable than ever. We've only managed to stay together because we have separate bedrooms, and I'm rarely home."

"Your home life sounds about as good as mine," Timothy said.

Roger frowned with one eye. "That doesn't sound too good. How is Jane?"

"She's diabolical, and she's driving me mad. I'm on the verge of leaving home."

"I thought it was your house?" Roger asked.

"It is."

Roger thrust out his jaw and drummed his fingers on the table as if he were playing the piano. "Then throw her out."

"I can't."

"Why not? I would."

"There's a chance that she might be ill." Timothy lit a cigarette. "How are the kids?"

"All right, I think. James has gone to live on a Scottish island, and Elizabeth's still working in Alaska. If it were not for my latest flame, I'd be a very lonely man."

Timothy smiled. "How old is she?"

"Thirty-five. I can't get twenty-year-olds anymore. And she's not a beauty by any stretch of the imagination. I was all right until I started gaining weight and losing my hair. The days of taking out a good-looking young woman have long gone. I'll end up having to pay for it."

"I'm thinking of getting rid of Jane and getting a blow-up doll," Timothy said. "It's the moaning that gets me down."

"Tell me about it," Roger said. "I don't even bother to talk to Bev anymore. Drink up. It's time to go. We have a lot to do."

They finished their drinks, and Timothy drove them to meet the other team members. They travelled in silence. Timothy had joined the army in his late teens and had enjoyed every minute. For the last fifteen years, he had been part of a five-man assassination team, and prior to that, he had spent over ten years in the SAS. Instead of retiring from the SAS, the team was asked to perform occasional operations, which always involved killing someone. He was now just an assassin, eliminating targets regarded as a threat to the state.

It was not as satisfying as regular SAS operations, but it was better than doing nothing. His boring life needed an occasional injection of excitement. It also paid the bills.

If only he could be young again and re-live his life. He would still join the army and the SAS, but he would not be railroaded into being an assassin. There was not enough action for his liking. For months on end, he did nothing, and then, for a few days or weeks, it was almost like the good old days. If he were to be honest about his feelings, it was time for him to hang up his gun. He had done more than enough for his king and country. According to Roger, the team was about to be disbanded, which suited Timothy.

They were a typical close-knit team and could trust each other one hundred per cent. Roger, the team leader, was a sex-mad alcoholic, which was why he never drove. Peter Bolt was fifty-one, six feet tall, slim, plain-looking, divorced and lived with his mother, his dogs and his horses. He was an electronics expert and was fluent in five languages. John Kent was fifty-eight, five-foot-six, well built, gay, as ugly as sin and lived with his sister in the winter and on his boat in the summer. He was an engineer. Matthew Jewson was fifty-four, five-foot-nothing, muscular, bald and an expert marksman. He was also a whizz-kid with computers.

Peter, John and Matthew were sitting on the deck of John's boat, waiting for them when they pulled into the Boat Inn public house car park in Knowle. John had a permanent mooring for his boat on the canal at the back of the pub. The fishing rods on display on the boat gave the impression that they were anglers enjoying some spare time.

Peter thrust cans of lager into Roger and Timothy's hands when they walked onto the boat. "Welcome aboard."

"I had expected this load of junk to have sunk by now," Roger said.

"It'll outlast you," John said. "What have you done to your eye?"

"I've had it out. It offended me."

"That reminds me of a joke," Peter said. "An old woman with six children to feed left the eyes in the fish so it would see her through the week."

No one laughed.

"What's the urgent job, Major?" Matthew asked.

"Let's go below. Roger looked at Peter. "Is it safe to talk?"

Peter nodded. "All the bugs on this boat crawl about and bite."

They walked down the steps into the cabin. It was a mess. There were magazines, empty beer cans and rubbish lying everywhere. Timothy perched his backside on the edge of the table, offered around cigarettes and lit up.

They were all hooked on the dreaded weed, except Matthew, who popped a piece of gum into his mouth.

"We'll be leaving in ten minutes," Roger said. "The target must be eliminated tonight."

"Bleeding hell," Peter said. "Why the rush?"

"The target's about to spill the beans on sensitive MI6 activities." Roger took a small package out of the bag he had with him and handed it to Timothy. "You're all familiar with the drug inside this syringe. It's our friendly little heart attack drug."

"We know all about that little drug," John said. "It'll cause death and then dissolve in the body and leave no trace, and the target will appear to have died from a heart attack."

"As I was saying," Roger said. "The target's fifty-eight, male, and will be leaving a hospital later this evening to drive three miles to his house."

"Where does the target live?" John asked.

"In Oxford." Roger took a map out of his bag and handed it to John. "The target's elderly mother is ill, which is why he's visiting her in hospital."

"Is she suffering from an MI5-induced illness?" Timothy asked.

Roger smiled. "Yes. It's almost impossible to hit the target at his house or place of work. He has to be hit while he's travelling in his car. He visits his mother at the hospital every evening. I'll show you where the hit will take place when we get to Oxford."

"Will the target be travelling alone?" Peter asked.

"Yes. If there's a passenger in the car, the mission is to be aborted. If the target is alone, there shouldn't be any problems."

Ten minutes later, they were travelling in the back of the custom-built Ford Transit van with John driving. Roger told them who would be doing what, and they then sat in silence.

When they arrived in Oxford, they spent an hour familiarising themselves with the route the target would be taking and then sat waiting in the van. These sorts of operations did not interest Timothy. They were too easy and did not raise the pulse sufficiently to provide the adrenaline rush he enjoyed, but he needed the money. If he did not take part in these occasional operations, he would have to get a proper job.

All joking and messing about had ceased. They were now serious professionals. Roger insisted on a high level of professionalism at all times.

Roger's mobile phone rang. He took it out of his pocket. "Yes?" He nodded and put his phone back into his pocket. "It's time for you to leave. The target has left the hospital."

They left Roger in the back of the van and drove off in the two cars that had been left for them. They never met anyone from MI5 or MI6. Roger was the only one who had any contact with them. He liaised with a controlling officer in MI5 known only as 'H'.

As far as the public was concerned, the assassination team did not exist. Officially, MI5 and MI6 did not have an active assassination team. Timothy suspected there were other assassination teams. The men in Timothy's team were paid £20,000 each for every operation they did and an annual retaining fee of £15,000. It was not a fortune, but they usually had at least one operation a year, and even if the operation was called off, they were still paid the £20,000.

They were using what they called a flashlight to disable the target. The flashlight was a powerful strobe light developed by the military for use against a target that needed to be kept alive. The flashlight not only blinded the individual for about a minute but also stunned them. The one they were using today could also cause eye damage and even permanent blindness, but because the target would be killed, there was no need to worry about eye damage.

They pulled up at a road junction. Timothy and Peter were parked opposite the junction and would operate the flashlight. John and Matthew were parked about thirty feet from the junction and would carry out the assassination. They were all wearing their disguises and gloves. Even their mothers would not recognise them.

While sitting in the car waiting for the target to arrive, Timothy thought back over his life. He had a working-class background and had spent his childhood years in Perry Barr, Birmingham. He had lived at number ten Tower Hill Road in a three-bedroom semi-detached house. The memories of his schooldays were now a bit of a blur. He had attended Dorrington Road Junior School and then went on to Birchfield Senior School. He had never been particularly clever, but he had an above-average IQ. His happy memories were of the hours he had spent playing with Daniel, his best friend, on the steep banks of the canal. They used to collect blackberries, and Daniel's mother would bake the most delicious pies in the world. They had been happy, carefree days.

Timothy joined the army at eighteen and served in the Falklands War and the Gulf War. He then travelled all over the world as an assassin. He travelled to Mexico, South Africa, Asia, and the Middle East. He had spent two years trying to assassinate Saddam Hussein. It had been a dangerous two years. Saddam had thousands of fanatical followers. It was their only failure. They also had two operations cancelled. It was very frustrating to have an operation cancelled when everything was set up.

Their most amazing assignment had been to assassinate Slobodan Milosevic. Peter and Matthew had spent ten hours in a two-man sniper hide that periodically flooded with sewage. They were then told that the operation had been cancelled. When they received the message to abort the operation, Matthew had Milosevic in his telescopic sights and had his finger on the trigger. Milosevic, who had been having a meal with his wife and son at the time, never knew how close he came to dying.

Timothy's private life had been almost as exciting. There had been dozens of casual girlfriends. His longest relationship was the three years he had spent with Jane. He had never wanted children, so moving from one girlfriend to the next suited him, although he would now like to meet someone he could spend the rest of his life with. He needed a best friend more than anything. It would also be nice to be loved.

"That looks like the target," Peter said. "The car's the right colour and make." He was looking through binoculars. "And it's the right registration."

Timothy aimed the flashlight, which looked like a cross between a gun and a camera, at the target as the car pulled up at the junction.

"All clear," Peter said.

Timothy fired the flashlight, and a beam of light lit up the target's face. John and Matthew leapt out of their car and ran to the target's car. It took them about six seconds to reach the car, three seconds to get into the car (John could get into any locked car in less than ten seconds) and three seconds to hold the target down and administer the drug inside the lower lip by using a syringe with a hypodermic needle. John and Matthew had closed the car door, so they did not attract undue attention when two cars drove past. They had used the drug before, and it only took about thirty seconds to induce a fatal heart attack.

Five minutes after the target had pulled up at the junction, they had assassinated him and were driving back to the Transit van. They did not speak. The operation did not end until they were back in the van and had taken off their disguises. Roger did not allow chit-chat.

A short time later, the two cars pulled up behind the Transit van, and they climbed out.

Roger climbed out of the back of the van. "Any problems?" he asked.

"No," John said. "It went like clockwork."

"I'll drive back," Matthew said.

The rest of them climbed into the back of the Transit van and made themselves comfortable on cushions. Peter passed around a packet of cigarettes, and they lit up. The back of the van contained cans of beer, fishing rods and fishing tackle. Night fishing was their cover in case the police stopped them, although up to now, the police had never stopped them.

"Was that our last job, Major?" Peter asked.

"I think so." Roger took out his flask and took a drink. "I'll have a chat with H."

"Do we get a retirement present like a gold watch?" John asked.

They smiled.

"I hope it is our last op," Timothy said. "I need the cash, but I've just about had enough. I'm finding it difficult to keep fit. If I have to run carrying anything heavier than a packet of fags, I'm fucked."

"I'm nearly sixty, and I've given up trying to keep fit," John said. "I used to be able to walk faster than I can run now. We're all getting old. God knows why they keep using us."

"It's because good old British Intelligence knows us and trusts us," Roger said.

"You can speak for yourself, John," Peter said. "I'm as fit as I ever was." He patted his flat stomach. "There's not an ounce of fat on me. I hope we have a few more ops. I need the cash."

"We should have been disbanded over five years ago," Roger said. "No one knows we exist except a few people at MI5 and MI6. Even the government is unaware that assassination teams still operate. My health is failing, and even if they want to continue to use us, they'll be out of luck. I don't think I'm up to another op."

They sat smoking in silence.

Timothy had been watching Roger as he spoke. The sparkle had gone out of his one eye. He was probably more ill than he was letting on. He now looked older than his fifty-three years. Timothy took a drag on his cigarette. Roger was not the only one who was changing. They were all getting old. Timothy was changing mentally as well as physically. He was no longer a staunch royalist and prepared to die for king and country. He had done his bit and now wanted a normal life with a normal woman, which ruled out Jane.

He chewed his lip. He had changed in more ways than one. One particular change was a little disturbing. About a month ago, he had been watching a television programme about babies and had suddenly been overcome with the desire to become a father. It had been a shock. He had never had the slightest inclination to have a child before. He had expected the desire to disappear, but if anything, it was now stronger than ever. It was very strange. Why had the need to procreate taken so long to appear? He was nearly fifty. He now had a strong desire to have a son and a daughter. If he did want to become a father, there were two problems he would have to deal with. One was age, and so he would have to get a move on; the other was finding a mother for his children.

His sudden desire to have children was another reason he needed to end his relationship with Jane. She had made it clear she was not the childbearing sort. To use her exact words, she would rather die than have a baby. Their desire not to have children had helped bring them together. It was now helping to drive them apart. Maybe his paternal instincts were just a passing fancy. Time will tell.

They spent the rest of the night sleeping on John's boat. It was cramped, uncomfortable and overrun with spiders. Timothy slept on top of the worktop with his legs across the cooker. He would be more comfortable sleeping on the floor, but would almost certainly be attacked by huge spiders.

At dawn, they said their goodbyes, and Timothy drove home. He was feeling randy and was hoping Jane would be in a receptive mood. He would know as soon as he saw her.

"I'm home," he said as he walked into the kitchen.

"I can see that," she snapped. "I'm not blind. I never know how long you'll be away."

His luck was out. She was still in a foul mood. "I was only away one night. I have to grab work when I can." He began to fill the kettle. "Would you like a cup of tea?" If he were nice to her, she might return to being a human being.

"No.

"Have you had breakfast?" he asked. "As a treat, I'll cook breakfast."

"I do not want you to cook me breakfast. And don't mess the kitchen up. I've just tidied up."

By the evil look in her eyes, she was still at bursting point. He was not up to any more arguments and unpleasant atmospheres. He put the teapot down. "Fuck it."

"And what do you mean by that?"

"I've had enough. I need a long holiday. I'm going to pack a few things and leave. I'll be away for a few days. I'll phone you."

"Don't bother. I'm beginning to enjoy my own company."

Twenty minutes later, after a severe tongue lashing from Jane while he packed his suitcase, he was driving away from his house. He switched on the radio. Just thirty minutes with Jane had convinced him that their relationship had ended. He would not be going back. What he had to do now was to decide where he was going to live.

His parents' five-bedroom house was quickly ruled out. His mother was in a nursing home, and as much as he loved his father, he was a nightmare to live with. His father hated music of any sort. He went to bed early and insisted on complete silence while he slept, which ruled out the television and the radio.

His father also had an infuriating habit of walking about and making strange sounds. It would not be so bad if he hummed, whistled or sang. The sounds he made were as if he had forgotten the words of a song, and there was never a tune to the sounds. He would say da da, de de and di di. It was extremely aggravating, and Timothy had never been able to understand how his mother had coped with it.

There were dozens of hotels and flats he could rent in the Midlands, but they were a bit too close to home. The further away he got from his problems, the better. He was approaching the M42. London suddenly seemed like a good place to live while he sorted out his life. He turned onto the M42 and headed south.

Chapter Two

It had been a long, tiring day, and Victoria Dixon felt exhausted. Being a nursery manager had its advantages (she loved working with children), but it also had its downsides. Each day left her mentally and physically drained. The last child left the nursery with her mother, and Assistant Manager Amy Price closed the door.

"I'm beginning to hate children," Amy said. She was a slim, pretty twenty-one-year-old.

Victoria smiled. "If they were all like George, I would as well. I've told his mother I'll give him one more week, and if he doesn't improve, she'll have to find another nursery for him."

Amy slipped on her coat. "I'll be glad when he goes. He always does the opposite of what I tell him. Are the decorators coming in over the weekend?"

"Yes, thank God," Victoria said. "I can't wait to have the purples and lime greens painted over. Do you want a lift?"

"No. My boyfriend's waiting outside in his brand-new car." Amy opened the door. "Bye."

"Bye, Amy."

Victoria's worries returned as she locked up and climbed into her car. Looking after small children was all-consuming, and while working, she did not have time to think about her problems, but they had now returned. She was thirty-four and in a rut. She sighed as she drove away from the nursery in Hall Green, Birmingham. Despite the impression she gave people, she was unhappy and frustrated. To be happy, her life needed two missing ingredients: a boyfriend and children. She desperately wanted a family of her own.

The first thing she would have to do if she wanted to get married and have children was to find herself a man, and not just any man. She needed a decent man she could trust and plan a future with. She was attractive, had a shapely figure and had no trouble attracting men. It was the sort of men she was attracting that was getting her down. Up until now, every man she had ever been out with had turned out to be a lying, cheating bastard. If she was going to be totally honest, what she needed most was to be loved.

Every weekend, she went in search of Mr Right with her mates and met all sorts of men, but most of them were not even remotely suitable. Her relationships with men she thought might be her type usually lasted for a few weeks until she saw the real man beneath the act. She was beginning to think that decent men did not exist.

She remembered an appointment she had made, and her spirits sank even further. She looked at her watch. She had arranged to meet her sister, Emma, at McDonald's restaurant in Solihull in twenty minutes. She now regrets agreeing to see her. It would be a waste of time. They would probably end up arguing. Her sister was as stubborn and unreasonable as she was pretty.

She drove to Solihull, parked her car and sat down in McDonald's restaurant with a coffee. Emma said she wanted to talk about something important. What could be important? It was probably something to do with their mother. Victoria had not spoken to her mother since leaving home and had no intention of speaking to her again. She chewed her lip and frowned. Perhaps her mother was ill. She might even be dying. As much as she disliked her mother, she would hate for her to have some incurable disease.

She stopped chewing her lip and frowning, and looked about to make sure that no one had seen her wearing what she called her deep-in-thought face. Thankfully, no one was looking at her. She had once caught herself in the mirror wearing her deep-in-thought face and had been horrified. She had looked like a demented witch.

At the next table, a young couple and their two children were tucking into burgers and chips. The children looked happy, and their parents were obviously deeply in love. Victoria was filled with envy. Life can be very unfair.

Emma walked into the restaurant and waved. Emma was thirty-six, immaculately dressed as usual, although she looked as if she had put on a few pounds.

"I'm sorry I'm late, Victoria," Emma said as she walked towards her. "The traffic was awful. I'll get a coffee."

Emma got a coffee and sat down facing her. "You look well, Victoria."

"I am well. What do you want to talk to me about? I hope it's not about Mum?"

Emma sipped her coffee. "I've not come to argue. I just feel I should try to get you and Mother talking again. You haven't spoken since you left home."

Victoria was relieved that her mother was not ill. "You're wasting your time."

"Why are you so stubborn?" Emma asked. "She is your mother, after all, and blood is thicker than water. Mother's ill and needs both of us."

Victoria began to worry. "What do you mean, ill? Has she got a serious illness?"

"No, but she's very depressed."

Victoria did not regard being depressed as an illness. "We all get depressed." She had never been close to her sister and never confided in her. Emma could not keep a secret and was a gossip, but the truth needed to be told if Victoria wanted to get her sister off her back. "Has Mum ever told you why we stopped talking?"

"I suppose so. I can't remember. I know you didn't tell me. You never tell me anything."

"That's because you're a blabbermouth. You're the worst gossip I've ever known."

Emma looked offended. "I am not. I can keep a confidence."

"No, you can't. You've never kept a confidence in your life. You couldn't; it would kill you."

"Let's not quarrel," Emma said. "We'll just have to beg to differ." She took out her cigarettes. "Why don't you talk to Mother? What possible reason could there be? Did you argue about something?"

"Yes, we did argue. You can't smoke in here."

"What did you argue about? I hope it had nothing to do with me?"

"It had nothing to do with you.

Emma put her cigarettes back into her bag and leaned back in her seat. "I wish I could give them up. It's a filthy habit. I've cut down to ten a day. Well? Are you going to tell me what you argued about?"

"I'm surprised Mum didn't tell you why we argued. It was because of Ben."

Emma looked surprised. "What did Ben do?"

"You and Mum think Ben's wonderful. Well, he isn't."

"We do not think he's wonderful," Emma said. "He's a bastard."

Victoria was shocked. "I thought you liked him?"

"I used to, but not anymore. He walked out on Mother a short time ago and moved in with a younger woman. It's what happens when you marry a younger man."

"Mum's only seven years older than Ben," Victoria said. "They used to look the same age."

"Mother's put on weight over the last few years, and she's aged dreadfully," Emma said. "She now looks fifteen years older than Ben. What did Ben do?"

"I don't know whether I should tell you. It's water under the bridge."

"I'd like to know. It might help me understand why you won't talk to Mother."

"He molested me."

Emma pulled her head back as if to bring Victoria's face into focus. "I don't believe you."

"I don't expect you to. Mum didn't believe me either. And stop calling Mum, Mother. We've always called her Mum."

"James believes that Mum sounds common," Emma said.

"Your husband was always a snob.

"He's not a snob. He has breeding. What did Ben do?"

"I don't want to go into the details." Victoria had never told anyone what had happened. "Ben's a child molester."

Emma frowned. "I find that hard to believe. He seemed normal to me."

"He's not normal. He's a pervert."

Emma leant forward. "What did he do?"

"I don't want to say."

"You can't just say that he's a pervert. It could mean anything. He could have just touched you, or he could have raped you."

If Victoria told Emma what happened, she would probably tell all and sundry, but it did not seem to matter anymore who knew. "He got me to wank him off."

Emma leant back in her seat as if she had been slapped in the face. She looked about. "Keep your voice down. When was this?"

"I don't know when it started. I was two and a half when Dad left. I don't remember Dad living with us. I regarded Ben as my father. I did it until I was about seven. It was just a game to me. I then watched a film about a man having sex with his daughter, and I realised that it was wrong to wank off your stepfather, and I told him that I didn't want to do it anymore. He used to give me sweets as a reward, and so I did it a few more times until my conscience kicked in."

"Did he have sex with you?" Emma whispered.

No. He used to touch me, but he just wanted to be wanked."

Emma pulled a face. "Don't say that word. It's disgusting. Did you tell Mother what he did?"

"Not until I was sixteen. I didn't go into details. I was embarrassed. I just told her that he made me touch his thing. She called me a liar, and we rowed for several weeks. It began to drive me mad, so I moved out. I haven't spoken to her since, and I don't intend to. When I was sixteen, I needed a mother. I needed Mum to believe me. I don't need a mother anymore. When did Ben move out?"

"A few weeks ago."

"It serves Mum right. If she had listened to me all those years ago and thrown him out, she would have found someone else by now."

"Ben never did anything to me," Emma said.

"It's because you went to live with Dad. You never lived with Ben."

Emma stared at her cup of coffee. "I don't know what to say. I wish you'd told me when you told Mother."

"I would have told you if we had been proper sisters. We were never close. I could never confide in you about anything."

Emma looked offended. "It's not my fault we were not close, and you could have confided in me. You just didn't want to."

"I did want to confide in you. When I was young, I needed a friend I could trust. I once told you a secret."

"When? What secret? I don't ever remember you telling me a secret."

"When I was thirteen, I kissed a boy. It was my first kiss. I told you, and I told you to never tell anyone."

"Oh, yes. I remember. I didn't tell anyone."

"You did. You told Mum. The day after I told you, Mum said to me, 'What's this I hear about you snogging a boy?' She gave me a lecture about how I should behave with the opposite sex."

"I only told Mother. I didn't realise she had told you what I had told her. I told her it was a secret."

"It was the last secret I ever told you."

They sat in silence for a while, sipping their coffees.

It had been ten years since Victoria's father had died in a car crash, and her childhood now seemed a lifetime away. "Did Dad ever talk about me?"

"I can't remember. I suppose he did. He was not a good father. I never really talked to him, not in the way I talk to Mother. He was either at work, out bowling or making models in the front room."

"I didn't know he made models. What models were they?"

"Models of boats. Some of them were quite big."

"Do you still see your stepmother and her daughter and three sons?" Victoria asked. "I suppose we should call them our half-sister and half-brothers."

"My stepmother died twelve months ago. She left me nothing in her will. Her children got everything. I see them occasionally. Will you speak to Mother? She needs you. I can only get to see her once a month."

"No. She was not there when I needed her."

Emma looked disappointed. "Is there any way you can forgive her?"

"No."

Emma stood up. "I'll have to go. I'm sorry I didn't keep your secret. I'll phone you.

Victoria watched her sister hurry out of the restaurant. They had never been proper sisters. From the day Victoria walked out of her mother's house, she had lived alone and had looked after herself. At times, she had felt like an orphan. Emma now lived in Derby, and it was probably the last time she would ever see her.

She sipped her coffee. It was cold. She did not feel sorry for her mother. Her mother had never loved her. When Victoria was young, her mother had tried several times to persuade her to live with her father and his new wife. Her mother had only been interested in dressing up and going out with Ben. Several evenings every week, Victoria had been looked after by a neighbour until she was old enough to be left on her own. Victoria had never met her half-sister and half-brothers and had no desire to. They were not and never will be a part of her life.

Emma was happily married to a decent man and had a large house, her own car and three children. Victoria was as pretty as her sister, had a similar figure and was more intelligent, so why was she still unmarried? Victoria had a house, a car, a career, and four close friends, but these were not what she needed. She needed a family. She needed children. She also needed to be loved by a man. What was wrong with her? What prevented her from getting a decent man? It was as if something was stopping her from achieving her dreams and being happy. Life can be so cruel.

She stood up and walked out of the restaurant. It might cheer her up to do some shopping. She needed to get a few things. Shopping was one of her few pleasures. What a sad person she had become. She walked into the first clothes shop she came to. It was pointless to blame anyone else. Her problems were of her own making. Her life was a mess because she made the wrong decisions. It was all down to the choices she made; it must be. She was dating the wrong sort of men. If she wanted a decent man, she would have to be more selective and more discerning, although she would never be able to settle for a man she did not fancy.

Her close friend Steven Hall would make a wonderful husband and would marry her tomorrow if she were so inclined. He had everything a woman could want. He was trustworthy, intelligent, handsome, had a good physique, and a good job. She just did not fancy him. He was more like a brother. If she married a man, she would have to be sexually attracted to him. She could not sleep with a man she did not find attractive, no matter how decent he was.

What she wanted and needed most of all was to fall in love with an attractive, kind man. The only escape she had from her lonely, sad existence was her novels. Every night in bed, she lost herself in a love story with a happy ending. If only life could be like a romantic novel.

Her phone rang. She took it out of her bag. "Yes?"

"It's Steven."

"Hello, Steve."

"Can I ask you a favour?" Steven asked.

"Yes, as long as it isn't for money." She almost added, or sex.

"Could I live in your spare room for a while? As you know, I'm buying a house. It needs rewiring, a new kitchen and a new bathroom, so I need to move out for a while."

She did not mind as long as it was not for months. "For how long?"

"About four weeks. I'll cook you a meal tonight as a bribe."

She smiled. "Okay. I'll be home in about two hours."

She bought some sexy underwear to cheer herself up, but it did not work. She drove home feeling just as depressed. What was the use of sexy underwear if you did not have a man?

*

At eight o'clock on Saturday evening, Victoria met up with her two mates, Katy Adkins and Rachael Barber, and they took a taxi into the centre of Solihull. It was Victoria's weekly attempt to find a man. It was also a break from work and an excuse to get a little drunk. Katy was twenty-six, tall, slim and could just about be called pretty. She was easy to talk to but was prone to tantrums and could be argumentative at times. Rachael was thirty-one, fat, small and plain-looking. She was fun to be with and had a good sense of humour.

"I'm desperate tonight," Rachael said. "I intend to get a man, and I don't care how ugly he is. I'll just close my eyes when we have sex."

They laughed.

"I'm feeling lucky tonight," Katy said. "I'm almost desperate. I'm willing to settle for a man who's rich, tall, well-built, wonderful and handsome."

"I'll settle for a man like that," Victoria said. "But I don't think that such men exist."

"I know they don't exist," Rachael said. "Men are never wonderful. All that you can hope for is that they don't fart all the time, and they have a thingy bigger than this." She wiggled her little finger.

Katy laughed so much she almost choked.

Victoria was acting happier than she felt. She would hate her friends to know she was desperate to get married and have a baby. There was no one she trusted enough to confide in. It would be nice to talk about her innermost thoughts and desires. To make things even worse, Steven had got himself a girlfriend. Victoria wanted Steven to be happy, but it would mean losing a close friend. His girlfriend, Rose, was small, slim and pretty. Steven had been taking Rose out for two weeks, and it looked serious.

They had a drink in the Barley Mow and then went to Rosie's nightclub. Victoria knew many of the people they met. The same men were there every week. They were either married, ugly, bores or rats. As usual, she hoped to meet her Mr Right. At ten o'clock, she began to lose heart. "I don't see any wonderful men," she said. "They're either too young, too old or too ugly."

"Don't look now," Katy said, "but we're being given the eye by three blokes at the bar. Two of them aren't bad looking."

Rachael and Victoria turned to look.

"I suppose I'll get the ugly one," Rachael said. "I wonder if he farts?"

Katy burst out laughing.

The three men walked up to their table.

"Hello, girls," one of the good-looking men said. "You look happy. What are you drinking?"

"We're always happy," Katy said. "Lager. Who do you support?"

"My mother and an ageing aunt," he said.

They laughed.

"I'm Richard," he said. "He's David, and he's Mark."

Richard was tall, well-built and had smiling eyes. He was well-spoken and well-dressed. Victoria was drawn to him immediately. Maybe this was her lucky night. "I'm Victoria."

"I'm Rachael."

"I'm Katy."

"We support Blues," Mark said. "I've always been a Blue Nose." He was tall, slim and average-looking but also well-spoken and well-dressed.

"Who do you support?" David asked. He was a carbon copy of Richard, without the smiling eyes.

"Blues," Katy said.

"We'll get the drinks," Richard said. The three men walked to the bar.

"What do you think?" Katy asked. "I think David fancies me. I caught him looking at my tits."

"They look well-heeled," Victoria said. "They're probably upper class and could be married."

"I fancy Mark," Rachael said. "I hope he likes buxom wenches."

The three men returned with the drinks and sat down.

"What do you do for a living?" Rachael asked.

"We're builders," Mark said. "We live in Sheldon. Do you live locally?"

"Yes," Victoria said.

They chatted and told a few jokes. They seemed like three decent men. Victoria was impressed with Richard. He would make a perfect Mr Right. She prayed that he was not married and would ask her for a date.

"Do you have boyfriends?" David asked.

"No," Rachael said. "So, we might be open to offers."

"I bet you've got girlfriends," Katy said.

"We haven't," Richard said. "And we're definitely open to offers. How would you three like to go for a meal with us on Wednesday evening?"

"It sounds like a good idea to me," Rachael said.

"Great," Richard said. "We'll meet you in the Barley Mow at eight. Better still, if we give you a lift home, we'll know where you live, and so we'll be able to pick you up on Wednesday."

"That sounds like a good idea," Katy said. "What sort of car do you have?"

"A BMW," Richard said.

"Are you drinking and driving?" Victoria asked Richard.

"No. This lager is non-alcoholic."

"And I only ever drink Coke," Mark said. "You three girls can go in Richard's car, and we'll follow in my car."

They left Rosie's and walked together to Richard's car.

Victoria felt a little queasy. She had probably drunk too much. She would feel better after a good night's sleep.

They climbed into Richard's BMW.

"This is a cracking car," Rachael said. "It must have cost a bomb."

"It did," Richard said as he drove off. "Will you give me the directions, Rachael? I'll take you home first."

Rachael laughed. "I'll give you anything you want, Richard."

Victoria was falling asleep and had to force her eyes open. The day was catching up with her fast.

*

Victoria woke up with a hangover. She lay in bed looking at the ceiling. Her throat was dry, her head was thumping painfully, and she felt sick. Sunlight was pouring in through her bedroom window, so it must be morning. She felt as if she had just closed her eyes.

She climbed out of bed, rushed into the bathroom and sat down on the toilet. Her headache intensified briefly and then slowly returned to a dull thump. She would have to cut down on the drinking; it was not worth all the pain. In slow motion, she flushed the toilet, slipped on her dressing gown and walked downstairs.

Steven was in the kitchen, washing up. "Good morning, Victoria. How would you like me to cook you bacon and eggs?"

"I wouldn't." She sat down at the kitchen table, and her cat, Sooty, jumped onto her lap. "I'd love a cup of coffee, though."

"I've already got the kettle on. I heard you flush the toilet. Did you have a good night out?"

"Yes." She stroked Sooty.

"And did you find a man?"

"I think so. We met three men. They're taking us out on Wednesday for a meal. How's Rose?"

"She's as beautiful as ever." He placed a cup of coffee on the table in front of her and looked up at the clock. "Look at the time. I'll have to rush. I didn't realise it was so late. I'm meeting Rose's parents today, and it wouldn't do to be late."

Victoria looked up at the clock. It was ten to one. "That isn't the time. The clock must have stopped. It probably needs a new battery"

He looked at his watch. "Your clock is working perfectly. It's exactly ten to one. I'm meeting Rose at one fifteen. I'm dreading meeting her parents."

She felt confused. "I've never slept in this late before. I'm usually up before nine."

He put on his coat. "It's because you were out all night."

"I wasn't out that late."

"You were. You weren't in when I came in, and that was about one-thirty."

She frowned. "I must have already been in bed. We only went to Rosie's nightclub."

"You were not in bed. Your bedroom door was open, and Sooty was sitting on your bed when I went to bed, and that was about two o'clock." He opened the door. "Bye. I might be late, so don't wait up."

"Bye."

She sipped her coffee and stroked Sooty. Steven must be mistaken about the time he went to bed. They left Rosie's at about eleven-thirty, and the journey home would have only taken about fifteen minutes in the car. She would have been at home before twelve. It was very strange. She could remember going out and meeting Richard, Mark and David in Rosie's and getting into Richard's car with Rachael and Katy, but she could not remember much else.

For several minutes, she sat stroking the cat and trying to remember. She had a vague memory of getting out of the car and feeling ill, but she could not remember going to bed. From now on, she would limit herself to four halves of lager.

While she walked upstairs and showered, she tried to remember how many drinks she had had last night. She had half a pint of lager in the Barley Mow and one, two, three more in Rosie's. She frowned. How could she have got drunk on two pints of lager? Even if she had four drinks in Rosie's, that would only be two and a half pints of lager. Three pints of lager usually made her tipsy, but she needed to drink at least five or six pints to get drunk.

The memory of a dream slithered into her thoughts as she stepped out of the shower. It was about Katy. She had dreamed of getting into bed with Katy. She smiled. In her dream, they had both climbed naked into a large bed. There was probably a meaning to the dream. Being naked in a dream was supposed to have something to do with insecurity. The dream was right. She did feel very insecure. Perhaps her date with Richard would bring a little security into her life. He was the sort of man she could marry.

She dressed, took two paracetamol tablets, and did the chores. The quicker she got them done, the quicker she would be able to sit down and relax. She filled the washing machine, switched it on, and began vacuuming the lounge carpet. The tablets began to work, and her thumping headache eased a little. As usual, Sooty attacked the vacuum cleaner as she moved about the lounge, ran off, hid, and then attacked again.

Her dream began to play on her mind. She had never dreamed of being naked before. And why would she dream of climbing into bed naked with Katy? It could have nothing to do with her sexuality. She was most definitely heterosexual. If two women were kissing on television, she would have to look away, and the thought of two women having sex made her cringe. There must be another reason why Katy was in her dream.

There was also a man in the dream. She stopped vacuuming and tried to remember the dream. The man was Richard. Mark and David were also in the dream. Why would she dream about Richard, Mark and David? She had only just met them. It was weird how the mind works when you are asleep.

She switched off the vacuum cleaner so that she could think. It was frustrating. She could remember only bits of the dream. The bits she could remember were very vivid and seemed almost real. She then began to remember more of the dream. She could now remember feeling Katy's breasts and then performing oral sex on her. Victoria's mouth dropped open, and the vacuum pipe fell from her hand. The dream was now becoming clear. Katy then performed oral sex on her. The men then had sex with them in different positions, and Victoria performed oral sex on Richard.

It was a very immoral dream. What she could not understand was why it seemed so real, as if it had actually happened. She began to worry. Nothing like this had ever happened to her before. A dream was a dream and very different to reality, so why did this dream seem real? She had never confused reality with a dream before.

She walked into the kitchen and made herself a cup of coffee. Perhaps she was losing her mind. There was no way she would get involved in group sex, and she would never have sex with a woman. Just the thought of touching a woman was repulsive, and she would rather die than perform oral sex on a woman. She had never performed oral sex on a man, although she probably would when she met Mr Right, but not on a first date.

She stared at the coffee swirling around in her cup. It was not a first date. She had not been out with Richard yet. It was a dream. It had to be a dream. She began to feel confused. Her mind was telling her that it was not a dream, and it had happened. She must be ill. She was probably going psychotic. She began to feel anxious. It could be the beginning of a nervous breakdown of some sort. Or maybe she had a brain tumour. She was now very worried.

"Calm down," she told herself. Her words sounded frightened. "I'm not losing my mind. I've just had a vivid dream." She sat down, and Sooty jumped onto her lap. She stroked Sooty and sipped her coffee.

If she was not losing her mind and did not have a brain tumour, what other explanation could there be? She was not drunk or on drugs, so why was she convinced that a dream had actually happened? And why was the dream all mixed up? If it were not a dream and it had happened, she would remember every detail. She could not remember going to a house and then into the bedroom with Katy and the men or getting undressed. And she could not remember getting dressed afterwards and going home.

She stood up, and Sooty jumped from her lap. She was now very worried. She must be going mad. The only other explanation was that someone had put a drug of some sort into her drink. She sat down and went to take a sip of coffee. The cup did not reach her lips and slowly sank back onto the table.

For several minutes, she stared at the picture on the wall. She could have been given one of those date rape drugs. Another part of the dream slipped into her mind. The three men had taken her and Katy into a large house. The next memory she had was getting into bed with Katy. They were both naked.

She could remember Richard squeezing her breasts hard. She touched her breasts. They hurt to the touch. She opened her blouse, pulled out her breasts and examined them. They were bruised. It had not been a dream; it had really happened.

The relief she felt at knowing that she was not going mad only lasted for a few seconds. It was then replaced by anger. How could they have done such a thing? Why would they drug two women for sex when there were dozens of women willing to do it without being drugged? They had set out that night to find a woman or women that they could drug and rape. The bastards. What sort of men were they?

There was no memory of Rachael being at the house. It was probably because they had not fancied her. The memories that were now drifting back into her mind were painful. While Richard was squeezing her breasts, she could remember seeing Katy performing oral sex on David. They had treated them as prostitutes, unpaid, unwilling prostitutes.

She stood up and began to pace up and down. What could she do? She did not know their addresses or their surnames. It would be pointless to go to the police. She was bursting with anger and frustration. There must be something she could do. Maybe Rachael could help.

She picked up her phone and phoned Rachael.

"Yes?" Rachael said.

"It's me. Did Richard, Mark or David tell you their last names or where they lived?"

"No. Why?"

"I need to trace them. Did they tell you where they worked?"

"No. They just said they were builders. We can ask them when we see them on Wednesday."

"We won't be seeing them on Wednesday," Victoria said. "How did you get home last night?"

"Richard gave us a lift. He dropped me off first. Can't you remember?"

"No. I think Katy and I were date-raped by Richard, Mark and David."

"Date-raped," Rachael said. "No. Surely not. They seemed like decent men. Are you sure?"

"Yes. Either that or I'm going mad."

"It's a good job I wrote down Richard's registration number," Rachael said. Now that I think about it, you and Katy were acting strange. I put it down to drinking too much."

"I only drank four halves of lager," Victoria said. "It takes more than that to get me drunk." She then realised what Rachael had said. "You wrote down Richard's registration number?"

"Yes. I don't know why. I've never done it before. I suppose it was because you were so drunk."

Victoria could not believe it. "You're an angel. What's the number? I want the bastards sent to prison."

Rachael told her the registration number, and she wrote it down. "Thanks, Rachael. I'll phone you later."

"Yes, bye," Rachael said.

Victoria felt euphoric. The police would now be able to find out who they were and where they lived.

Victoria's phone rang. She picked it up. "Yes?"

"It's Katy. Do you fancy going for a drink? I need the hair of the dog."

"Yes. I'll meet you at The Crown pub in thirty minutes."

"Okay. You sound as if you also need the hair of the dog. I'll see you in thirty minutes."

Thirty-five minutes later, Victoria walked into The Crown public house in Solihull and saw Katy sitting at a table. She looked ill. Victoria bought half a pint of lager and sat down facing her.

"I'm never getting drunk again," Katy said. "I feel like shit, and I've got a terrible headache."

"Can you remember how much we had to drink last night?" Victoria asked.

"No. I can hardly remember anything about what happened last night."

Victoria felt disappointed. She had hoped that Katy would remember what had happened. "Do you remember meeting Richard, Mark and David?"

"No."

"Try and remember, will you? It's important."

While Katy stared at the table, obviously trying to remember, Victoria drank the entire half-pint of lager. It would help if Katy also remembered what had happened.

"Oh, yes. I remember now," Katy said. "We did meet three blokes, didn't we?"

Thank God for that, Victoria thought. "What else can you remember?"

"Not a lot." Katy sipped her drink. "I wish this fucking headache would go. I've already had four paracetamol tablets."

"What do you remember about going out last night?" Victoria asked.

"I remember going to Rosie's, and I now remember the three men, but I don't remember anything after that."

"Do you remember what the three men looked like?" Victoria asked.

"Yes. They were good-looking blokes."

"See, you can remember if you try. What else can you remember?"

"I can't remember anything else. Why can't you remember what happened? You were there."

"It's important that you remember what happened. Try and remember?"

Katy finished off her drink and stared at the table. "I can remember a few things. I can now remember meeting Richard, Mark and David and going somewhere with them. Fucking hell. Did we have sex with them?"

"Yes. What else do you remember?"

"It's coming back to me now. We must have been blind drunk if we had sex with them on the first date. I can now remember what happened. Fucking hell. I'm broad-minded, but I've never done anything like that before. Where did we go? Did we go back to your house?"

"No. I don't know where we went."

"We must have gone to one of their houses," Katy said. "I bet they got us drunk on purpose. The bastards."

"Have you ever had group sex and sex with a woman before?" Victoria asked.

"No, I have not. I'm a total heterosexual. Although I did sleep with two brothers once when I was drunk. Have you ever had sex with a woman before?"

"No. It was the first time for me as well." Victoria was pleased that Katy could now remember what had happened. They would now both be able to make statements to the police.

"What's wrong with men?" Katy said. "I would have slept with David if he had taken me out. There was no need to get us drunk. There's no way I'm going out with them on Wednesday."

Victoria was seething with anger and had a burning need for revenge. "I need another drink, but I'm driving. They did not get us drunk. After we left Rosie's, do you remember having any more drinks?"

Katy shook her head. "No, but I don't remember much of what happened. I don't even remember going home. I do remember feeling sick, so I must have been drunk. And I would never have group sex and sex with a woman unless I was absolutely blind drunk."

"They drugged us," Victoria said.

"What?" Katy stared open-mouthed at her. "What do you mean, drugged us?"

"They drugged us so that they could have sex with us. That's why we're finding it difficult to remember what happened. Even if I was drunk, I would not have group sex with three men and a woman. I would rather die."

Katy looked shocked. "Fucking hell. The bastards. We could get pregnant or get AIDS."

"I remember them putting on condoms, so we should be all right," Victoria said. "I want them arrested and put in prison."

"We don't know where they live," Katy said. "And we only know their first names."

"Rachael wrote down Richard's car registration number," Victoria said. "The police will be able to trace them. We can go to the police station now and make a statement."

Katy frowned and began to bite the knuckle of her right hand. "Will we have to go to court?"

"Yes. I'm not letting them get away with raping me."

Katy looked worried. "It'll get into all the papers. I couldn't bear everyone knowing what we did."

Victoria would also hate people to know what had happened, but she was willing to put up with it to get them convicted. "I know how you feel, but it has to be done. The bastards deserve ten years for what they did to us."

Katy shook her head. "I can't do it. I want to, but I just can't."

"We can do it together," Victoria said.

"We need to think about it first," Katy said. "There's no rush."

"There is. We need them arrested." Victoria stood up. "You can think about it. I'm going to the police station. I'll see you later."

Victoria drove the short distance to Solihull Police Station. She could understand why Katy was reluctant to report the incident to the police. It would be embarrassing if what happened to them were to get into the newspapers, but it had to be done. She was determined to testify against them, so they were sent to prison. She could not live with herself if they got off scot-free.

She parked her car and walked into the police station.

"Can I help you?" a fat Asian woman receptionist asked.

"I've been date-raped. I need to speak to someone."

"Will you take a seat?" the receptionist asked in a calm voice as if she had heard it all before. "I'll get someone to see you."

Victoria sat down. She would hate for everyone to know what the men had done, but the need to hurt them was very powerful. She could not let them get away with it. If they got what they deserved, they would get at least ten years.

A female police officer walked up to her and smiled. “I’m WPC Banks. Could you follow me?”

Victoria followed her into a small interview room. She began to feel nervous.

WPC Banks closed the door, and they both sat down.

“I need to take a statement from you,” WPC Banks said. “Tell me your name and address, and what happened?”

Victoria told WPC Banks her name and address, and what had happened. WPC Banks wrote it down, and Victoria signed it.

“I want the bastards arrested,” Victoria said.

“It’s good for you that they used condoms,” WPC Banks said. “You don’t have to worry about catching AIDS or VD, but it’s bad for your case against them. It’s very difficult to get a guilty verdict without forensic evidence. It’ll be your word and Katy’s word against theirs.”

“I don’t care. I want them arrested.”

“We have dozens of date rape cases a year,” WPC Banks said. “But they very rarely get to court, and it’s rarer still to get a conviction.”

Victoria was surprised. “Why?”

WPC Banks leaned back in her seat. “Usually, the men cannot be traced. In your case, we might be able to trace them, but it’ll still be your word against theirs. Having two witnesses might help. The main problem is the embarrassment it will cause. It will get into the newspapers, and everyone will know what you’ve told me. Are you prepared to go all the way? If you’re going to drop out halfway, it’s better not to get started.”

“I’ll go all the way,” Victoria assured her. “I want the bastards sent to prison.”

WPC Banks stood up. “Then leave it with me. We’ll do all we can. And don’t forget to get photographs of the bruises on your breasts.”

Victoria left the police station and drove home. She felt as low as she had ever felt. Why were men such bastards? If she were a man, she would go after all three of them and make sure they never date-raped a woman again.

Chapter Three

London was a lonely place. Timothy had spent several days walking along crowded streets and drinking in public houses. He felt as lonely among crowds of people as he did when he was alone in his small hotel room. London was not for him. It was also an expensive place to live. A small taxi ride costs an arm and a leg, and he had not been able to find a cheap café that served decent food.

It was nine-thirty in the morning. There was a threat of rain in the grey clouds that rolled across the sky. He was once again walking through the crowded streets and feeling as lonely as ever. It was time for some positive thinking. He had already decided to move on, but where to?

He eventually found himself in Trafalgar Square. He sat on a bench and watched a small boy feeding the pigeons. It would be nice to be young again, without worries and responsibilities. He lit a cigarette and watched the tourists taking dozens of photographs of the lions and Nelson's Column. He was not one for taking photographs. One of his pet hates was looking through other people's photograph albums.

His phone rang. It was Jane, and so he ignored it. She was probably going to apologise for how nasty she had been, but it was now too late for words. He had no intention of ever speaking to her again. Their relationship was well and truly over.

It was pointless to keep putting it off. He had to decide what he was going to do with his life and where he was going to live. He sighed. It was hopeless. He had no enthusiasm for anything, which was probably because of the tablets he was taking. They not only took the edge off his lows but also blunted his highs. Perhaps it was best to go back to the Midlands. He was running out of tablets and felt guilty about not seeing his parents.

He smiled. The little boy who had been feeding the pigeons was crying. A pigeon had defecated on his head, and the white, creamy excrement was running down his face.

"Don't cry," the boy's mother said as she wiped his face with a tissue. "It was a naughty pigeon."

"The pigeon who did that was a stool pigeon," Timothy said to the woman.

"Pardon?" the woman said, and she stared at him with a blank expression on her face.

"It was a joke," he said.

When the penny dropped, she smiled and shook her head. "Your jokes are as bad as my husband's."

Timothy stood up and walked slowly back to his digs. It was time to leave the metropolis and return to familiar surroundings. His movements were laboured as if he were a clockwork toy that needed winding up. In slow motion, he packed his few possessions into his suitcase, paid his bill and drove back to Birmingham. He drove in the slow lane of the motorway. It was pointless rushing when you have nowhere to go and all the time in the world to get there.

For the first time in his life, he felt alone in the world. It was a painful feeling and much worse than just feeling lonely. He needed a family. He needed someone to care for him and to worry about him. He needed to be loved. As soon as he had found himself a place to live, he intended to sort out his life. In a short time, his parents would be dead, and he would have no one to care whether he lived or died. What he needed most was a friend.

It was three-thirty when he reached Birmingham. It was raining. After checking that Jane was still living in his house (her car was parked in the drive), he had a meal in a cafe. He could not bring himself to tell Jane to leave his house on the off chance that she was ill. His movements were still laboured, as if his body was unable to get out of first gear. He was moving and doing things as if he were a ninety-year-old man.

After eating his meal, he drove around looking for a cheap hotel. He had not realised how much Birmingham had changed. Parts were now made up almost entirely of blacks and Asians. His green and pleasant land was slowly disappearing. If the foreigners continued to have more children than whites and refused to integrate, there would eventually be no white people left.

He drove out of the centre of Birmingham and booked into a hotel in Sheldon. He was not a racist, but he would feel uncomfortable living among blacks and Asians. His spirits lifted slightly. Even though foreigners were slowly taking over Birmingham, there was something special about the Midlands. The people were friendlier, and there were fewer tourists. It was the nearest thing to a home he had.

For over an hour, he sat by the window in the tiny lounge of his hotel suite and watched the traffic driving up and down Coventry Road. He was drowning in loneliness. Time seemed to stand still. If you were lonely and lived to be a hundred, you would probably feel as if you had lived forever. He must have had a reasonably happy life. His forty-eight years had flown by. His school days seemed like only a few years ago.

This would not do. He stubbed out his cigarette in an ashtray and stood up. He would have to keep active. He forced his clockwork legs to move, left his digs and climbed into his car. It was about time he visited his mother. Knowing that his mother would spend the rest of her life in a nursing home did not sit well in his mind, but what could he do? He could not look after her. She needed specialist care. What he could and should do was visit her more often.

He drove to the nursing home in Solihull and found his mother sitting in a wheelchair in the garden. He kissed her on the cheek. She was seventy and thin. "How're things?" he asked.

"Could be better. You haven't visited me for over three weeks. How are you feeling? Are you still taking the tablets?"

"Yes. I'm doing fine." He sat down on a low wall next to her wheelchair. "You're getting to be a bit of a character."

"What do you mean?"

"You're wearing an expensive trouser suit. You have a shawl around your shoulders. You're dressed like a film star."

She frowned. "What's wrong with that? I always take care with my appearance."

He pointed to her slippers. "Then why are you wearing pink slippers with a rabbit's head on the toe?"

She looked down and smiled. "My friend Violet was given them by her granddaughter, but she refused to wear them. It upset her granddaughter, so I said that I would wear them. Violet doesn't know how lucky she is to have a beautiful granddaughter."

"Are they treating you well?" he asked. He needed to change the subject from grandchildren.

"Yes. They're very good here. Do you like my new glasses?"

"Yes. They make you look beautiful."

She looked over her glasses at him. "I think you might need glasses. Have you been to see your father?"

"No. Not for weeks."

"Then go and see him. Something's bothering him. I think he's ill."

"I'll go and see him tomorrow."

She looked him up and down. "You look untidy. You need a shave, and you don't look happy. How's Jane?"

"Moaning as usual."

"It's her hormones," she said. "All women have hormonal trouble. I used to drive your father to distraction."

"You still do."

She smiled. "Your father's the one with the odd habits. When you were young, I remember you saying that your father only knew the first two bars of a song."

"His dar dars and de des still drive me mad," he said. He took out his cigarettes and lit up.

"I thought you were giving them up?"

"I will one day." He could put his mind to most things and had a strong willpower, but not when it came to cigarettes.

She looked worried. "Smoking will eventually kill you."

He nodded. "I know. It's a filthy habit. As soon as I get my life sorted out, I'll pack them up."

"When are you getting married?" she asked.

"Never. At least not to Jane. I've walked out on her."

"Oh, dear. I was hoping for a grandchild. I know you don't want children, but I was hoping you would have an accident."

He smiled. "I'm not one for accidents, at least not those sorts of accidents." He took a drag on his cigarette. It would probably be better to tell his mother that he now wants to have children. It would cheer her up. "I've had a change of heart."

"What about?"

"I've decided I do want children."

She stared at him. "Are you serious? You shouldn't joke about things like that."

"I'm not joking. I do want children."

"Why? What made you change your mind after all this time?"

"I don't know. It's a bit of a mystery. There's one problem, though."

"Don't tell me that you've had that operation?"

"No. I can father a child. I just can't find a decent woman that doesn't resemble Frankenstein."

"I find that hard to believe," she said. "You have your father's good looks. I suppose being nearly fifty doesn't help. Why don't you join one of those dating agencies? There must be hundreds of decent women looking for a husband."

He frowned. "I couldn't." He did not like the idea of joining an agency. It offended his masculinity.

"Why not? What's wrong with dating agencies?"

"It would be as good as admitting that I'm not capable of finding a woman, which is true, but it's not something I want to advertise."

"At least give it a try. What have you got to lose?"

"Nothing, I suppose. I'll think about it."

"I would if I were you. If you get a move on, your father and I might get to see our first grandchild. It would be wonderful. We only have a few years left." She lifted her hands and examined them. "I hate being old. I've stopped looking in the mirror. I used to be beautiful. I now look like a witch. If it wasn't for my hands, I could fool myself into thinking that I didn't look too old. My hands are very old. They're wrinkled and covered in those brown spots."

"You do not look like a witch," he insisted. "You only look forty-five."

She smiled. "I wish I did. Being old would not be so bad if I had my health. I used to be so active. Being partly paralysed is worse than getting old."

They talked, or at least his mother did, mostly about their childhoods. He let her talk. She seemed to live in the past, which was understandable. It would depress her if she dwelt too much on what the future had in store for her. Two hours later, he stood up. "I'll have to go. I think I left the kettle on."

"Your jokes are as bad as your father's. Make sure you join that dating agency. And if you find a young woman, bring her to meet me. I'll soon tell if she's suitable."

He kissed her on the cheek. "You've still got your looks. You're by far the best-looking chick here."

She smiled. "I now feel a little better. Go and see your father, and don't forget to tell him that you want to have children. It'll make his day."

"I will. Bye."

"Bye. Take care."

"I will."

He drove to the nearest public house. He was starving but also needed the comfort of alcohol, which he hoped would kick the hell out of his worries.

*

Victoria had to force herself to get up and go to work. She had not slept for more than three hours. The date rape had been playing on her mind. Why were men so disgusting? They did not have to use drugs to have sex. It was just a laugh to them. It helped a little to know that the men who had raped her would be going to prison. They would not be laughing then.

The day flew by. Working with small children was enjoyable and was the highlight of her dull life. It was the evenings and the weekends that dragged their feet.

Steven was cooking a meal when she returned home. It was nice to have someone she could trust in the house. "That smells nice," she said.

"It's curry. I hope you're hungry?"

"I'm starving. How was Sunday?"

"Great. Rose has marvellous parents, and I hit it off with her brother. I've already decided to marry her. That is, if she'll have me."

She sat down at the table. "I am pleased." She would like to talk about being date-raped, but decided to leave it for a few days. "Rose will jump at the chance of marrying you. I wish I could meet a decent man. I must be doing something wrong."

"You only go to Rosie's," he said. "It's no wonder you don't meet any decent men. Decent men wouldn't be seen dead in that place."

"I agree, but where can I go?"

He thought for a few moments. "I don't know. Somewhere where decent men go."

"And where would that be? Where do decent men hang out? I have no intention of going to a football match."

"I suppose it is difficult. If I were you, I'd join a dating agency. You can specify exactly what you want in a man. You might end up with a rich, handsome man."

She smiled. "I'll probably get a pervert."

"You can go out with dozens of men until you meet someone suitable," he said. "Just think of all those free meals."

"I suppose I could give it a try. What I need is a mature, professional man, and as long as he's rich and handsome, I'll overlook the odd bad habit."

"Put the kettle on," he said. "I'm about to dish out the grub."

Chapter Four

Timothy's days were boring, his evenings stressful, and his nights painful. He had spent the last three evenings in several bars trying to find a woman and had failed miserably. The young women ignored him, and women in their thirties were invariably with men. His only success was a proposition from a prostitute and a sixty-year-old pensioner. It was time to take drastic steps and take his mother's advice.

The dating agency he decided to use was above a shoe shop on New Street in Birmingham. It took him fifteen minutes to pluck up the courage to walk up the stairs. When he walked into the office, he was confronted by an overweight thirty-year-old woman. She smiled at him.

"Can I help you?" she asked in a very deep voice.

He felt embarrassed and only just managed to resist the powerful urge to walk back out of the office. "I've never been in a place like this before. I'm not sure I'm doing the right thing."

"If you're looking for a rewarding relationship, then this is the place to be," she said. "Take a seat."

He sat down in front of her desk. She was probably thinking that he was a failure and was resorting to desperate measures to find a woman, and he felt that he needed to offer some explanation. "I've just split up with a woman, and I don't want to wait years to find someone suitable."

"There's no need to feel uncomfortable," she said. "I'm sure we can find someone suitable. All you need to do is fill in a form. Do you have a photograph that was taken recently?"

"Yes."

He filled in a form, gave her the photograph and paid the twenty-pound registration fee. He was promised three photographs in the post, and if he decided to go out with one of the women, it would cost him ten pounds. It could work out to be very expensive.

Two days later, he received three photographs of suitable women in the post. Two of the women claimed to be in their early thirties but looked to be at least forty-five. The other woman was thirty-one and looked promising. He paid the ten pounds, and a meeting was arranged. The agency did not give out phone numbers or addresses in case things did not work out.

He met the woman outside the art gallery in Birmingham on Saturday evening at eight o'clock. She was tall and slim, and more attractive than in her photograph. They shook hands.

"I'm Tim," he said.

"I'm Debbie. Where are we going?" She had a high-pitched voice.

"Shall we go for a drink?" he said.

She linked arms with him. "I know just the place. What do you do for a living?"

"I blow up buildings." He was being led along like a little boy.

"How thrilling. It must be a very rewarding job. Is it dangerous?"

"It can be." He was already going off her. She was trying to talk posh but was not quite making it, and her high-pitched voice was grating on his nerves. He had a feeling that she was as rough as rough could be. They had a couple of drinks and talked about their lives. She liked to talk and told him all about her family and her two failed marriages. She had two children and did not want any more. By ten o'clock, he was getting bored and decided to leave.

"It's been nice meeting you, Debbie," he said. "You've given me plenty to think about."

She smiled. "I've already made my mind up about you. You'll do for me. The acid test will decide if we're made for each other."

"What's the acid test?"

"Sex. Are you willing to give it a try?"

He was flabbergasted. "I … er …" She had a decent figure and large breasts, and he was sorely tempted. "Do you mean, have sex?"

"Yes. You can come back to my flat if you like. I gather you do fancy me?"

"Yes. You're a very attractive woman." He had not had sex for what seemed like years, and his resistance was minus one. "When?"

"Now. There's no time like the present."

"Okay. Lead the way."

She did. It was disconcerting to be led along as if you were blind. They took a taxi to her flat in Acocks Green. It was small, and the furniture had seen better days, but it was clean and tidy.

"I'm sure you'll be won over after we've had sex," she said. "I'm adventurous and willing to try anything."

It looked as if he was going to get his ten pounds' worth. "I'm sure I will."

She pushed a condom into his hand and led him into a small bedroom. They undressed down to their underwear, and he rolled the condom onto his erect penis. The lights were dim, and he could only see the outline of her body. It was probably just as well.

"Do you want my legs in the air, or shall I bend over?" she asked. "I don't want to be too adventurous on our first date."

"The legs in the air will do just fine," he said. He had the feeling that he was with a prostitute.

She lay down on the bed and lifted her legs. "Just help yourself."

He did. She had large, soft breasts, and within a few seconds, he had forgotten about her rasping voice. There was nothing quite as enjoyable as a woman's body. He did not bother about foreplay and selfishly thrust into her. His climax shuddered through his body.

"I can tell you enjoyed that," she said. "Did it pass the acid test?"

"It certainly did." He rolled off her and climbed off the bed.

"I think we were made for each other," she said. "Do you want a cup of coffee?"

"Yes. That would be nice."

She slipped a dressing gown on and left the bedroom.

He took off the condom and got dressed. She was a good person, and he felt guilty about taking advantage of her. He lit a cigarette and followed her into the kitchen. "What do you do for a living, Debbie?"

"I'm a health visitor. Do you have milk and sugar in your coffee?"

"Yes, please."

They chatted while drinking coffee, and he left her thinking he would phone her. She was nice enough and would soon find a man, but she was not his type. He intended to phone the agency and ask for three more photographs to be sent to him.

*

Victoria was sitting in the lounge of her house. Her phone rang. She picked it up. "Yes?"

"It's Emma. How are you keeping?"

"I'm fine. What do you want?"

"Mother would like to speak to you."

"I don't want to speak to her."

"It's different now," Emma said.

"How is it different?"

"Mother believes you now. We both do. We both believe that Ben did what you said he did."

"It's too late," Victoria said. "She should have believed me when I first told her."

"I know," Emma said. "I phoned Ben and spoke to his new girlfriend and told her what he did to you. She didn't believe me, but it will make her think. Could we meet in Solihull? I could bring Mother."

Victoria was undecided as to what to do. It was nice to be believed, even if it was nearly eighteen years too late. "I'll think about it. I'll phone you."

"I hope you agree to talk to Mother," Emma said. "It'll be nice to talk over old times."

"Yes. Bye."

Victoria put the phone down and sat looking at Sooty, who was playing with a ball of paper. It was eight o'clock in the evening. The television was turned down low, a half-empty bottle of red wine was on the coffee table, and an unopened romance novel lay on her lap. Her life was being wasted. She had to find a decent man.

She had joined a dating agency and had received three photographs of men. They were all totally unattractive. She had asked for three more photographs. She was hoping that one of them would be attractive. Being in love was not all-important, as long as she fancied him and he was decent and kind. If she did not have a child soon, she would be too old.

*

Timothy was sent three more photographs of women. Two were ugly, and one was pretty. The following Saturday, he met the pretty one. Her name was Jackie. She was twenty-six, had a nice figure, was well dressed and spoke without a strong accent. She was very attractive and seemed perfect for him. They talked over a drink for an hour. The more they talked, the more interested he became.

"I play tennis, and I go swimming every week," she said. "Are you the sporty type?"

"I work out a couple of times a week, and I play golf now and again. I do a bit of portrait and landscape painting in my spare time."

"I'm no good at art," she said. "Do you want to see me again?"

"Yes, I do."

"I'll give you my phone number." She wrote her phone number on a piece of paper and handed it to him. "What church do you go to?"

"I don't go to church."

She sat back in her seat as if he had slapped her face. "You don't go to church. I thought you were a Catholic?"

"No. I don't believe in God."

She snatched the piece of paper out of his hand and stood up. "There's been a terrible mistake. I would only consider a relationship with a Catholic.

The agency has made a mistake. I told them that the man must be a Catholic." She hurried out of the pub without saying goodbye.

He felt bitterly disappointed. He intended to contact the agency and amend his requirements to include women who were not religious and who wanted children. It was a pity about Jackie; she seemed like a nice person.

*

On Wednesday evening, Victoria went to meet a man from the dating agency. Her spirits were high. She was determined to be optimistic. She had made an effort with her appearance. She had her hair cut and highlighted, and was wearing a new dress. When she met him, she could not believe her eyes. He was as good-looking as he had appeared in his photograph. He was well-built, about five feet nine inches tall, and dressed in an expensive suit. He looked middle to upper class and seemed ideal. They shook hands.

"Hello. I'm Victoria."

"Hello, Victoria. I'm Craig. Shall we go for a drink?"

"Yes. That would be nice."

They sat down in the nearest pub and chatted about their lives. The attraction she had felt for him slowly disappeared. He was manly-looking but had effeminate mannerisms. Now that she had met and talked to him, there was no way she could ever find him attractive. It was a pity. He was a lovely person and would make some woman a good husband.

At the end of the evening, she did not have the heart to tell him that she was not interested in him, so she took his phone number and promised to call him. She drove home feeling depressed. It had been a waste of time. Perhaps she was destined never to find a man.

That night in bed, she tried to use her vibrator, which she used several times a week, but vivid, horrible pictures flashed into her mind. She put the vibrator back in the drawer. How could she climax when all she could see were pictures of the three bastards who had raped her? Sex was never going to be the same again.

Chapter Five

On Tuesday, Victoria had a visit from Detective Sergeant Harris. He was short, bald and wore glasses. He looked more like a bank manager than a police officer. They sat down in the lounge of her house.

"Have you arrested them?" she asked.

"Let me explain a few things. The three men are from well-to-do families in Knowle. One is a law student; one is the son of a police sergeant, and the other is the son of a judge."

She was a little surprised. "I didn't think they lived in Sheldon. It doesn't change anything. It doesn't matter how well off they are. They still raped me and Katy."

"I know, and I believe you. The problem is, the good lady judge is willing to swear that all three men arrived at her house at midnight on the dot on the evening that you claim they raped you. The CCTV in Solihull showed you walking with your two friends and the three men to Richard's car at eleven thirty-five. According to your statement, Rachael was dropped off at her home, and the three men took you and Katy somewhere and raped you."

She nodded. "That's exactly what happened."

"Let me finish what I was saying. If the three men arrived home at twelve o'clock, they would have had just enough time to drop you and Katy home and then drive to Knowle, and they would have had to put their foot down. I drove from your house to the judge's house in Knowle at eleven forty-five last night, and it took me eighteen minutes."

"What are you saying?" she asked. "They did rape us. The judge is lying to protect her son."

"That may be the case, and we might have a case if Katy had backed you up."

She frowned. "What do you mean? What did Katy say?"

"In Katy's statement, she claims that the men dropped you both off at the corner of your road, and you both walked home."

She could not believe it. "She's lying. She also remembers them raping us."

"For what it's worth, I believe you, but what can I do? The CPS has decided that there is insufficient evidence, and so the men will not be prosecuted."

She felt upset and frustrated. "This is all very wrong."

"The men claim that you are accusing them of raping you because they would not take you out. They claim that all they did was give you a lift home."

She began to feel angry. "It's all lies. So, they'll get away with it?"

"We'll keep your statement on file in case someone else accuses the men of raping them." He stood up. "I'm sorry. There's nothing more I can do."

As soon as the detective had left, she phoned Katy.

"Yes?" Katy said.

"How could you lie to the police? Because of you, the police are not prosecuting them."

"It's for the best. I had to lie. I couldn't go to court and tell them what happened."

Victoria had never felt so angry before, and she felt like screaming. "Because of you, they're getting away with it and will probably do it again."

"I would like them to be sent to prison, but how could we live with everyone knowing that we were gang-raped? We would never get decent boyfriends, and our reputations would be mud."

"Sod our reputations," Victoria screamed. "They're rapists and deserve to go to prison."

"I know you're upset, but you'll thank me in time," Katy said. "Rachael agrees with me. It's something we have to forget. From now on, we must not put our drinks down. We'll talk about it on Saturday."

"No, we won't. I don't ever want to see you again. You're no friend of mine." She ended the call and threw the phone onto the settee. The problem with mobile phones is that you cannot slam them down.

She opened a bottle of wine and drank a large glass in one go. Her life was going from bad to worse. She had been date-raped, and the men responsible would not be going to prison; she had lost her two best friends and would be seeing very little of Steven from now on. And she did not have a boyfriend. If she knew where the three bastards who had raped her lived, she would exact some revenge. She felt vulnerable, weak and lonely.

*

On Saturday, Victoria went to meet a man the agency described as highly suitable. He seemed quite attractive in his photograph, but she was not holding her breath. She expected to find something wrong with him. He would either not show up, be four feet six tall, or be wearing a wig. She should not be going out. She was not in the mood to meet even highly suitable men. As far as she was concerned, all men were bastards, especially the attractive ones, but she had to do something now that she was not going out with Katy and Rachael.

The highly suitable man was waiting for her outside the entrance to the Barley Mow, as arranged. He was tall, well-built, looked good for forty-eight and was almost handsome. She held out her hand. "I'm Victoria."

Timothy was pleased with what he saw. He shook her hand. She was petite, about four-foot-ten, had short dark hair, big blue eyes and a little girl's figure. "I'm Timothy, but I like to be called Tim. Do I call you Vic?"

No one had ever called her Vic before. "You can call me what you like." He had a masculine voice and appeared to be a confident person. It was time to see if he had a sense of humour. She looked him up and down. "There must have been some mistake. I requested a man no older than eighteen and no taller than five feet two inches. You must be at least six feet, and it's been a long time since you were eighteen."

"I'm five-foot-ten and a half, and I agree, there has been a mistake. I ordered a six-foot blonde with huge bazookas."

She could not help smiling. He was grinning like a Cheshire cat and had passed the 'sense of humour test.' "Shall we make the best of it and go for a meal?"

"Why not? Do you know a cheap place?" She was very attractive and had a knee-buckling smile.

"No, but I know a dear place. I'll lead the way."

She analysed her feelings for him as they walked to the restaurant and chatted to see if he passed the 'Do I fancy him test.' He was doing just fine.

"I haven't done very well from the dating agency," he said. "So far, I've had a sex maniac and a religious nutcase."

"I've been unlucky as well," she said. She decided not to ask him how he had discovered that the woman was a sex maniac. "I've only met one man. He was very nice but effeminate. My man must be butch."

"I'm very butch." He looked about. "If you want, I'll kick an old lady on the leg to prove it."

"There's no need. I can see that you're all man."

They had only known each other for a few minutes, and he was already enthralled by this vivacious, petite young woman. She had a bubbly personality and was attractive and sexy, but was it all an act? Time will tell. Women, he was only too aware, could be very good actresses.

She began to relax and enjoy herself as they walked towards the restaurant. They talked as if they had known each other for years. For the first time in a long time, she felt happy, and her many worries drifted away.

She led him into a Chinese restaurant he had never been to before. A friendly Chinese waiter showed them to a table and handed them each a menu.

"I'm not au fait with Chinese food," Timothy said.

"Au fait?" she said. "What does that mean? Are you showing off?"

He smiled. "I'm trying to. I don't want you to think I'm thick."

"There's no need to worry. I can tell that you're a very intelligent man. Did I tell you that I'm a compulsive liar?"

He smiled. "I'm always totally honest, except when I lie."

"We're talking a load of nonsense," she said. "Shall we order our meal?"

"Why not?" He liked her mad sense of humour.

They ordered their meals and sat drinking wine. It was time for one of his jokes. "I used to be a dustman."

She could not tell whether he was being serious or not. "Did you?"

"Yes. I used to empty the bins from behind this restaurant. One day, I couldn't find the bin, so I said to a Chinese man, where's your bin? The Chinese man said, I've bin on holiday. No, I said, where is your wheelie bin? The Chinese man said, I've weely bin on holiday."

She began to laugh. It was a very good joke. "I'd be careful what you say about the Chinese in here. You could end up eating cat instead of chicken."

They had a very enjoyable meal and left the restaurant at ten thirty. He liked everything about Victoria, especially her warm and genuine smile. She seemed to like him, and he was hoping she would want to see him again. "Would you like to go out with me again?" he asked.

She nodded. "When?" She was pleased that he wanted to see her again.

"How about Thursday evening? We could go for a drink."

"Okay. We'll meet outside the Barley Mow at eight."

"Do you want a lift home?" he asked.

"No thanks. I'm in my car."

They said goodbye, and he walked to his car. It had been a very enjoyable evening. As much as he wanted sex and a relationship with an attractive woman, he also wanted a friend. Victoria could be the one for him.

*

Victoria drove home feeling happy. Timothy had passed nearly all the tests. He was interesting and had a sense of humour, and she fancied him. God, did she fancy him. There was only one more test. What was he like in bed? It would be just her luck to discover that he suffered from premature ejaculation or wore women's underwear.

*

On Monday, Timothy drove to his house. Jane was at work, and he was able to load his clothes and some of his possessions into his car without speaking to her. He was not in the mood for a row. He left a note saying that it was over between them and that she could stay until she found a place and wished her well. He then drove back to his lonely hotel room and unpacked. Even though he hated being lonely, it was ten times better than being with Jane. Loneliness did not throw things at you.

He sat down on the bed and lit a cigarette. All he could think about was his date with Victoria on Thursday. She was very attractive and would be perfect for him. He frowned. When he met Jane, he thought she would be perfect for him. For some reason, Jane had changed from an angel into a devil. If Victoria eventually changed into a devil, he would forget about women and get a blow-up doll.

*

Victoria returned home from work on Monday and found Steven singing as he cooked a meal. "You seem happy," she said.

"I am. I'm over the moon. Rose said that she loved me, and I asked her to marry me. We're getting engaged next month and married next year. We could have a double wedding."

She smiled. "I'm pleased for you, but I doubt there'll be a double wedding. I've only just met Tim. I don't know anything about him. All I said was that I liked him."

He pointed the spatula at her. "There's been a change in you. I can see it in your eyes. I think you're really keen on this bloke."

"I've only seen him once. I'll know more on Thursday."

"I can hear two lots of wedding bells," he said.

She dug him in the ribs. Steven was a wonderful person, well-built and as good-looking as Timothy, but for some reason, she was not attracted to him. He lacked something that Timothy had in abundance. It was probably something related to his character. She tried to think what that something could be. The only difference she could think of was that Steven was boyish, and Timothy was manly. She was probably attracted to Timothy because she needed a man in her life, not a boy.

That night in bed, she was able to use her vibrator while thinking about Timothy, and it worked.

*

On Thursday evening, Timothy met up with Victoria in the Barley Mow, and they sat down with a drink. She looked extra special. "You look nice," he said.

"Thank you." She was pleased that he found her attractive. "Have you blown up any buildings today?"

"No. It's not a nine-to-five job. I might not work for months, and then I could be working day and night for three weeks. Some jobs can take months. I have to travel all over the world."

"It sounds interesting," she said.

"It is. I enjoy blowing up buildings. I just don't like the travelling, and I'm seriously thinking of doing something different."

She wanted to know all about him, but first, she wanted their cards laid out on the table. "What are your future plans?"

"I don't really know."

"The reason I joined the dating agency was because I wanted to find someone to spend my life with," she said. "It's no good for us to get to know each other if we're going in different directions."

He nodded. "I agree. What do you want to know about me?"

"The most important thing to me is to have children. Do you want to get married and have a family?"

"Yes. As far as children are concerned, we are definitely going in the same direction. What else do you want to know?"

"Are you religious? She was praying that he was an atheist. If he was religious, it could spoil their relationship before it got started.

He shook his head. "No. Are you?"

"No." She breathed an inner sigh of relief. She could now relax and see where their relationship took them.

He lit a cigarette. "We seem to be going in the same direction. What do we do next?"

She sipped her drink. He seemed very relaxed in her company. "We need to get to know each other. I don't want to wait forever to find my Mr Right, and I think we should see as much of each other as possible so that we'll either fall in love or lose interest. Do you agree?"

"I do. Shall we go out tomorrow night?"

She smiled. "I didn't mean we should see each other every night. We could spend the weekends together and perhaps one night in the week?"

He had an idea. "We could go on holiday together. A week in, say, London would allow us to really get to know each other."

"That's a good idea. He must like her if he was prepared to go on holiday with her. "I could do with a holiday, and I've always wanted to do a bit of sightseeing in London. When were you thinking of going?"

"We could go next week. If you can get time off work?"

"I could get time off work. I'm owed a week's holiday. Okay. Next week it is. Will we be driving, flying or going by train?"

"We could go in my car. Do you want me to book the hotel?"

She nodded. He was obviously keen on her, and she was certainly keen on him. It seemed too good to be true. But was he being honest, and was she seeing the real Timothy, or was he full of baloney? If only she could read his mind.

The evening flew by, and it was suddenly ten-thirty. "I think it's time I went home," she said. "I have to be up early for work tomorrow."

He stood up. "I'll walk you to your car."

They left the public house and walked to the car park. He was hoping to kiss her goodnight. "I enjoy your company, and I'm looking forward to our holiday together."

"I also enjoy your company. I think we should give each other our phone numbers."

"A good idea."

They exchanged phone numbers, and he kissed her briefly on the lips.

"I'll phone you," he said.

"Yes. Goodnight."

"Goodnight," he said.

She climbed into her car and drove off. The kiss had sent her pulse racing, and she was already looking forward to their holiday together.

*

On Friday, while Victoria was at work, her phone rang. She picked it up. "Hello."

"Hello, it's Tim."

"Hello, Tim."

"I've booked the hotel," he said. "Can you be packed and ready for me to pick you up at eight on Saturday morning?"

"Yes. Where are we staying?"

"I can't remember. It's a dead cheap place. Are you at work?"

"Yes, and I'm very busy. I'll have to go. I'll see you on Saturday."

"Yes. Bye."

Victoria put her phone down. It was nice to know that someone was thinking about her.

"Was that your new bloke?" Amy asked.

"Yes."

"Are you still going on holiday with him?"

"Yes. We're going on Saturday. I'm really looking forward to it. I could do with a break. Will you be able to manage?"

"Of course. Just forget about this place and enjoy your holiday. What's his name, and is he Good-looking?"

"Tim and he's dead gorgeous."

Amy smiled. "You lucky devil."

*

Timothy could not stop smiling. He was happier now than he had ever been. Going on holiday with a young woman had never affected him like this before. It must be because he was getting old. Or he could be going mad. Or it could have something to do with a petite young woman with a knockout smile.

He chewed his lip. It was Friday. If he was going to London on Saturday for a week, he should go and see his mother today. He should also go and see his father. It had been months since he had seen his father. He phoned his father. There was no answer. He began to worry. Perhaps his father had been taken ill and was in hospital. He phoned his mother.

"Yes?" she said.

"It's Tim. How are you?"

"I'm fine. Why are you phoning? You don't usually phone."

"I've just phoned Dad, and he didn't answer."

"That's because he's gone into Birmingham for some tests. He won't be home till late. Why were you phoning him?"

"I was going to pay him a visit. He wasn't in the last time I went to see him. I'm going to London for a week, and I thought I'd see both of you before I go."

"You can come and see me," she said. "Why are you going to London?"

"I'll tell you all about it when I see you." It would give them something to talk about.

"You can bring me a box of tissues and a packet of chocolate digestives," she said. "When will you be coming?"

"I've got a bit of shopping to do first. It'll probably be about three."

"If it's nice, I'll probably be outside."

*

Victoria left work a little early. She had so much to do. She could not believe that she was going on holiday with a man who seemed perfect for her. She must be dreaming. Steven was ironing his clothes when she walked into the house. "Why if it isn't Steven," she said. "You can do my ironing if you like?"

He smiled. “No thanks. I hate ironing. I’m just praying that Rose likes it. It’s the one chore I hate.”

“I’m glad you’re here,” she said. “I need to ask you a favour. Could you look after the place while I’m away and feed the cat?”

“Yes, of course. Where are you going?”

“To London. I’m going for a week.”

“Who are you going with? Have you made it up with Katy?”

“No. I’ll never speak to her again for as long as I live. I’m going with Tim.”

He stopped ironing and put his hand on his hip. “You are going with Tim. You’ve only just met him.”

“I know. We want to get to know each other as quickly as possible to see if we’re suited.”

“You must like him,” he said. “I knew when I first went out with Rose that she was the one for me. Do you have that feeling about Tim?”

She nodded. “I’ve never been this sure about a man before. I hope I’m not wrong. One thing for sure, I’ll know after spending a whole week with him.”

“You certainly will. I hope it works out for you.”

“So do I.”

Chapter Six

Timothy lit a cigarette. He was packed and ready to go on holiday and was drinking a cup of coffee. It was seven o'clock on Saturday morning. He suddenly realised that he did not know where Victoria lived. He smiled and picked up his phone.

*

Victoria was in the kitchen of her house, drinking a cup of tea. Her phone rang. She picked it up. "Hello."

"Hello, Vic. It's Tim."

"Hello, Tim. I hope you're not on your way. I've only just got up."

"No. I haven't left yet. I need to know something."

She began to worry. "What do you need to know?" Surely, he was not going to change his mind about the holiday.

"If I'm going to pick you up, I need to know your address."

She smiled. "I thought you knew where I lived. It's ninety-three Castle Lane. I should just be ready by eight o'clock."

"Great. I'll see you then."

*

The sound of Victoria's voice had thrilled him, and Timothy was eager to see her. He filled a bowl with milk and muesli and placed it in the microwave. He had not felt so excited in years. The last time he felt so alive and happy was when he qualified as a member of the SAS. Being badged had been very special to him.

The microwave pinged, and he took the bowl out and placed it on the table. While the milk soaked into the muesli, he sat smoking and thinking. As well as being excited, he was also a little apprehensive and worried that Victoria might not be the dream come true that he thought she was. She was good company, extremely attractive, and would make a wonderful mother, but was he seeing the real Victoria? It could all be an act. The real Victoria could turn out to be a right cow. He would probably know, after the first few days of their holiday, what she was really like.

*

Victoria had just finished packing and was checking her reflection in the mirror when the doorbell rang. She opened the door. It was Timothy. "Hello, Tim. I'm all packed."

"Hello, Vic. You look fantastic."

She smiled. "Thank you. Could you carry my suitcases? I think you're stronger than me."

"I'll see if I can manage."

He put her two large suitcases into the back of the Range Rover, and they climbed in. As he drove off, it began to rain. He switched on the windscreen wipers. "What sort of music do you like? I've got loads of cassettes. I'll let you be the DJ."

She put on a Kenny Rogers cassette. "I like most kinds of music, although I don't like opera, and I'm not too keen on classical music."

"Touché," he said.

She glanced at him. "Are you just being polite, or do you really dislike opera and classical music?"

"I always say what I mean. I don't know anyone who likes opera and classical music. I like sixties and seventies music, Elvis, the Beatles and even Cliff Richard, at a push. It's probably because I'm old."

"I also like the sixties music," she said. "And everyone likes the King. I see you've got some Abba cassettes. I love Abba."

"So do I. I even prefer them to the Beatles. They're a very underrated group."

"I'll put an Abba cassette on next," she said.

They drove onto the M42.

"Can I ask you a question?" he said.

She stared at him. He sounded serious. "Yes."

"Do you act when you meet someone for the first time? When I first met Jane, I thought she was wonderful, but she was acting. It took months for me to see the real Jane. I now think she's horrible."

"I'm nervous when I meet someone for the first time, but I don't think I put on an act. I can confidently say that you're seeing the real me, for what it's worth." She was hoping he liked what he saw.

"I hope so." He glanced at her. She had beautiful eyes. "The reason I asked is because I think you're wonderful. I just hope to God that I'm seeing the real you."

She was thrilled. "I'm pleased that you think I'm wonderful. I'm not wonderful, but you are seeing the real me. What I want to know is, am I seeing the real Timothy? I don't even know your surname."

"It's Freeman. What's your name?"

"It's Dixon."

"Freeman and Dixon," he said. "We sound like a firm of solicitors. You are seeing the real me."

"We know very little about each other," she said. She was hoping that the hint would prompt him into talking about himself.

"I'll tell you my life story, and then you can tell me yours," he said. "We should be in London by the time we finish. I was born at a very early age, and I was very immature when I was six."

She smiled as she listened to him. She even liked the sound of his voice. "That's enough of the jokes. I'd like to know your real-life story."

After they had told each other their life stories, which took just under an hour, they sat in silence and listened to a variety of cassettes.

He felt perfectly relaxed in her company. Relationships were very strange, and the outcome was always impossible to predict. You could never tell how things would turn out. He had only just met Victoria, but he had a good feeling about her. She would be a perfect partner for him.

They had not spoken for some time. She glanced at him. He seemed to be deep in thought. "A penny for them."

"I was thinking about what a shapely bum you have."

She punched him on the arm.

"If you want to know, I was thinking about relationships. We don't have any say in whether we're going to like someone or not; it just happens."

She frowned. What he said did not make sense. "What do you mean? If we don't decide who we like, then who does?"

"No one else is involved. Love and hate are mostly predetermined by our genes."

"That's about as clear as mud. Try explaining what you mean in words of one syllable."

"When we meet someone, we begin to like them or hate them. It's a natural process. We cannot say before we get to know them that we're going to dislike or like them. And we cannot say that we're going to fall in love with someone. You cannot change your feelings that develop about someone. You cannot force yourself to love someone, and you cannot force yourself to hate someone; it just happens."

She thought about what he had said. "I see what you mean. You don't consciously decide to like someone or dislike them. Although I don't believe that it's predetermined by our genes. We probably have an in-built picture of the person we will fall in love with; a complete picture of their personality and their looks, and if the person doesn't fit that picture, we don't fall in love with them."

"You could be right. I'm looking for someone to love, but I can't make it happen. I can get to know as many people as possible, but I don't have any conscious say in what my feelings for them will be. I'll either fall in love or not. I don't even know what this person I'm going to fall in love with will look like. I might think I prefer blondes with a big bust, but I could end up falling in love with a brunette with a small bust."

I hope so, she thought. "Do you think everyone has a predisposed template that the person must measure up to if they're going to fall in love with them? It sounds a bit weird."

"It does sound weird. It might not be that rigid and could work on a points system. For example, you get two points for blue eyes but only one point for brown eyes. Two points for being a brunette and one point for being a blonde. Two points for not being religious and minus ten for being religious, and so on. It would all depend on your personal beliefs, likes and dislikes."

"It probably does work something like that," she said. "When the points reach a hundred, you fall in love. If the points only get to ninety, you remain friends, and if the points go into minus, you begin to hate them."

"I think you're right," he said. "Each person has a different system for deciding on what points are given, which is why one person will hate a particular person, and someone else will love them."

She already knew how complicated people and relationships could be. They had been in London for over thirty minutes and were now in Mayfair. "Are we near the hotel yet?"

"Yes. It's just up the road."

They parked in the hotel car park and carried their luggage into the hotel foyer. It looked quite posh. She began to worry that he had booked just one room in the name of Mr and Mrs Smith. "I hope we have separate rooms?"

He grinned. "I tried to get the bridal suite, but it was already booked. Don't worry, we have separate rooms."

They checked into the hotel and unpacked in their respective rooms, which were on different floors. Her room had a large bed, a television and plenty of wardrobe space. The en-suite bathroom was luxurious and had a bidet, a bath and a shower. They met in the lobby thirty minutes later.

"I have a lousy view from my room," he said. "All I can see is a brick wall and a roof."

"I'm on the top floor," she said. "I can see right across London. I'm starving. Are we going to eat?"

"Yes. This seems like a decent hotel. Shall we eat here?"

She nodded. If her feelings were anything to go by, he had already amassed over ninety points.

They had steak and chips, followed by ice cream and apple pie for dessert. They washed it down with a bottle of wine. Even though at times they sat without speaking, there was no uncomfortable atmosphere. He had never felt so relaxed with a woman before. "Shall we go for a walk?" he suggested when they had finished their wine. "The sun's shining."

"Yes. After that long drive to London, I think I need to stretch my legs."

They left the hotel and walked towards Piccadilly Circus. The streets were crowded. He held her hand. It felt small. A need to protect her flowed through him. It was a new experience for him. "What are we going to do while we're in London?" he asked.

"We could make a list. We could go to the Tate Gallery and the British Museum."

"I've always wanted to go to Madame Tussauds," he said. "And I've never been to the Tower of London."

"We could also go to a theatre," she said. "We need to get a visitor's guide to find out what's on."

They stopped for coffee and eventually ended up walking along the side of the Thames as the sun sank over the tops of the buildings.

"I'm enjoying our little holiday," she said.

"So am I. Shall we go and find a restaurant? I'm in need of sustenance."

"A good idea."

While eating their meal, they made a list of what they intended to do. The Tower of London was at the top of the list.

"I booked separate rooms, but it doesn't mean I don't want to sleep with you," he said. "Sex, they say, is the acid test of a relationship." A mental picture of Debbie lying on her bed with her legs in the air flashed into his mind.

"I suppose it is, but we'll be keeping to separate rooms. I want to use this holiday to get to know you completely. We'll then give our relationship the acid test, but only if we fall for each other." She was already falling for him.

He was disappointed, but was hoping she might change her mind after a couple of days. He hated sleeping alone, especially when he was with such an attractive woman.

It was eleven-thirty, and they were travelling in the hotel lift to their separate rooms. They were both very tired and were almost falling asleep on their feet.

She was tempted to ask him to come to her room to see the view and to have a cup of coffee, but she decided against it. She was determined not to sleep with him while on this holiday. If she were alone with him in her room, her resolve might weaken.

When the lift stopped at his floor, he pulled her into his arms, hugged her, and kissed her gently on the lips. He did not want to put pressure on her, so he kept his hands away from her nice bits. "Goodnight, sweetheart," he said.

"Goodnight," she said. "I'll see you in the dining room tomorrow at eight o'clock."

"Eight o'clock. He pressed the button to keep the lift doors open. "I'll need a bit of a lie-in. Driving always tires me out. Can't we make it ten o'clock?"

"No. We have a full day ahead of us. We'll meet at nine o'clock to give you a bit of a lie-in, but don't be late."

"I'll try not to."

He stepped out of the lift. As he walked to his room, he took stock of the situation. Things could not be better. He not only fancied Victoria, he also liked her and enjoyed her company. If she were not acting, she would do for him. He wondered if Debbie had found a suitable man. She was a good person, and he hoped she would eventually be as fortunate as he appeared to be.

*

Victoria undressed, slipped on her nightdress and crawled into bed. They had been together all day. By now, their psyches would be totting up the points. The way she felt about him, he already had nearly a hundred points. She was lonely and was frightened that she would rush into the relationship and fall in love with falling in love. Despite her need to love and be loved, she was determined to take her time and let her feelings develop naturally. She was also determined to be in love with him before she slept with him. If only she knew how he felt about her.

*

Victoria woke up at ten to eight in the morning. She climbed out of bed and danced around the room. She had not felt this good in a very long time. She thought back. The last time she had been this happy was when she had fallen in love with Richard, a boy who had lived on her road when she was fourteen. The one-sided love affair lasted for about three months. Her phone rang. She picked it up. "Yes?"

"It's Amy. I can't find the keys to the office."

"They're in the peg bag. Are there any problems?"

"No, so stop worrying and enjoy yourself. Is Tim as nice as you thought he was?"

"Even nicer. He's a dish. We spent the whole day together, and I'm liking him more and more."

"Did you do it last night?" Amy asked.

"No. I wanted to, but I don't want to rush things. I don't want our relationship to be just sexual. I've decided not to sleep with him while we're on holiday. By the end of the week, I'll know the real Timothy, and if he's the right one for me, I will then sleep with him."

"I hope it works out," Amy said. "I'll see you next week."

"Yes, bye."

*

Timothy overslept and woke up at nine-fifteen. He jumped out of bed. He should have arranged for an early morning call. He showered and dressed in record time and ran downstairs without waiting for the lift. Victoria was waiting for him in the dining room, sitting at a table. He spread his hands as he walked towards her. "I'm sorry I'm late. Have you been waiting long?"

"Yes, and I'm starving."

He kissed her on the cheek and sat down. "I'm usually very punctual. I must have been extra tired." He picked up the menu. "Let's order."

They ordered a traditional English breakfast and a pot of tea.

"According to the weather forecast, it's going to be a nice day," she said.

"According to how the woman I'm sitting with looks, it's going to be a wonderful day.

She smiled. "So, you haven't gone off me yet?"

"Far from it." He looked about, as if he were worried that someone might hear what he was about to say. "Don't tell anyone, but I think you're spiffing."

"It's no good trying to impress me with your big words. I'm only a working-class lass."

"And I thought you were a princess."

"We're talking nonsense again," she said.

He smiled. "I know. It's great, isn't it?"

She felt totally relaxed in his company, as if she had known him for years. If this were a dream, she did not want to wake up.

They had breakfast and went for a walk. The sky above them was bright blue.

He held her hand. "The weather forecast was right."

"Yes. She was conscious of his hand. "It's a perfect day for sightseeing. Where are we going first?"

"We could visit Madame Tussauds first."

By the time they had walked around Madame Tussauds, Victoria was forced to admit that she had fallen for Timothy lock, stock and barrel. He had already amassed a hundred points. The feelings she had for him were unmistakable and frighteningly powerful. He was laughing at one of his jokes. He had wonderful eyes. The most important thing was, she trusted him completely. She would trust him with her life.

Why had she fallen for Timothy and not for one of the hundreds of men she had met before? What was different about him? He was good-looking, but she had met dozens of good-looking men. Whatever it was that made a person fall in love had happened to her. What was alarming was how quickly it had happened. She glanced at him. Was he also falling in love with her? It was obvious that he desired her and liked her, but did he love her? One thing for sure, she was not going to sleep with him until he had fallen in love with her.

They walked out of Madame Tussaud's. He looked at her. "How do you feel?"

"What do you mean?" Surely, he could not tell that she had fallen for him.

"About going to the Tower next?"

"Oh. I think I need a drink first."

They had two drinks and took a taxi to the Tower of London. It was later, while they were drinking coffee, that it hit him. The feelings he had were very powerful. As Victoria drank her coffee, he glanced at her. He had never felt like this about anyone before. She was beautiful.

He sipped his coffee. Why had it taken so long for him to fall in love? He was nearly fifty and had had dozens of girlfriends. Why should it happen now? And why should he fall in love with Victoria? It was a bit of a mystery. His love for her was amazing, and he had not even slept with her. Perhaps this feeling that was overwhelming him would go when he had slept with her, and perhaps it would not. He prayed that he would always feel this way about her.

They visited the Tate Gallery in the afternoon and then had a meal at a posh restaurant. It was such a warm evening, they decided to give the theatre a miss and have a walk along the side of the Thames. They strolled along arm in arm in silence.

He would have to tell her how he felt. It might persuade her to sleep with him. It took three drinks in the lounge of their hotel before he had plucked up sufficient courage. It was eleven o'clock in the evening. He held her hand. "I need to tell you something."

He looked very serious. What he was about to say was probably going to upset her. "You're married?"

"No. I've never been married. Why did you think I was going to tell you that I was married?"

"I don't know. You looked very serious. What do you want to tell me?" He still looked serious. "Is what you're going to say nice or horrible?"

"It's nice. What would you have done if I'd told you that I was married with four kids?"

"I don't know. Just tell me what you've got to say."

"I think I've got to know you by now, Vic. Do you like me calling you Vic?"

"Yes. Just get on with it." She was bursting to know what he needed to tell her.

"I think I now know the real you." He was looking into her eyes. She had beautiful eyes.

"You do know the real me." He was probably going to tell her a joke. "What do you want to tell me?"

"I've fallen in love with you."

She stared into his eyes. "Have you?"

"Yes."

Her mind seemed to swirl around. It was what she had been praying for. "How do you know?"

"What do you mean?"

"How do you know you've fallen in love with me? Have you fallen in love before?"

He shook his head. "No. It's all new to me."

"So how do you know it's love? It might be desire."

"It's not desire. I began to desire you when we first met, and I'm an expert at desiring attractive women. This is very different."

She was thrilled by what he was saying, and she wanted to hug him. "Explain how you feel."

He leaned back in his seat and had a drink of lager. "It's difficult to explain."

"Then how do you know it's love? Tell me why you think you love me?" She had to know exactly how he felt.

"It's more than love. I've loved before. Until now, I thought I'd been in love at least three times. I now realise that I've never been in love." He looked up at a large chandelier. "The feeling is sort of steady and very powerful. It's unmistakable." He spread his hands. "I just want to spend the rest of my life with you."

"I'm glad you've fallen for me," she said. "When did I get the hundred points?"

"While we were at the Tower."

"You got the hundred points when we were in Madame Tussauds," she said. "I hope it's the real thing."

"So do I." He was pleased that she had also fallen in love with him. "I hope our love lasts forever. What has always amazed me is how two people who believe that they've fallen in love can fall out of love very quickly and end up hating each other. It doesn't make sense."

"I don't think those people were ever in love," she said. "They might have loved each other, but they were not in love. You could never hate someone you've fallen in love with."

"That's what I believe. He looked at his watch. It's getting late." He was hoping to be invited up to her room.

"Yes." She stood up. "It's been a long day."

He stood up. "Are you going to invite me up for a cup of coffee?"

"No. I'm too tired to fight you off."

"Then don't fight me off."

"I don't want to rush our relationship," she said. "I need a few days to get used to the idea that we're in love. It's happened so quickly."

"I suppose I can wait a few days," he said.

She smiled. He looked so disappointed. "I suppose I could rush our relationship a little and invite you up to my room tomorrow night."

He grinned. "It's a date."

*

They spent the next day sightseeing. She could tell what was on his mind. It was also on her mind. As much as she desired him, she was worried that sex would not be perfect. It would be a disaster if they did not satisfy each other. Her worries about sex were deferred for at least five days by the arrival of her period late in the afternoon. She left it until they were having a drink in the lounge of their hotel at eleven o'clock, before telling him.

"I've had a visitor," she said.

"What visitor?"

"I have the same visitor each month. He usually stays for about five days."

"Oh, no," he groaned.

"You'll have to wait," she said. "You can come to my room for a coffee if you like. We can sit on the balcony and admire the view."

They took the lift to her floor, and he followed her into her room. "We should have come last week."

“Be patient,” she said. “Five days is not forever.”

Chapter Seven

Timothy and Victoria's holiday came to an end, and they drove back to the Midlands on Saturday afternoon. He was sexually frustrated but was trying not to show it. Their holiday together, apart from not having sex, had been a total success. He had found the woman of his dreams. She was everything he wanted. If the sex was right between them, he intended to ask her to marry him and start a family. Even if sex was a flop, he still intended to marry her, or at least to ask her. He could not live without her. She was now a permanent part of his life, or at least he hoped so.

"Will I see you on Sunday?" he asked.

"No. I need a day to sort myself out and get things ready for work."

He felt disappointed. "I hope you're not going off me?"

She smiled. "No, not yet. I'd love to see you, but I've got a pile of washing and ironing to do. You can take me out on Monday. We can go back to your hotel room and spend the night there if you like."

"I do like, although don't expect much. The hotel's a bit of a dump."

He dropped her off at her house, took her luggage in and drove off. His whole life had changed. Instead of drifting through life like a ship without a rudder, he now had plans and dreams. Life could not be better.

*

Victoria sat down at the kitchen table. Sooty jumped onto her lap. "I've met a wonderful man, Sooty."

She stroked the cat. Timothy had only just left, and she was already missing him. He was the man she had spent her whole adult life looking for. He would make a perfect husband and father. Her one worry was sex. She had small breasts, and her bum was bigger than it used to be. When he kissed her goodbye, he had a good feel of her body and seemed to like what he felt. Everything would be revealed and resolved on Monday night.

*

On Monday afternoon, Timothy went to see his father. After ringing the bell and banging on the door for five minutes, he began to worry that something serious had happened. He walked into the back garden and found his father in the greenhouse. "Keeping busy, Dad?"

"Oh, hello, Tim. Yes. I like to keep active. How're things?"

"Fine." The sight of his father dismayed him. He looked old and haggard, and for the first time, he looked his age.

"Let's go in the house and have a cup of tea," his father said.

"I could do with a cuppa." Timothy followed his father into the house and sat down in the kitchen. The house looked as it did twenty years ago.

His father looked over his glasses at him. "You look better than when I saw you the last time. Are you feeling more like your old self?"

"Yes. I feel really happy. I've met a woman. Her name's Victoria."

"What happened to Jane?" his father asked as he filled the kettle.

"I've finished with her. We were not right for each other. I've just spent a week with Victoria in London. I'm going to ask her to marry me."

"I'm pleased you've found someone," his father said. "A man needs a woman. It can get very lonely on your own."

Timothy felt that his father was hinting that he did not visit him often enough. "The last time I called to see you, there was no one in. I was also intending to visit you when you went to Birmingham for some tests."

His father nodded. "Your mother told me that you were finishing with Jane. She also told me that you were thinking of having children. You've left it a bit late."

"I know. I must be going mad." Timothy lit a cigarette. "What's wrong?"

His father put the tea bags in the teapot and turned to look at him. "What do you mean?"

"Are you ill? You don't look well."

His father sat down. "I've not felt well for a long time. I suppose I knew I had something. I've now had it confirmed."

"How serious is it?" Timothy asked.

"The doctor said I've only got a few months to live. It's cancer. I might last a year."

"Have you told Mum?"

"No."

"You should tell her. She needs to know."

"It will depress her if I tell her. She's only got me. You rarely visit her."

"I'll make an effort to see her more often. Mum already knows you're ill."

"How could she?" The kettle boiled. His father stood up and poured the boiling water into the teapot. "I haven't said a word."

"Mum's not daft. You look ill. You look half dead."

His father smiled. "I am half dead." He leaned on the worktop. "I suppose I should tell her."

"You should." He felt sorry for his father.

"I'll tell her today," his father said. "I suppose she has a right to know."

Timothy stood up and hugged his father. His father's body felt thin and bony. "If I get a move on, you just might see your first grandchild."

"You're not even married yet." His father patted Timothy's back, released him and put milk and sugar into the cups. "Even if you got married tomorrow, I'd still have to wait nine months. It's good to know that you'll be having children. It's cheered me up."

*

Victoria was a nervous wreck when Monday evening arrived. She had a shower, put on her sexiest underwear and her favourite dress, and met Timothy in the Barley Mow. He was smiling. She felt like saying, Let's have sex before our meal to get it over with. "Where are we going for a meal?"

He kissed her on the lips. "You look delicious. To that place just off Mell Square. Let's have a drink first."

She watched him get the drinks. She felt like a sixteen-year-old girl on her first date. It was not that sex frightened her. She knew all about men and what they liked. What worried her was the need to totally satisfy a man who had popped into her life as if in answer to a prayer. It was very important to her that sex with Timothy was perfect.

He placed the drinks on the table and sat down. "Tonight's the night."

"I know. I'm just praying that you're not a bondage freak or wear women's underwear under your jeans. If I see a whip or handcuffs, I'm off."

He smiled. "You have no need to worry. I'm quite normal. I like tits and bums and things like that. I also like different positions. I'll show you what I mean later."

"I bet you will," she said.

During their meal, he tried to engage in a meaningful conversation, but was not doing very well. All he could think about was having sex. Several times, he lost his train of thought and finally gave up talking and sat listening to her. She had beautiful, full lips. He had always liked women with full lips. Thin lips make a person look mean.

"Are you listening to me?" she asked.

"Yes. At least I'm trying to. What were you saying?"

She shook her head. "It doesn't matter."

"Shall we make a move so that I can have your body?" he asked.

"Why not? I've got nothing better to do." She finished off her wine and stood up. He stood up, held her hand and led her out of the restaurant like a virgin being led to the sacrificial altar. The touch of his hand sent a tingling sensation through her body.

He could not wait to get his hands on her body, but tried not to rush as they walked to his car, and he drove at a reasonable speed to his hotel. "Don't expect much," he said.

"Why? Aren't you very good at sex?"

He smiled. "I was referring to my hotel suite. I'm pretty good at sex. I've been known to make it last for two minutes."

She smiled. He seemed very confident about having sex. "It looks as if we're in for a wonderful time."

"My hotel suite is little more than a bedsit, and it's a bit of a dump," he said. "I can't afford a penthouse suite. It has a small bathroom, an average-sized lounge, and a small bedroom."

"As long as the sheets are clean, I don't mind," she said.

"Clean sheets and a clean duvet cover were put on this morning," he said. "I've also put a bottle of wine and a strawberry cheesecake in the fridge."

She felt nervous as they entered his hotel suite. It was a bit of a dump, and the décor was only meant to be seen at night with the lights turned down low. It could also be tidier.

He led her into the bedroom. "This is the bedroom," he said.

"I thought it was when I saw the bed. Shall we get undressed?"

"Yes. I've got a condom under the pillow." He began to get undressed. He was watching her as she took off her coat and then her dress. He was not concentrating on what he was doing, and as he tried to pull off his trousers while standing on one leg, his foot caught, and he fell onto the bed.

She burst out laughing. "Do you want any help?"

He stood up. "I think I can manage." She was standing by the bed, wearing pants and a bra. "You look beautiful."

"You're just saying that."

"I'm not." He threw his trousers across the room and climbed onto the bed. "Come here, and I'll show you how I feel."

She climbed onto the bed, and he pulled her into his arms. He kissed her on the lips and squeezed her breasts. Their tongues touched, and her world turned into liquid pleasure. She had never felt like this before. Her body was burning with a powerful need.

He rolled on the condom and climbed on top of her. Foreplay would have to wait. He was bursting with desire. She looked good enough to eat. He pulled her pants to one side and pushed into her. His desire was now out of control.

She bit his neck and dug her nails into his back as her body filled with desire. She could feel him thrusting deep inside her. For several seconds, the pleasure was so great it was almost painful. Her body and mind then exploded and shattered into a thousand pieces. "Ohhh," she cried softly. "Ohhhhh. Ooooohhhhh."

He pushed deep into her, squeezed her breasts and climaxed. It was as fantastic as he had expected it to be, and the power of the ejaculation shook his body.

When his body and mind had returned to normal, he kissed her neck. "I'm sorry I rushed things. It barely lasted two minutes. I needed you so much. I think you just managed to climax."

"I did." She hugged him. "I also needed you." He had passed the last test with flying colours.

"I think you'll do for me," he said.

"And you'll do for me."

"I'd like to ask you to marry me, but I don't want to get out of bed to get down on one knee," he said.

She was thrilled. He had obviously enjoyed the sex as much as she had. "You can do it lying down if you like."

He took her hand. "Will you marry me and spend the rest of your life with me and let me make love to you every night and sometimes in the day?"

She kissed him on the lips. "Yes. Will you get off me? I can hardly breathe."

He rolled off her, and they lay side by side. "This flat is a right dump," he said.

"It might help if you tidied it up." She frowned. "What is that on the light shade?"

"It's one of my socks. I was in a hurry to get undressed."

"I think you need a woman to look after you," she said.

"You could be right."

She hugged him. She had never been happier. She had found her Mr Right.

Chapter Eight

Timothy was sitting in the lounge in Victoria's house, listening to a cassette. They had been living together for six weeks and had not argued once. She had not changed and was still attractive, sexy and fun to be with. It had been a long time since he had felt so happy and content with his lot in life. The cherry on his cake of happiness was sex. It was amazing and was even better than with Jane. They had sex nearly every day, in various positions and in different places. The most unusual place to date was on the grass in the sunshine next to the River Avon in Stratford-upon-Avon. What he enjoyed the most was just being with her. They often had long discussions, but even when sitting with her without speaking, he felt content.

Victoria walked into the room. "Are you still listening to Roger Whitaker? You'll wear that cassette out."

"It helps me relax. Are you cooking, or are we going out for a meal?"

"I'm cooking." She stared at him. "It's not healthy for you to spend most of your time sitting down. You need to be more active."

He had to agree. He was putting on weight. "I intend to start going to the gym again."

She sat down. "I think it's time to make plans. We're in love, and we get on together perfectly."

He turned the volume of the cassette down. "What plans?"

"First, we need to buy a larger house. You can sell your house, and I'll sell mine. We should then be able to afford a house in Dorridge."

He sat watching her as she flicked through the pages of the television magazine. She was a very attractive woman. "Jane still lives in my house."

"Then tell her to leave. She's had plenty of time to find a place. When we have a bigger house with a nice garden, we can get married. We can start for a baby whenever you feel up to it."

He smiled. "Do I have any say in these things?"

"No. It's all been decided."

His phone rang. He took it out of his pocket. "Yes?"

"It's Roger. I'll be at your golf club in thirty minutes."

"I'll be there." Timothy put his phone back into his pocket. "I'm going out. It could be work."

"I hope not. You could be away for weeks. I thought you were going to look for another job."

"I am. I'll tell him that this will be the last job." He stood up. "I just don't know what else I can do. I have very specific qualifications. I'll get Thursday's newspaper and see what jobs are on offer. I won't be long."

"What about your meal?" She dreaded the thought of him going away for weeks on end.

"I'll get something at the club."

Roger was waiting for him in the golf club lounge, sitting at a table. He looked like a tired old man. "What are you drinking, Major?"

"A fruit juice. I'm not allowed to drink alcohol."

Timothy bought the drinks and sat down. "Did you tell H we wanted to call it a day?"

Roger nodded. "I did, and H agreed and said that we could disband. Two days later, he phoned me and asked us to do just one more job. I tried to put him off. I even told him that I was not one hundred per cent fit, but he said that it was very important, and so I said we would do it."

"It has to be the last job," Timothy said.

"It will be. I can guarantee it."

"What's the job?" Timothy asked.

Roger lit a cigar. "I'm not supposed to smoke. How can I live without smoking and drinking? Fuck the lot of them." He blew out a cloud of smoke. "This op is different. I don't know all the details yet. H said that when we know who the target is, we can pull out if we want to."

Timothy frowned. "Why would we want to pull out? We've never refused an op before."

"It must have something to do with the target. I think the target's well-known. It won't bother me. A job's a job. We drive to London on Monday. Be ready by zero six hundred hours."

"I'll be ready. How long will we be away?"

"I don't know. H said it could be a few days, weeks or even months."

"Fucking hell," Timothy said. "I'm getting married. This must definitely be the last job."

"It will be." Roger frowned with one eye. His black eye patch made him look like an actor. "I thought you said you'd walked out on Jane, and now you're getting married. Why the change of heart? I never took you to be the marrying sort."

"I'm not getting married to Jane. I don't intend to speak to her again. I've met someone else, and I've promised her that I'll be getting a regular job. And anyway, we're all too old now. They should get themselves a younger team."

"I agree," Roger said. "I can promise you that it will be the last op. We'll be getting £100,000 each for this op. I suppose it's some sort of bonus for all the hard work we've done in the past."

"A hundred grand will be a nice retirement bonus," Timothy said. "It's better than getting a watch."

Roger leaned back in his seat. "I'm not doing it for the money. I'm doing it for H. He's been good to me over the years. According to H, this op is extremely important to him and to national security. If the target is not eliminated, there could be anarchy."

Timothy could not understand how one person could cause anarchy. "I wonder who it is?"

"God knows. The target, apparently, wants to bring down the monarchy."

Timothy lit a cigarette. "I used to be a royalist. I don't give a damn now. I don't think it would make the slightest difference to this country if they were to get rid of the monarchy. The Queen is little more than a tourist attraction and a diplomat, and if they did get rid of the monarchy, there's no way it would cause anarchy."

"You've certainly changed your tune," Roger said. "You used to worship the Queen."

"I know. I've changed in many ways. Don't get me wrong; I don't hate the royals; I just see them now as ordinary people."

"They're far from ordinary," Roger said. "They're very rich and very powerful."

Timothy blew out a cloud of cigarette smoke. "I agree, but they don't have the power and influence they used to have."

"Maybe not, but they still have considerable power and influence, and I would not like to cross them."

Timothy has a drink of lager. "I used to be proud of this country. Not anymore. It's now full of foreigners who have allegiance to other countries. Most of Birmingham is now black and Asian. Enoch Powell was right; the streets of this country are already running red with blood."

"It's not the blacks," Roger said. "They regard this as their country, and they've integrated. It's the Asians with their own language, dress and religion that's causing the trouble. They regard white people as trash. They have a word for us that's as derogatory as nigger is to the blacks. I forgot what it is. I think it's kaffir."

Timothy nodded. "I know what you mean. Asians do think that they're better than us. This country will end up divided into no-go areas. There'll be areas for whites and areas for Asians. I dread to think where it will all end."

Roger sipped his orange juice and pulled a face. "The future's something I'll not have to worry about. Sod it. I need a proper drink." He stood up. "Do you want a refill?"

"Yes, why not?" Timothy watched Roger walk to the bar. He had lost weight and now looked more like a pensioner than a film star. He felt sorry for him.

Timothy returned to Victoria's house at nine-thirty. She let him in, and he followed her into the lounge. "I forgot my key," he said.

"Was it work?" she asked.

"Yes." He sat down. The television was not switched on. "It's quiet in here."

"I was reading." She sat down, and Sooty jumped onto her lap. She began to stroke the cat. "When will you be leaving?"

"On Monday. I told him that it was definitely my last job."

"How long will you be away?"

"I'm not sure. It might only be for a few days, but it could be for several weeks."

She felt disappointed. "I'm not looking forward to sleeping on my own. Did you really tell him that it would be your last job?"

"Yes. We'll get married as soon as I get back. That's if you still want me?"

"I've got no choice. All the intelligent, handsome men are already married."

"Thanks a lot," he said.

"You can make a cup of tea," she said. She was pretending to be happy, but was far from feeling it. She hated the thought of spending even one night on her own.

*

Victoria got up with Timothy at four-thirty on Monday morning, and while he packed his things, she cooked him breakfast. She felt miserable. "If you are away for weeks, will you be able to come home on the weekends?" she asked.

"No. When we start a job, we work non-stop until it's finished. It's a very complicated process wiring up buildings to be demolished."

"Where is this job?" she asked.

"I'm not sure. I haven't been told the details. Our first stop is London. I've been told to take my passport, so it's probably abroad."

The Transit van pulled up outside Victoria's house at exactly six o'clock.

Before leaving the house, he kissed and hugged her. "I'll phone as soon as I know what's happening."

"Be careful, and don't blow yourself up," she said.

"I'll try not to," he said as he opened the front door.

She watched him walk down the path with his suitcases and climb into the back of the van. She was going to miss him.

Timothy closed the van door and made himself comfortable on a cushion next to Roger, John and Peter. Matthew was driving. "It's about time we had proper seats in here."

"It beats taking the bus," John said. "Major says that you're getting married, Tim?"

"Yes. I'll be getting married when I finish this op."

"Is she beautiful?" Peter asked.

"I think so."

"Have you met her mother yet?" John asked.

Timothy shook his head. "No."

"I would if I were you," Peter said. "You'll then know how she'll look in a few years."

"My mother-in-law used to work at the airport," John said. "She used to kick-start the Boeing 747s."

"My mother-in-law looks like a Boeing 747 in high heels," Peter said.

They were all tired, so the jokes quickly dried up, and they slept during the journey to London. They booked into a hotel, and Roger went to see H. London seemed less friendly without Victoria. They watched a film and drank coffee. Timothy was eager to know who the target was. He was also hoping the operation would only take a few days.

Roger returned at nine-thirty. He switched off the television and sat down. "There's been a change of plan. The op's been postponed. It's too risky to hit the target in this country and has been rescheduled for a later date." He looked at Peter. "Is it safe to talk?"

Peter nodded. "Is it the same target?"

"Yes. We'll be going to France in about a week. The target's a woman. She's a celebrity. Does anyone have a problem with that?"

No one spoke.

"Who is the target?" John asked. "Is she a film star?"

"She's more famous than a film star. It's Princess Diana."

Peter laughed. "Like fuck it is."

Roger pulled a cigar out of his top pocket, looked at it and then put it back. "I'm serious. The target is Princess Diana."

They sat in silence for a few seconds.

Timothy was shocked. "Why? Why in God's name does she need to be killed?"

Peter put his cup of coffee on the table. He looked amazed. "Why the fuck do they want her dead?"

"I had a long chat with H," Roger said. "Apparently, for some time, Princess Diana has been hell-bent on discrediting the Royal Family. She's a loose cannon. They have her house and car bugged, and they know every word she says and who she meets. They now believe that she's obsessed with bringing down the monarchy."

"How the fuck can she destroy the monarchy?" John asked. "She might be a loose cannon, but she's no match for the Queen."

"I think she's already done all she can do to discredit the royals," Timothy said. "Did you see that Panorama programme on television when Martin Bashir interviewed her? It's obvious that she hates Prince Charles and the Queen. She's already rubbished the royals. What else can she do?"

"She intends to get married again and have a baby," Roger said.

Peter looked confused. "And what harm can that do? Most women want to get married and have children."

"She intends to marry a Muslim," Roger said.

Timothy was against hitting Princess Diana. He regarded her as a decent woman. "That's not reason enough to want her dead."

"How can marrying a Muslim bring down the monarchy?" Matthew asked.

"If she marries a Muslim," Roger said, "she'll have to become a Muslim and bring up her children as Muslims. They think she's planning to marry Dodi Al-Fayed."

John took a cigarette packet out of his pocket. "There's got to be something more to it than just marrying Dodi Al-Fayed and becoming a Muslim. This is bullshit."

"That's what I thought at first," Roger said. "It's very complicated. If she marries a Muslim and has children, they will be half-brothers or sisters to William and Harry, and so when William becomes king, he will not only have a Muslim stepfather, he'll also have Muslim siblings."

Matthew looked shocked. "Fucking hell. I see what you mean. There's no way the Royal Family will welcome Muslims into the fold. If Dodi and Diana did get married, the entire Al-Fayed family would be present at royal functions, and that would include Mohamed Al-Fayed."

"There'll be fucking riots," John said. "Most people in this country hate Muslims."

"They'll not be able to make William king if he has Muslim brothers and sisters," Roger said. "I'm not keen on hitting Princess Diana, but I can understand what harm she could do to the Royal Family by marrying a Muslim."

John offered Timothy and Peter a cigarette, and they lit up.

Timothy could now understand why they wanted Princess Diana dead. The country was full of racists, and if she did have Muslim children, it could cause anarchy. Even so, it was one operation he would rather not be a part of.

Peter got a can of lager out of the fridge. "I need a proper drink. I'm sick of coffee."

John, Matthew and Timothy also got a can of lager out of the fridge, and Roger made a cup of coffee. They sat drinking in silence for a while.

"Who wants her dead?" Peter asked. "Is it the Queen, Prince Charles or MI5?"

Roger shook his head. "God knows. My relationship with H is on a need-to-know basis. I would guess it's a decision made by the men in grey suits, known affectionately as the palace protectors. They're a fanatical lot."

"The Queen and Prince Charles hate Princess Diana," Matthew said. "I bet they've got something to do with it. And with Princess Diana out of the way, Prince Charles will be able to marry Camilla. We'll probably end up with a Queen Camilla."

Timothy had a long drink of lager. He felt like getting drunk. The thought of killing Princess Diana had upset him, and he was glad that he was still taking antidepressants. "I don't think killing Princess Diana is the answer. It could cause more problems than it solves. What will her two sons think when they find out?"

"They will never know," Roger said. "Her death is to be made to look like an accident."

"They'll eventually find out what happened," Peter said. "The world was told that JFK was killed by Lee Harvey Oswald and that it was not a conspiracy. Everyone now knows that the FBI and the CIA conspired to kill him and then tried to cover it up. There's even talk of the mafia being involved."

"JFK upset the powerful arms dealers, who were set to make billions out of the Vietnam War, and so they killed him," John said. "Princess Diana has upset powerful monarchists, and so they intend to kill her. The moral is, don't upset powerful people."

Roger pointed a finger at them. "There must be no loose ends. It has to appear to be an accident. There can be no slip-ups. The job has been given to us because we're the most efficient and trusted team in the country. They've decided that it'll be a car accident. They've already decided on how and have selected several likely locations. They'll be contacting us in a few days, so be packed and ready."

"Now we know why they're paying us a hundred grand each," John said.

The team drove back to the Midlands in the van. The others did not seem too bothered about the high profile of the target, but Timothy was. It disturbed him. He was convinced that if they made an effort, the palace protectors could find another way to prevent Princess Diana from marrying a Muslim and having his children. He suspected that powerful people wanted her dead and that any excuse would be good enough.

*

Victoria could not sleep. After spending several hours in her large empty bed, she got up, made a cup of coffee and sat in the lounge, watching the television with Sooty on her lap. She missed Timothy and was praying that he would only be away for a few days. It was just after two am, and a film had just started. She was hoping the film would take her mind off her worries.

Her phone rang. She picked it up. "Yes?"

"It's me," Timothy said.

"Are you all right?" she asked.

"Yes. I'm very happy."

"I'm pleased you've phoned me, but why are you phoning at two in the morning?"

"I didn't realise it was so late."

"When will you be coming home?" she asked.

"Any second now."

She frowned. "What do you mean? Where are you?"

"Looking through the window at you."

She turned around and smiled. He was grinning at her through the lounge window. She put the phone down, ran into the hall and opened the front door. "I didn't expect you for weeks." She threw her arms around him and hugged him. "I don't want you to go away again."

"I have to." He walked inside and closed the door. "The job's only been postponed. I'll be going away in a few days. They need to sort out the contracts."

She felt disappointed. "For how long?"

"I don't know."

She watched him take off his coat. "I hope it will be the last time you will ever leave home?"

"It will be."

"I want you to get a job in the Midlands," she said. "I don't want to sleep alone."

He kissed her on the lips. "Don't worry. I've told them that it'll be my last job. Is there any chance of a cup of tea?"

"I'll make one," she said. "Do you want anything to eat?"

"No. I want a drink, and then I want you."

She smiled.

Chapter Nine

Timothy was sitting in bed, smoking. It was eleven o'clock in the evening. Victoria had just gone to the toilet. He sighed. The knowledge of who the target was had been playing on his mind. He had always regarded himself as a hard man, and he was not used to being plagued by his conscience. It was probably because he had grown to like Princess Diana. His logical mind told him that if Princess Diana did marry a Muslim and had children, there was a possibility that it could bring down the monarchy, and it could even cause anarchy, but it still felt wrong.

Princess Diana had grown up and was no longer a spoiled little rich girl. She was now a decent woman and did a considerable amount of charity work. His argument against killing her was that the monarchy would eventually fall, with or without Princess Diana's help, so why kill her? Either way, it was not his problem. He was there to just do or die.

Victoria walked into the bedroom, climbed into bed and cuddled up to her dream man. They had just made love without using a condom. "Is it more enjoyable for you to make love without using a condom?" she asked.

"Yes."

"Why?"

"I don't know. It just is. I suppose it's more natural."

She was beginning to worry about him. There was something on his mind. Perhaps he was not ready to start a family. "Do you want a baby?"

"Yes. Of course I do. I can't wait."

She kissed his shoulder. "Good." Something else must be bothering him. He was probably worrying about his father, who only had a short time to live.

She fell asleep with his arms around her.

She opened her eyes. Timothy was saying something. "Pardon?"

"It has to be done," he said.

She looked at the clock. It was three o'clock. "What has to be done? Why can't it wait till tomorrow?"

"I don't have a choice," he said.

"What are you talking about?" she asked. "It's the middle of the night. Can't we talk about it tomorrow?"

"The monarchy will fall," he said. "There'll be anarchy."

She suddenly realised that he was talking in his sleep. She smiled. "Go to sleep."

"It's the last op," he said. "Give me the gun. I'll do it. The target is a woman. The op could take several weeks."

She frowned. "What's an op?"

"It must look like an accident," he said. "Diana could bring down the monarchy."

"Who is Diana?" she asked. She was probably an ex-girlfriend.

He began to roll his head from side to side. "It's wrong to kill a woman. It has to be done. It's the last op."

She sat up. What was he talking about? Who was going to kill a woman? Was someone going to kill Diana? If only he would answer her questions. "What woman is going to be killed?"

He lifted his head off the pillow as if he were looking at someone. "Die, lady, die," he whispered. He then turned over and began to snore.

She lay down. Why would he dream about a lady called Diana? Surely, he was not dreaming about Princess Diana? Who would want to kill Princess Diana?

*

After cooking breakfast and while drinking a cup of tea in the kitchen, Victoria thought about what Timothy had said in his sleep. She looked in the lounge to check where he was. He was sitting in the conservatory, reading the newspaper. She picked up the dictionary and looked up the word op. There were six meanings. In the context of how Timothy had used the word op, it was probably an abbreviation for operation. It was his last operation. Op was an unusual word to use.

She then looked up the word target, in case there was more than one meaning. There were ten meanings, although the most likely meaning of the word target was something people aimed at. She felt just as confused. If only she could ask someone what the words meant. Steven. He might be able to help her.

She picked up the phone and phoned Steven. She moved nearer to the window so that she could see Timothy.

"Hello?" Steven said.

"It's Victoria. I wonder if you could help me with a quiz question."

"I'll do my best," he said."

"What does op mean? And could there be another meaning for the word target?"

"Op is probably a shortened version of a word. And the only meaning I know for the word target is a thing you aim at."

"The question was something about a woman being the target," she said.

"Oh, I know," he said. "It sounds as if the woman is a target for an assassin. The army uses the word op to mean operation. Does that help?"

"Yes, thanks. How are you keeping, and how is Rose?"

"We're both fine. Are you still in love?"

"Yes."

"It's wonderful, isn't it?" he said. "I told you I could hear wedding bells. We'll have to get together and go for a drink."

"Yes, we will. I must dash. Bye."

"Bye," he said.

She put the phone on the table and sat staring at Timothy. He used to be in the army. Surely, he was not involved in an assassination? He was not the sort of person to kill someone, especially a woman. Then why was he talking about it in his sleep? A cold shiver ran down the skin on her neck. He was about to go away on his last job. Could it be his last op? Surely, he was not going to kill a woman? And who was Diana?

She sat watching him light a cigarette. He was good and kind and could never kill anyone. Or could he? She had only known him for a short time. She needed to know more about him, and his mother was the best person to talk to. No. Jane would know more about Timothy than his mother. She stood up. "I'm going shopping. I won't be long."

"Okay, he said. "I'll see you later."

Victoria drove to Timothy's house and knocked on the door. It was opened by a slim, blonde woman in her late thirties. "Are you Jane?" she asked.

"Yes. What do you want?"

"Could we talk?" Victoria said. "I'm Tim's girlfriend."

Jane looked her up and down. "You look very young." She stepped back and opened the door wide. "Come in.

They sat in the kitchen, and Jane made them a cup of coffee. "How long have you been going out with Tim?" Jane asked.

"About three months. I'm pretty keen on him, and I wanted to know all about him. I'd hate to find out he's married with ten kids."

"Tim's never been married, and as far as I know, he doesn't have any children. I fully understand how you feel. I was led up the garden path by a man. I fell for him, and he turned out to be married. I've just found out that his wife has died, and we've decided to give it another try. To be honest, I've never stopped loving him, which is why it would never have worked out for Tim and me. How is he?"

"He's fine."

"Does he still go off every few months?" Jane asked.

"Yes. He's promised to get another job."

"I know all about his promises," Jane said. "He only does what he wants to do. And he never puts anything away after him."

Victoria smiled. "He also talks in his sleep."

Jane nodded. "I know. He started talking in his sleep when he began taking antidepressants. It drove me mad. I then found that he only talks in his sleep when he's lying on his back. Push him onto his side, and he stops."

Victoria did not realise that he was taking tablets. "What did he talk about when he talked in his sleep?"

"Things that were bothering him. He talked about his dog dying and about his mother being ill."

"Is he really an explosives expert?" Victoria asked.

"I think so. He knows all about them sort of things. He used to be in the SAS. I think he still goes on SAS missions. He came home once with what looked like a bullet hole in his arm."

Even though Victoria was shocked, she tried to act as if she knew that Timothy still went on SAS missions. "He's promised to get a regular job. I don't want him doing anything dangerous."

"It's about time he settled down," Jane said. "I hope you don't expect to have children. Tim has no intention of becoming a father."

"I do want children," Victoria said. "Tim's changed his mind. He now wants children."

Jane looked shocked. "I am surprised. Tim's always said that he didn't want the responsibility of children."

They talked for about fifteen minutes about men, children, and life in general, and Victoria returned home. She was angry and upset. She felt that Timothy had deceived her by not telling her everything about his life. She let herself into the house and found him in the kitchen, reading a magazine.

He looked up and smiled. "Hello, sweetheart. Do you want a coffee?"

"Yes." She sat down at the kitchen table. She felt let down by him. He had not been totally honest with her.

He frowned. She looked upset. "Is anything wrong?"

"Yes. We need to talk."

He poured the boiling water into the cups. "What about?"

"About honesty. If we're going to spend the rest of our lives together, we need to be honest."

He placed the cups of coffee on the table and sat down. "I am honest."

"Why didn't you tell me that you were on antidepressants?"

He shrugged. "I'm not proud of relying on tablets. I didn't want you to know. I didn't want you to think I was a weak man. How did you find out?"

"I went to see Jane. We had a long chat."

He was surprised. "What about?"

"Mostly about you. You didn't tell me that you were in the SAS?"

"Didn't I? I thought I did."

"You told me that you were in the army, but you didn't mention the SAS."

"Not telling you something is not the same as lying," he said.

"It is if it's important. I need to know that you're being totally honest with me."

"I am," he insisted. "Why are you so upset about me not telling you that I'm on tablets and that I was once in the SAS?"

"It's not just that," she said.

He frowned. "What do you mean? What else haven't I told you? What has Jane told you?"

"Did you know you talk in your sleep?" she said.

He shook his head. "No. Do I?"

"Yes. According to Jane, you started talking in your sleep when you began taking the antidepressants. I've spent last night listening to you."

He suddenly became alarmed. "What do I talk about?"

"About what you do when you go on ops. You don't go blowing up buildings, do you? You go with your SAS friends."

He sipped his coffee. He needed to be careful about what he said. "I am an explosives expert. I've told you what I do." He would have to find out just how much she knew.

"No, you haven't," she said. "I want to know the truth."

He chewed his lip. This was very awkward. The house could be bugged. "I'm not supposed to talk about the things I did in the SAS. If I did, I would get into serious trouble. And I've already told you I'm packing in my job."

"I know what you do when you go on your ops," she said.

He was now very worried. "People say all manner of things in their sleep. It's just another form of dreaming. What did I say I do on these ops?" They were in serious trouble if she knew that he was an assassin.

"You only talk about facts. Jane said that you talked about things that were worrying you. You talked about your mother being ill and about your dog dying."

He began to panic. She might have heard him talk about his assignment to kill Princess Diana. If the house was bugged and she said that she knew about the assassination, she was as good as dead. He stood up. "I don't want to row."

"Where are you going?" she asked.

"Into the garden."

"I want to talk," she said. "This is important."

He walked out of the back door. "Then come into the garden."

She followed him outside and down the path. "Why are we going into the garden? I don't want to argue with you. I just want to know what's going on." She began to feel annoyed. He obviously had no idea how hurt she was at being lied to. "I know what you do."

They were now far enough away from the house. He turned around. "And what's that?"

"You're an assassin. And don't even begin to lie to me."

He sat down on the bench and lit a cigarette. If he lied to her, he could lose her. She was too important to him. But if he told her the truth, she could be killed. "What exactly did I say in my sleep?"

"It's a bit jumbled up. You talk in odd sentences. You say things like, It's my last op. The target's a woman. Are you an assassin?"

"Have you told anyone about what I've been saying in my sleep?" he asked.

She was beginning to get really annoyed. "No. And will you please answer my question?"

"Let's assume that I am an assassin. The people who employ me will probably have the house bugged, and if they do, they'll now know that you know what I am."

She looked at the house. She had not thought about it being bugged. "So?"

"If they realise you know I'm an assassin, you're as good as dead."

She sat down on the bench. She began to worry. "Why would they kill me?"

"They will kill both of us."

"You came out of the house so they would not hear us talking," she said. "So, you are an assassin?"

"I love you, and I don't want to lie to you. It's very dangerous for me to talk about what I do. We could both end up dead."

She was now very frightened. "Would they really kill me for knowing what you do?"

He nodded.

"What can we do?" she asked.

"I don't know. It might already be too late. They might have heard me talking in my sleep, and if they were listening to what we said in the kitchen, they would have guessed from what you said that you know what I do."

She tried to think back. "All I said in the house was that you talk in your sleep. I didn't say what you said."

"You were upset," he said. "You mentioned the SAS. I suppose you could be upset about me doing dangerous things. When we go back into the house, we'll pretend that I mentioned an old girlfriend's name in my sleep. Pretend that I talked about Katy in my sleep."

"I need to know," she said. "I need to know everything."

"There's no need for you to know. This is my last op."

Victoria felt confused and frightened. "I didn't realise that the house could be bugged. I wish now that I hadn't heard you talking in your sleep. Do they usually bug the houses of SAS men?"

"I don't know." He flicked his cigarette nub into a flowerpot. "But it's possible, so it's best not to talk about what I do."

"I know who the target is," she said.

He stared at her. "I hope to God you don't?"

"I do. It's Princess Diana."

He put his head in his hands. "Oh, no. That's fucked it." He looked up at her. "Have you said anything to anyone about me being an assassin and about the target being Princess Diana?"

"No. Why do they want to kill Princess Diana?"

"Did you say anything to Jane?" he said.

"No. I haven't told anyone anything." She then remembered her phone call to Steven. "I did ask Steven if he knew what the words target and op meant. I made out it was a quiz question."

"Oh, bleeding hell," he said. "It's going from bad to worse. Let's hope the house and the phone aren't bugged."

"You did not answer my question," she said. "Are they planning to kill Princess Diana?"

"If we're going to talk, we'll have to get well away from the house," he said. "Let's go for a drive, but don't talk in the car. When we get into the house, ask me about Katy and pretend to be annoyed."

She followed him down the path and into the house. She was shaking with fear. "It's no good saying that you haven't seen Katy for years," she said. "You must have seen her if you talk about her in your sleep."

"Let's go for a ride," he said. "I've told you, I haven't seen Katy for three years. She's probably married by now."

They left the house and drove to the park. She felt confused and frightened. They did not speak until they were sitting by the lake. "What made you become an assassin?"

He shrugged. "It just sort of happened."

"I didn't think you were the sort of person to kill someone."

"I'm not a murderer. Killing is what you do in the army. It's what I'm trained to do. When I joined the SAS, I continued doing the same things I did in the army. Killing is what military people do."

"Yes, but only in a war. Why are you still killing people?"

"I don't know. I wish I'd packed it in years ago."

"What sort of people have you killed?"

He held her hand. "I don't intend to tell you any more than you already know. You already know too much. I love you, and I don't want to lose you. I know that you're upset by what I do. I just hope it's not changed things between us. Will you be able to live with a man who is an assassin?"

She pulled her hand away. "I don't know."

The predicament they were in was serious, and it began to get to him. He could feel his depression fighting with his tablets. He was on the verge of losing the most precious thing in his life, and there was nothing he could do about it.

"How can you tell if our house is bugged?" she asked.

He thought for a few seconds. "I know someone who could tell in a few minutes. I'll give him a call." He took his phone out of his pocket and stared at it. "No. I can't call him. They might think I have something to hide if I have the house swept for bugs." He put the phone back into his pocket.

"So, we have no way of knowing whether someone is listening to our every word?" she asked.

"No. We just have to be careful about what we say." He thought for a few moments. "It's very unlikely they've bugged my car and your house. It's possible, but very unlikely. They would also have to bug the houses and cars of the other members of the team if they felt that they could not trust us."

"It would be very time-consuming to listen to all of you for twenty-four hours a day," she said.

"They have automated recording systems that listen for certain keywords," he said.

"How many are in your team?" she asked.

"You don't need to know."

They sat in silence for a while, watching the ducks. She felt confused and very worried. "I'd hate to think people are listening to what we say." She leaned back on the bench. She could not believe that Timothy and his army mates were going to kill Princess Diana. "Who wants Princess Diana killed?"

"I don't know."

She was shocked. "You don't know? Who gives you your orders?"

"It's better that you don't know the details. These decisions are made by British Intelligence. We just follow orders."

"Why could they possibly want to kill Princess Diana?" she asked.

"They believe she's determined to bring down the monarchy. How much does Jane know about me?"

"She knows that you were in the SAS, but she doesn't realise that you're an assassin. How can Princess Diana bring down the monarchy?"

"She intends to marry a Muslim and have his children. If she does, her children will be brought up as Muslims."

She frowned. "How can that bring down the monarchy?"

"It's a bit complicated." He lit a cigarette. "If Princess Diana marries a Muslim, she'll have to convert and become a Muslim. When Prince William becomes king, he'll have Muslim brothers and sisters. I don't think the monarchy would survive having Arab Muslims as part of the Royal Family."

"That's not reason enough for them to kill her," she said.

"I agree."

"Then don't do it." She was determined to persuade him not to commit what she considered a crime.

"I don't want to do it, but I don't have a choice."

"You do have a choice. We all have a choice about what we do. Just tell them that you don't want to do it."

He had a drag on his cigarette. "It's not as easy as that. If I refuse to go on the op, they might kill me."

"Why would they kill you?"

"If I refuse this op, it would show that I was against Princess Diana being assassinated. They might worry that I would do something to protect Princess Diana or spill the beans to the press. I would be seen as a weak link in the chain."

She felt frightened and frustrated. "I like Princess Diana, and I don't believe that the monarchy would be affected by her having Muslim children. I don't think people care about the monarchy anymore."

"Most people in this country are racists," he said. "It could cause riots. Could you imagine a young woman in a burka or a hijab in royal photographs?" He suddenly realised the implications of talking in his sleep. "Fuck it."

"What's wrong?" she asked.

"The other members of the team might hear me talking in my sleep."

"According to Jane, you only talk in your sleep when you lie on your back. She used to push you onto your side to shut you up."

He breathed a sigh of relief. "I'll have to remember to sleep on my side. I'm glad this is my last op."

"So am I. I feel sick. I'm worrying so much. I also feel frightened."

He held her arm. "Try not to worry. Just remember not to talk about what I do unless we're in the open. Do you still love me?"

"Yes. I just don't know if I can live with you."

That was not the answer he wanted. "I still love you."

His phone rang. He took it out of his pocket. "Yes?"

"It's Roger. We'll be picking you up in an hour."

"Okay," Timothy said. "I'll be ready." He put the phone back into his pocket.

"Are you going?" she asked.

"Yes. They're picking me up in an hour."

"Oh, no," she said. "Tell him that you're ill. I don't want you to go."

"I have to." He stood up and walked towards his car. "If I could get out of going, I would."

She followed him. "You don't have to go. Tell them that you've hurt your back."

"I can't."

"Isn't there anything you can do?"

"No. I could make some excuse and not go, but it would put our lives at risk. I don't want to kill Princess Diana. We'll have to hope that they abort the mission."

She held his arm. "Don't get into the car yet. What do you mean, abort the mission?"

"They might decide not to kill her and cancel the op."

"I don't want to live with the knowledge that you've killed a good person like Princess Diana. I don't think I could live with it. It'll tear me apart. If you love me, you'll do something."

He looked down at her. He loved her more than he could ever put into words. "There's nothing I can do. I'm just a very small cog in a very large machine. The best I could do is to try to sabotage the mission in some way to delay it. It would be very risky, and I'd only be delaying the inevitable. If they want her dead, she will be killed."

"Do what you can to save Princess Diana, but don't take any risks. She would rather them kill Princess Diana than Timothy.

He looked at his watch. "I'll have to be going. When we get back into the car, be careful what you say."

They drove back to her house in silence.

Her happiness had been shattered by a world she did not know existed, an evil, murderous world, and the man she loved lived in that dark, secret and very dangerous world.

They climbed out of the car.

She followed him into the house and watched him push a few things into a bag. "I don't want you to go." She had the feeling that someone was listening to their every word.

"I have to." He could sense that her love for him was slipping away. "It's the last time I'll have to go away. I've made a list of some jobs I intend to go after when I get back. I'll never be going away again."

"If you love me, you would stay." She was worried that he would get killed and she would never see him again.

He turned to look at her. It was probably already over between them. She was looking at him in a strange way. "I hope we can work things out when I get back. I don't want to lose you."

"How long will you be away?" she asked. She had to be careful what she said.

"I don't know. It could be weeks. It could even be months."

She was shocked. "Months. A few days would be bad enough. If you love me, how can you go swanning off for months on end? How can I live with such a selfish person? Tell the people you work for that you're not going."

"I can't. I've already told them that I won't be working for them anymore, but I've promised to do this one last job."

She began to feel angry. "Do you realise what I'm going through? We're supposed to be planning our marriage and selling our houses. You're not the man I thought you were."

"I am. I've not changed." He stood by the window. "We'll sort things out when I get back."

"It's impossible," she said. "Everything was perfect, and now this. Isn't there anything you can do?"

The Transit van pulled up outside. "No. I have to go." He hugged her, kissed her and left the house. She had not kissed him or hugged him in return. If she still loved him, she would have hugged him.

She stood by the window and watched him climb into the van. This could be the last time she would ever see him. Tears began to roll down her cheeks. She ran to the door, opened it and ran outside. "I love you," she shouted. The van was driving away. "Take care," she whispered. "You're all I've got."

She watched in a trance-like state as the van drove away. Why was there a need to kill people? What prevented people from living in peace? The world was supposed to be civilised, but there are more conflicts and problems now than ever before. Several powerful emotions were ripping her apart. Fear for both of their lives, anger that he had lied to her, confusion as to why he could not pretend to be ill, and frustration that she had no control over what was happening.

Chapter Ten

Timothy lit a cigarette and made himself comfortable in the back of the van with Roger, Matthew and Peter. John was driving. "Fancy meeting you lot here," Timothy said in a pathetic attempt at a joke. He did not feel like joking, but forced himself to be friendly.

"We have to dispose of the target ASAP," Roger said. "The target's sleeping with Dodi and could be pregnant."

"What's the plan, Major?" Timothy asked.

"It's all been arranged. We'll discuss it later. Give me your phone."

Timothy handed over his mobile phone. His head was full of worries. If Victoria's house was bugged, and they knew that she knew about the operation, what would they do? They would assume that he had broken the cardinal rule and talked about their operations, and they would probably make some excuse and pull him off the assignment. Or they could just kill him. They could also kill Victoria. What a mess.

Timothy laughed at a joke that Matthew had told, even though he had only heard the punch line. If he remained part of the team, it would mean that they did not know that Victoria knew who the target was. He would relax if he were still alive in a couple of days.

"I was attacked by a gang of thugs a couple of days ago," Peter said. "They were making a nuisance of themselves outside my mother's house, so I told them to fuck off, and they threw bricks at me. I had to run for my fucking life. The cheeky bastards. Some of them were no more than fourteen. My mother phoned the police, and the bastards broke every window in her house."

"What did the police do?" Matthew asked.

"Fuck all as usual," Peter said. "They warned me not to do anything. This country's going to the dogs."

"I know what I would have done to them," Roger said.

"Don't worry, they won't bother my mother again," Peter said. "I caught up with the four ring leaders and broke their toes with a hammer."

"The police are too soft on thugs," Roger said. "They should lock them away as soon as they cause a nuisance, even if they're only ten. They'll then learn to behave themselves. What we need is another prime minister like Margaret Thatcher."

"No, we don't," Timothy said. It might help him forget his troubles if he got involved in the discussion. "Thatcher wanted a police state. If she had stayed in government, we would have ended up with a dilapidated National Health Service and a second-rate education system."

Matthew nodded. "You could be right. Thatcher widened the gap between the rich and the poor."

Roger put an unlit cigar in his mouth. "I can't light it, but I like the smell. I think Thatcher did a good job. She took on the trade unions and won. The unions were ruining this country."

Timothy had to agree, but it was the only good thing she did.

The discussion eventually dried up, and they travelled the rest of the way to Weymouth in silence.

If only Timothy could turn back the clock. He would then refuse to become a part of the assassination team and would now be living a normal life. He would now be at home with Victoria, and she would not be on her own, worrying about him. Although she might not be worrying about him. She had acted odd just before he left. She might not love him anymore and could already be planning a new life for herself. It would be difficult for any woman to accept that the man they loved was an assassin and was on his way to kill the most loved woman in the world. It would be understandable if Victoria did not want to see him again.

On the car ferry to France, they played cards. Timothy could not concentrate, and he lost twelve pounds. All he could think about was Victoria. By the way she had acted, he had sensed that her love for him had died. It was understandable but very painful. How could a woman love an assassin?

When they reached France, it was raining. They drove in the Transit van through the rain to Paris. A discussion broke out, and they discussed Global Positioning Systems and private security work. After a while, the conversation dried up, and they sat in silence.

When they reached their destination, it was still raining, and they got drenched as they carried their possessions into a dilapidated hotel. Their apartment had seen better days. They had a bedroom each but would have to share the bathroom, kitchen, and lounge.

"I'll make the coffee," Matthew said. We'll need to do some shopping tomorrow."

Roger sat down in a large armchair in the lounge. "I don't have to go through the rules. No one makes any calls home or to anywhere until we're back in England. We cannot afford any cock-ups."

Timothy lit a cigarette and sat down. "How long will we be here, Major?"

"If things go according to plan, for about two weeks, but it could be months. We'll have to stay until the job's done. There'll be no drinking. We need to be able to move out at a minute's notice, day or night."

John looked disappointed. "No booze. Surely a glass of wine won't do any harm?"

Matthew placed his bag on the table. "I work better when I've had a drink." He took a bottle of wine out of his bag. "What do I do with this? I've also got a dozen cans of lager."

Roger pointed a finger at them. "This op is too important for any cock-ups. Limit yourselves in any one day to a couple of glasses of wine or two cans of beer."

"Thank God for that," John said. "I can't sleep unless I've had a drink."

Roger looked at his watch. "It's late. Try to get some sleep. We'll be going over the details tomorrow."

Timothy stood up. "I'm knackered. I think I'll turn in." He left them in the lounge and unpacked his possessions in his tiny bedroom. He was relieved to have his own room; nevertheless, he intended to sleep on his side with a bag against his back so he could not roll over. He could not risk talking in his sleep.

*

Victoria could not sleep. She lay in bed, staring at the ceiling. Her life was in tatters, and her dreams were falling apart. How could everything that seemed so perfect go so wrong? Why did Timothy have to be an assassin? And why was he on a mission to kill the world's most famous woman?

She got out of bed, put on her dressing gown and walked downstairs. One minute, she hated Timothy for destroying her dreams and plans, and she never wanted to see him again. Then, the next minute, she realised how much she loved him and that she could not live without him, and she was desperate for him to return home safely. But even though she loved him, she was not sure that she could live with an assassin who had killed Princess Diana. The knowledge would tear her apart and could destroy their relationship.

She made a cup of coffee and sat in the kitchen. The house felt empty and sad. All she wanted was a normal life with a normal man and to have normal children. How could she live with a murderer? What had she done to deserve all these problems? She felt so confused and frustrated, and the tears came in a flood.

*

It was nine-thirty in the morning. Timothy walked out of his bedroom and into the lounge of their apartment in Paris. John, Peter and Matthew were watching the television. "Morning," Timothy said.

"You look like death, Tim," John said.

"I feel like it." Timothy sat down in front of the television and lit a cigarette. The news was on. The newsreaders were speaking French. Timothy was fluent in French. The news was about Princess Diana and Dodi Al-Fayed.

Peter was watching the television. He was also fluent in French. "It's her own fault. She's a typical woman scorned. If she'd just got on with her life and not continually rubbished the royals, we wouldn't be here."

John shook his head. "That's not the reason we're here. The royals can look after themselves. It's her determination to marry an Arab and have kids that's caused the trouble. The Fayeds are Muslims, and the British public has no time for Muslims. Muslims don't mix with us. They wear different clothes, speak a different language, and are fanatically religious. They don't even drink, and they think they're better than us."

"That's the difference between blacks and Muslims," Matthew said. "The blacks think they're as good as us, but the Muslims think they're better than us. At least, that's the impression you get. You can say what you like about Christians or Jews, but if you say anything about Muslims, you'll have to watch your back. The bastards will kill anyone who criticises them. If you're white and speak English, they'll regard you as an evil Westerner and will bump you off as soon as look at you."

"I don't go into shops owned by Muslims anymore," John said. "They piss me off. They'll suddenly start talking in their language. I told them once that it was an insult to talk in their language in front of an English person. They could be saying anything."

Timothy took a drag on his cigarette. He was not a racist, but there was more than a grain of truth in what they were saying. Even if Princess Diana did not marry a Muslim, there would probably still be race riots in a few years. White people now fear Muslims, and hate always comes with fear. There was no way that the Muslims would ever peacefully co-exist with white infidels. The aim of Muslims is to take over the world by any means, convert everyone to Islam and instigate Sharia law.

The television was now showing pictures of the Al-Fayeds' yacht, the Jonikal, anchored off Cala di Volpe, a private resort in Sardinia. The newsreader was saying that they expected an announcement over the next few days about Princess Diana and Dodi's engagement.

The door opened, and Roger walked in. He handed the van keys to John. "Go with Peter and get the two bags and the box out of the van that's in the garage, and bring them here. And make sure you lock up the van."

John and Peter walked out of the room.

"The target is in Sardinia," Timothy said.

Roger looked at the television. "I know. She certainly gets about. Whose turn is it to make the coffee?"

Matthew stood up. "I'll do it. You lot always make it too strong."

Roger sat down at the table and rubbed his leg. "I think I've twisted my knee. I've never seen H looking so worried. He's under a great deal of pressure. It's crucial that the target is eliminated ASAP, and it must appear to be an accident. What amazed me was being told that if we fail in eliminating the target in what looks like an accident, she is to be shot."

Matthew looked shocked. "Fucking hell. If she's shot, everyone will know she's been assassinated."

"Yes, but they won't know who pulled the trigger," Roger said.

Mathew handed Roger and Timothy a cup of coffee. "But they might suspect us."

"If by us you mean British Intelligence, I doubt it," Roger said. "They'll probably think she was killed by some madman, like that madman who killed John Lennon."

John and Peter walked into the lounge and placed two travelling bags and a large box on the table.

"Why the arsenal, Major?" John asked.

"It's to make sure we don't leave any loose ends. If the police stop you and you cannot talk your way out of trouble, you'll have to shoot your way out. You cannot be taken into custody. And don't take off your disguises until the op's over. There will be cameras everywhere." He handed out handguns. "And make sure you wear your vests at all times." He placed a high-velocity rifle with telescopic sights on the table. "And let's hope you don't have to use this."

Timothy checked the handgun he had been given. It was loaded. "If we shoot our way out of trouble after the target's dead, they'll know it was not an accident."

Roger nodded. "I agree, but it'll be a disaster if ex-SAS men are arrested. Just make sure everything goes according to plan. I've had a long talk with H. Like us, he wants to retire. His orders are to hit the target ASAP. From reading between the lines, I suspect there's another team involved. They're probably operating in the South of France."

Timothy was hoping that the other team would hit the target first. He could then go home and forget about assassinations.

Roger sipped his coffee and pulled a face. "You make a diabolical cup of coffee, Matthew."

"I know. It tastes like shit. I don't think I boiled the water. What I want to know, Major, is, why are we hitting the target in France? Only Tim and Peter can speak French."

"French law will make it easy to cover up any mistakes we make and will allow us to hide facts from the public. They don't have public inquests in France, although there's bound to be an inquiry, so we need to be extra careful."

"What's the plan, Major?" Peter asked.

"The target is to be killed in a traffic accident."

"Have they picked the location?" John asked.

"Yes." Roger took a map out of one of the bags and laid it on the table. "There are six possible locations in and around Paris."

They gathered around the table. It was a map of Paris.

Timothy was surprised that they were intending to hit the target in a city. "Wouldn't it be less conspicuous if we hit the target in the country, Major? There are bound to be witnesses in the centre of Paris."

"The target is not expected to be travelling long distances in a limo. Most of her journeys will be between the Ritz hotel, Dodi's apartment and restaurants." He pencilled a circle around six locations on the map. "It's been decided that these six places are the most suitable. It has to look like an accident, so we can't shoot her or ram her car over a cliff or into a river."

Peter frowned. He looked confused. "Then how the fuck are we going to kill her?"

"H and his fellow conspirators have come up with a simple plan that should work. It's similar to the initial plan we intended to use against Milosevic."

"Even if we use the strobe light to blind the driver and cause an accident, it doesn't mean the target will die," John said. "We intended to finish off Milosevic with a bullet. If the target doesn't die in the accident, how are we going to kill her?"

"We'll then use the heart attack drug," Roger said. "They'll assume that her injuries caused her to have a heart attack."

John sat down. "She's a bit young to have a heart attack. That drug is usually used to kill middle-aged and old people. From what I know, she's very fit."

Timothy was against using the heart attack drug. It would be a mistake. "Princess Diana is a keep-fit fanatic, and I don't think we should use the heart attack drug."

Roger picked up his cup of coffee and put it down again. "Then let's hope she dies from her injuries, and the drug is not needed. I need a decent cup of coffee."

"I'll make it," Timothy said. He switched on the kettle. "There are two problems with the plan, Major. We should not use the heart attack drug because people might suspect she was killed. And Mercedes has seat belts and airbags, so she might not sustain any injuries."

"The target rarely uses a seat belt in the back of a limo," Roger said, "and so it's almost certain that she'll sustain some injuries. The strobe light will be used to blind the driver when the limo is driving near a solid object." He pointed to the map. "For example, the Alma tunnel has been selected as one of the locations for the accident. There are concrete pillars in the tunnel that are not protected by barriers. If the limo hits the pillars, the target will be severely injured. She might even be killed."

"I know the Alma tunnel," Peter said. "It's an accident blackspot."

Timothy handed around cups of coffee and sat down. He was still not happy with the plan. To kill or seriously injure Princess Diana, the limo would need to be travelling over sixty miles an hour, and the speed limit in the Alma Tunnel is about thirty miles an hour.

Roger sipped his coffee. "That's better. Strong and hot. We'll go through the plan in detail later. When the target returns to Paris, she's bound to travel from the Ritz Hotel to Dodi's apartment in Rue Arsene Houssaye, and hopefully to other destinations. When they do, we must be ready."

Peter looked at the map. "When they travel from the Ritz to Dodi's apartment, they won't have to travel anywhere near the six locations. They'll travel along the Champs-Élysées."

Roger nodded. "I know. We'll know before they start each journey where they'll be going and the route they'll be taking. We'll have to hope that they'll eventually travel through one of these six locations. If they don't, we'll have to resort to plan B." He tapped the high-velocity rifle with his finger.

Timothy was amazed that they were even considering shooting Princess Diana. They must be desperate to make sure she dies. "How long have we got before the target has to be shot, Major?"

"They didn't give me a deadline. We have about three weeks."

"Who will be doing what, Major?" John asked.

"Your job will be to drive the car and make sure that the target's limo is in the right position for the strobe light to be used." He pointed to the Alma tunnel on the map. "If they travel through the Alma tunnel, you'll be positioned at the entrance to the tunnel to make sure that when the strobe light is used, the limo is just a few feet from the concrete pillars.

Timothy could see another flaw in the plan. "There's no guarantee the limo will hit the pillars. When we use the strobe light, the driver will hit his brakes and keep the limo in a straight line."

"The strobe light will stun the driver as well as blind him for at least a minute," Roger said. "The one we'll be using is more powerful than a normal strobe light. The driver will not know who he is or what he's doing for about thirty seconds. They've conducted extensive tests. The driver will probably release the steering wheel with both hands, and there's a fifty per cent chance that he'll not brake or take any evasive action for several seconds. And seconds are all we need. When the limo enters the Alma tunnel, Peter and Matthew will be just in front of them on a motorbike. As the limo pulls alongside John's vehicle, Peter will use the strobe light and drop a modified stinger under the limo's wheel. The stinger's been designed to act as a ramp and steer the limo into the pillars. Peter and John will continue driving out of the Alma tunnel. Tim, who will be following behind the limo on a motorbike, will pick up the stinger and, if necessary, inject the heart attack drug into the target. The procedure's the same at each location."

"There's a lot that could go wrong," John said. "It's a bit iffy."

"What about the CCTV cameras, Major?" Timothy asked. "They'll see everything."

"Not everything. If they're working, and there's a good possibility that they won't be working, the cameras in all six locations are not pointing directly at where the crash will take place. They'll just see the limo, paparazzi on motorbikes and John in a Fiat Uno just before the accident. They won't recognise John because he will be wearing his disguise. Peter, John and Tim will be carrying cameras and masquerading as paparazzi, and they will be wearing crash helmets."

"A Fiat Uno," John said. "What happened to the Aston Martin?"

They all smiled.

"We are using the Fiat Uno, so everything will look normal," Roger said. "It must look like an accident. The simpler the plan is, the better it will look, and after the accident, there'll be nothing left to suggest foul play."

"It sounds too simple to me," Peter said. "I'm sure they could come up with something better."

Timothy had no confidence in the plan, and he expected something to go wrong. "What speed do you expect the limo to be travelling at the time of the accident in the Alma tunnel?"

"The paparazzi will keep to the speed limit because of the CCTV cameras, but the limo will travel much faster. The faster, the better. They expect the limo to be travelling between sixty and seventy mph. It's unlikely that anyone will survive if they hit a concrete pillar or a solid object at sixty mph. If they're travelling less than fifty mph, they might not be killed. If the target's still alive, you will have to use the drug, Tim."

Timothy looked at the map. There was a hospital very near the Alma Tunnel. "I know we can hide the needle mark with a cut, but the drug can be detected in the body for about an hour." He pointed to the map. "The hospital's only a few minutes' drive from the Alma tunnel. If the target is only injured and I have to inject her, when she is taken to the hospital, the first thing the doctors will do is take a sample of blood so that they can match it to give a blood transfusion. If they do, they will detect the drug."

"We have been assured that the target will not reach the hospital for at least sixty-five minutes," Roger said. "She'll not be taken to the nearest hospital. Whichever of the six locations is used for the accident, she'll be taken to the Pitie-Salpêtrière hospital. By then, she'll be dead, and the drug will have dissolved."

John looked at the map. "There are two hospitals nearer to the Alma Tunnel than the Pitie-Salpêtrière hospital? How can they guarantee she'll be taken to the Pitie-Salpêtrière hospital?"

"I don't know," Roger said. "They obviously have agents or people on their payroll working there."

"How many agents are involved in the op?" Matthew asked.

Roger leaned back in his seat. "I've no idea. It could be a dozen. Several top MI5 officers are in France. They have a top security man at the Ritz feeding them inside information, and they probably also have top police, ambulance drivers and doctors on their payroll. The men in grey suits who protect the royals are not the only ones who hate the target. The arms manufacturers in America stand to lose millions because of her anti-landmine work."

"It was the USA arms manufacturers who were behind the assassination of JFK," John said. "They would have lost billions if JFK had called off the Vietnam War."

"JFK did call the soldiers home from Vietnam," Peter said. "But as soon as he was killed, they sent the soldiers back. Arms manufacturers are not the sort of people to upset. My motto is to never upset powerful people."

Roger stood up. "I need the loo. We'll order something to eat, and then go through the plan step by step. We'll need to travel to all six locations. We have a great deal of work to do." He walked out of the room.

Timothy leaned on the windowsill and looked through the open window across an overgrown orchard. A lump of sadness filled his chest. How did he get into this mess? He hated the idea of killing Princess Diana, but it was something he would have to learn to live with. What he could never learn to live with and would never recover from was losing Victoria. She had become his reason to live.

Chapter Eleven

Victoria had a day off from work. She was too worried to work and would not be able to concentrate. She also wanted to visit Timothy's father to find out what sort of person Timothy was. It was difficult to believe that at this very moment in time, some men were trying to kill Princess Diana. What was impossible to accept was that the man she loved was one of the assassins. She was hoping that they would call off the assassination or that Timothy would be able to stop it.

She drove to Timothy's father's house and knocked on the door, not knowing what to expect.

A stern-looking old man opened the door. "What do you want?" he asked.

"I'm Victoria. I'm Tim's girlfriend."

His face lit up with a smile. "Oh. I'm pleased to meet you. Come on in. I'll put the kettle on."

She followed him into the kitchen. The house was untidy, very old-fashioned, but reasonably clean. "I hope I'm not intruding."

"Of course not. Call me George. Sit down. Do you want coffee or tea?"

She sat down. "I don't mind. I take milk and one sugar." She found herself liking George. He had friendly, smiling eyes.

"We'll have tea then," he said. He filled the kettle. "Where's Tim?"

"He's gone on one of his trips. He calls them ops."

George stared at her and frowned. "Did he tell you what he does?"

"No, but he talks in his sleep. I now know what he does, and I'm worried to death. I wish I didn't know."

"Life's very complicated and contains stingers as well as flowers," he said. "Does he know that you know what he does?"

"Yes. He's told me all about it."

George put tea bags into two cups. "I am surprised he told you. He must trust you completely. I gather you don't like what he does?"

"I hate it. I thought I knew him, but now I'm not so sure. How can I live with a man who does what he does?"

"It's better not to talk about his job," he said. "It could put his life in danger. Soldiers are trained to kill. They kill people with the permission of their government. It's a messy business."

She was not sure whether George knew Timothy was an assassin. "It's wrong to kill."

He nodded. "I agree. I've killed twenty-three people at least."

She was shocked. "Are you serious?"

"Yes. I was in the Second World War. I was in Dunkirk. I was rescued by an old man and a boy of no more than fifteen on a small boat. I was only a kid myself."

"War's different," she said. "We're not at war now."

The kettle boiled, and he poured boiling water into the cups. "We are always at war. We were defending our country in the Second World War; today, the soldiers are still defending our country. Even in peacetime, we need soldiers. What soldiers are told to do will not always be right. Politicians and generals make the decisions about when they fight and what they do."

"How did you kill twenty-three people?" she asked.

"When I landed in France on D-Day, I was asked if I was a good shot. I said I was, and I became a sniper. It was dangerous work. We had to get close to the enemy and try to kill the officers. I soon learned not to hide in bushes and old buildings. After I shot one of them, they would shoot at anything that could conceal a man. I used to dig a hole and cover myself in grass and twigs. Then, after shooting someone, I would remain where I was until it became dark. My main worry was dogs. It wouldn't take five minutes for a dog to find me. I used to cover myself in cow dung and hope the dogs wouldn't sniff me out. I was proud of what I did."

"I think war is different," she said. "When we're not at war, we have no right to kill people."

He smiled. "If we had killed Hitler before the war started, we would have saved millions of lives. Tim will be retiring soon. You'll then be able to forget all about it and have a family."

"I'm not sure I can forget about it," she said. "I love him, but I'm not sure I can live with him. How can a killer be a loving father and husband?"

He handed her a cup of tea. "I was."

They talked about Timothy's childhood and some of the things he did while growing up, and she went home feeling even more confused. According to his father, Timothy was a fine, upstanding person.

*

Timothy and the team spent three days familiarising themselves with the roads and the one-way systems around each of the six locations designated as suitable sites to kill Princess Diana. They rehearsed the accident at each site. Timothy was unable to see how he could sabotage the plan. If he were on the back of the other motorbike, he could drop the strobe light or misplace the stinger. It would be risky and would look suspicious, and he would only be able to use the cock-up spanner once, but in the end, it would all be a waste of time. If they failed in creating an accident, they would resort to plan B. It did not matter what he did. The target would eventually die.

That evening, he had a meal with Roger in a restaurant. After eating the meal, they sat drinking coffee.

"What's bothering you, Tim?" Roger asked. "You're not yourself."

Timothy did not know what to say. "I suppose I'm missing Victoria." He smiled. "I've never been in love before."

Roger sipped his coffee and stared at Timothy. "There's something else. Are you having second thoughts about the op?"

"No. I don't like the idea of killing a woman, but I can understand why she must die."

"She's an adult," Roger said. "She knows all about the men in grey suits who protect the monarchy. She's said many times that she expects to be killed. If she wants to live, she should not be planning to marry a Muslim and have his children. It's her decision. She has two sons. One of them will one day be king, so why isn't she thinking of them?"

"I agree with you. She should be thinking of them. I've just had enough of ops. I want to settle down. I've decided I want children. I must be mad."

Roger smiled. "You are mad if you want children. It's our last op, and it'll soon be over."

Timothy could not sleep that night. Up until now, he had been convinced that he did not have a conscience. He had been wrong. He did have a conscience, and it was now spewing out a constant stream of advice as if it were a well-meaning friend. In reply to his conscience, he would say that if he did not kill Princess Diana, someone else would. And if he left the team and went home, they would probably call in Paul Johnson, a reserve SAS officer to take his place. And to leave the team now would be tantamount to signing his own death warrant.

He had no choice. If he did not kill Princess Diana, someone else would, and he would also be killed. Either way, she would die. To leave the team would be throwing his life away. And even if he could find a way to sabotage the mission, he would only be delaying it. His one hope was that the operation would be aborted.

Someone knocked softly on his door. "Yes?" Timothy said.

The door opened. It was Peter. "I thought you'd be awake. I could hear the television."

"I never sleep well on ops," Timothy said.

"Neither do I," Peter said. "Do you fancy a game of cards?"

Timothy shook his head.

Peter sat on the bed. “I’m glad it’s the last op. I’m too old for all this excitement.” He offered Timothy a cigarette. “There’s one thing worrying me.”

Timothy took a cigarette. “And what’s that?”

“When the op’s over, they might think of bumping us off to cover their tracks.”

“Take out insurance,” Timothy said. “I have. They’re in for trouble if they bump me off.” He had not taken out insurance, but because the room could be bugged, he did not want them to know.

“I intend to,” Peter said. “I would like us all to keep in touch so that if anything happens to any one of us, the others can take action.”

“I agree,” Timothy said. “You can’t trust anyone.”

Peter smiled. “You can’t trust the men in grey suits, and that’s for sure.”

They smoked and talked about the missions they had been on for about an hour. Peter left at two-thirty, and Timothy eventually fell asleep at three-thirty.

*

It was eight o’clock in the morning. Timothy was sitting in the lounge of their apartment in Paris with Matthew, John and Peter, watching the television. He was drinking orange juice. He was sick of coffee.

Roger walked into the room and sat down in an armchair. “I’m knackered. The target and Dodi are flying to Paris today. I’ve called in Paul Johnson. His job will be to take out the backup car.”

Matthew looked annoyed. “Not Paul. He’s a total prat. If he takes the piss out of me again, I’ll blow his fucking brains out.”

“Paul hasn’t got any brains,” John said.

They laughed.

“You won’t be meeting Paul,” Roger said. “They hope to delay the backup car in some way, but if they’re unable to, Paul will be needed to crash into it and disable it.”

“It could be weeks before the target travels to one of the six locations,” Matthew said.

“Then we’ll have to resort to plan B,” Roger said. “Let’s go over plan A in the Alma tunnel.”

“It’s a simple plan,” John said. “I get to the Alma tunnel just before the limo containing the target. We’ve rehearsed it five times at each location, so there shouldn’t be any problems. I then drive into the tunnel, slow down, and give the limo just enough room to pass me. Then, after the accident, I drive to the garage."

Roger nodded. He looked at Matthew. "And what's your job?"

"Me and Peter will follow the limo from the Ritz hotel. When we reach the Place de la Concorde, we'll overtake the limo and keep in front of the limo along the Cours la Reine. We'll keep about thirty feet in front of the limo as we enter the Alma tunnel."

"And what's your job, Peter?" Roger asked.

"I keep in touch with John and tell him when to begin to move. I use the strobe light as we pass the Fiat Uno and enter the Alma tunnel, and then I drop the stinger under the wheel of the limo. We did six dummy runs in a country lane. I don't see any problems. We then drive to the garage."

"Roger turned to Timothy. "And you?"

"I follow the limo when it leaves the Ritz and follow it to the Alma tunnel. After the accident, I pick up the stinger and make sure that the target's dead. If she's alive, I inject her into an open wound, if possible, and then drive to the garage."

Roger rubbed his hands together. "It couldn't be simpler. Just make sure that nothing goes wrong. Get something to eat and be ready to move out at a minute's notice."

Roger left the apartment, and they sat smoking and watching television. Timothy's thoughts turned from the operation to Victoria. He was now convinced that she no longer wanted anything to do with him. She had made it very clear that she could not live with a murderer. He had never considered himself a murderer, but he could understand how she felt. He hated the thought of living without her. He would have one last talk with her when he got back home to see if he could persuade her to give their relationship another chance, but if he failed, and she was still being awkward, he would sod off.

*

Victoria went shopping with Steven and Rose to try to get her mind off her problems. It was proving very difficult. Her worries followed her around from shop to shop. It would help if she could talk over her problems with someone. At this very moment, Timothy and his friends could be killing Princess Diana. If she told Steven and Rose, they would think she was mad.

Steven frowned and stared at Victoria. "Are you all right? You don't look very happy."

"I'm sorry if I'm ruining your day. I'm feeling a bit low."

"You're not ruining our day," Rose said. "We all have bad days."

"Are you worried about something?" Steven asked.

Victoria decided to tell them at least a part of the truth. "I'm having second thoughts about Timothy. I'm not as confident as I used to be about us being happy together."

"Time will tell," Rose said. "You'll either go off him or find that you cannot live without him."

Steven pointed. "Let's go into that pub over the road. A drink might cheer you up, Victoria."

The drink did not help. Victoria returned home feeling even more worried and depressed.

That evening, she sat watching the news channels. If anything happened to Princess Diana, it would be on the news. She was surprised to discover that Princess Diana and Dodi Al-Fayed were in France, and if Timothy and his friends intended to kill her, Timothy would also be in France. According to the newsreader, Diana and Dodi were in love and would soon be announcing their engagement. There was even a rumour that Princess Diana was pregnant. It seemed so wrong to kill such a good person who, after all of her problems, was now happy and in love.

She opened a bottle of wine. She needed a good night's sleep and intended to get one, even if she had to drink two bottles of wine. It took three large glasses of wine to take the edge off her worries. She now felt slightly more optimistic. Hopefully, Timothy would return home in one piece, and Princess Diana would not be killed.

*

It was four-thirty in the afternoon. Timothy was bored out of his mind. He was sitting in the lounge of their apartment in Paris and for the last hour, had watched John, Peter and Matthew play cards. He stood up. "Who wants a coffee?"

The three men shook their heads.

"I'm sick of coffee," Matthew said.

Timothy walked into the kitchen. He was also sick of coffee and took an orange juice carton out of the fridge. He walked into the lounge, sat down and had a drink.

The door to the apartment opened, and Roger walked in. "We've had a good piece of fortune. Dodi and Diana arrived at Le Bourget airport at three twenty-two this afternoon. The SPHP, the French diplomatic bodyguards, were waiting to escort them, but Dodi sent them packing. We can gather from this that Dodi's not taking their security seriously. When the limousine drove off, neither Dodi nor Diana was wearing their seat belts. They're now in the

Imperial Suite at the Ritz. Our man at the Ritz was on holiday, but he's now on his way to the hotel. Everything is now ready."

Timothy was eager to get the job done. "When do we move out, Major?"

"As soon as we get word from our contact at the Ritz. We need to know the route and the destination in advance so that we'll know which location to use for the accident. I don't want you lot hanging about outside the Ritz for days on end."

John placed his playing cards on the table. "I'm sick of playing cards and I don't fancy being cooped up in here for God knows how long. We could be here for months."

"You'll only have to stay here for two weeks at the most," Roger said. "H has just told me that if the target cannot be killed in an accident in the next two weeks, we'll have to resort to plan B."

"I can see us ending up using plan B," John said.

"I'm not convinced the stinger will work," Peter said. "How thick is it?"

"I've been told it's only a few inches thick," Roger said.

"If it's too thick, it'll puncture the tyre and damage the wheel," John said. "They'll then have proof that the limo went over something."

"It's been thoroughly tested," Roger said. "It's been designed not to damage the wheel and to act as a ramp to steer the vehicle to the left. I'll be picking up the stinger later today."

"Even if the stinger does damage the tyre and the wheel, it won't make the slightest difference," Timothy said. "If the limo hits something solid like the pillars in the Alma tunnel at over fifty mph, the car will be a write-off. It'll resemble a pile of scrap metal."

Peter shook his head. "It all sounds a bit dodgy to me. Surely, with all the modern technology, they could think of something better."

"That's what I thought at first," Roger said. "I've since changed my mind. A simple plan will make it look more like an everyday car accident." He lit up a cigar. "What makes the plan brilliant is its simplicity. The strobe light will blind and stun the driver. He'll feel as if he's been punched in the face, and for a few seconds, he won't know who he is or where he is and will probably let go of the steering wheel. If the stinger is dropped in the right place, it will cause the limo to veer to the left and hit either the pillars, the bridge or the walls, depending on the location. And if the limo is travelling over fifty mph, the target should be killed. If not, Timothy will administer the heart attack drug. There will then be no evidence to prove that it was not an accident. All great plans are simple."

John opened a bottle of beer and took a drink. “It’s my last bottle. “I don’t regard the plan as simple. Shooting her from the top of a building would be simple.”

Timothy had a drink of orange juice. He would have to get a few bottles of beer. “What happens if I can’t find the stinger? It could end up under the wrecked limo.”

Roger stood up. “It’s been designed to look like a draught excluder that you put at the bottom of a door. If it gets left at the scene, it won’t be a disaster. I have to go out. I need to speak to H. Put on your disguises and vests and be ready to move out.”

*

It was ten-thirty in the evening. Victoria was sitting in her lounge watching the news on television. Dodi Al-Fayed and Princess Diana had arrived in Paris and were staying at the Ritz Hotel. She used the remote control to flick through the other news channels. It did not seem possible that Princess Diana was about to be assassinated. It was wrong. No one should be killed for speaking their mind. Princess Diana might have once been a spoilt little rich girl, but not anymore. She was now a good person doing charity work, and if she managed to get landmines banned, thousands of lives would be saved.

She stood up and began to pace up and down. She must do something, but what? She picked up her mobile phone. If she told the police, they could warn Princess Diana. She hesitated. Timothy had told her that the police could trace mobile phone calls. Even if she told the police that Princess Diana was about to be killed, they would probably not believe her, but if Princess Diana was killed, they would want to know how she knew that it would happen. They would then find out about Timothy.

She put her mobile phone down. She would be risking Timothy’s and her life if she told anyone. There was nothing she could do.

*

Timothy was sitting in his bedroom at their apartment in Paris. It was two o’clock in the morning. He was smoking and flicking through the news channels on the television. If they were successful in killing Princess Diana, there was bound to be an inquest, and some people would suspect an assassination. Princess Diana was loved by millions, even though very few of them knew her. She suffered from bulimia and depression, but had courage. Despite her illnesses, she had fought back against the Royals. Prince Charles and the Queen must be amazed at her resilience. It was a pity she had to die.

No one likes to be hurt, and it is natural to want to fight back, but it is not without risks. Sometimes, the risks are too great, and it is better to take it on the chin. JFK took on the mafia, J Edgar Hoover and the arms manufacturers. He made enemies of many powerful men. He probably thought he was too powerful to be killed. He took the risks and paid the price. Princess Diana took on the Queen and Prince Charles. It was very risky, and she was about to pay the price. It was a dog-eat-dog world. Or to be more correct, a man-eat-man world. Since the beginning of time, mankind has strived for power and will kill to get it and kill to keep it. What a sick, pathetic creature the human being is.

Chapter Twelve

Victoria was standing by the window in the lounge of her house, sipping sherry and watching Sooty in the garden. It was one o'clock in the afternoon. Why was life so complicated and confusing? There was a good side to people, but also a bad side. World War I was supposed to have ended all wars. Since then, there have been dozens of wars and conflicts. Why do people think that going to war will solve their problems? People are educated and know how horrible war is, so why do they feel the need to fight and kill each other? It is all so pointless.

Sooty began to stalk a bird on the lawn. She reached to open the window to warn the bird, but it was too late. Sooty pounced, grabbed the bird and ran off into the rose bushes. She sighed. She loved Sooty, even though he had a dark side and could kill. She also loved a man who had a dark side and could kill.

The more she thought about life, the more confusing it became. A part of her mind wanted to believe that there was a loving God in a place called heaven and that everyone had a guardian angel to protect them, but what proof was there that such a God existed? Everyone suffered, some more than others, and little children and babies died every day. Many babies were born deformed. If there was a loving God, there would be no pain or suffering. And if there are guardian angels, they are doing a lousy job.

Sooty appeared, sat on the lawn and began to clean himself. He had probably eaten the blackbird. Almost everything about nature was nasty and violent. The oceans were full of creatures with mouths full of giant teeth. A loving God would not have made carnivores. There is no need for animals to kill other animals so that they can eat meat. They could all be herbivores.

She was thinking too much. It did not help to ask unanswerable questions. What was clear in her mind was that there was no need for people to kill. There was also no need to kill Princess Diana. Victoria walked towards the kitchen. She needed another drink.

*

Timothy, John, Matthew and Peter were sitting in their apartment in Paris, watching television and drinking beer. It was five-thirty in the afternoon.

Roger walked into the apartment. He looked tired. "I feel diabolical. I'm sure I'm coming down with something."

"Is it time for us to move out, Major?" John asked.

"Yes. It's time to leave. It'll help if you have some practice at being a paparazzo and following the target. I'll keep in contact with you by phone. We don't have any details yet, except that the target's expected to leave the Ritz sometime this evening."

Timothy followed the others to the lock-up garage at the rear of the hotel. The garage was ideally situated and was not overlooked. They all knew exactly what they had to do.

"Do you think we'll make the hit tonight?" Matthew asked.

"I doubt it," Peter said. "We could be following the target around for the next two weeks."

"I think we'll end up using plan B," John said.

Matthew and Peter climbed onto one of the motorbikes and drove off. Timothy climbed onto the other motorbike, and John climbed onto the pillion seat.

"Don't go too fast," John said.

John was a daredevil when it came to motorbikes. He had once clocked one hundred and eighty miles per hour on the M1.

"I'll try not to," Timothy said.

Timothy dropped John off to collect the Fiat Uno, which was parked in another lock-up garage and drove towards the Ritz hotel. When they eventually hit the target, and the operation was over, they would not return to the apartment. They would meet up at a third lock-up garage, leave the motorbikes and the Fiat Uno and drive back to the ferry in the Transit van. Everything was always meticulously planned.

Timothy drove slowly to the Ritz Hotel. There were paparazzi everywhere. He would hate to be famous and have to deal with them every day. He stopped his motorbike in the Place Vendome in front of the Ritz Hotel and cut the engine. He sat astride his motorbike and acted as if he were one of the paparazzi. He had a camera around his neck and hoped he looked the part. Matthew and Peter drove past. He ignored them.

"I think they're about to come out," one of the paparazzi said to Timothy in French.

"You could be right," Timothy said in French.

Timothy's phone rang. He took it out of his pocket. "Yes?"

"Where are you?" Roger asked.

"Outside the Ritz. I'm hoping to get a few photographs of Princess Diana."

"I've had H on the phone," Roger said. "He's under pressure to get the job done. I've told him that things cannot be rushed and that it could take weeks. He's reduced the two-week deadline to five days."

Timothy was shocked. “Five days. I don’t think we can do it in five days.”

“Neither do I,” Roger said. “We have five days, and then we use plan B.”

“Why the rush?” Timothy asked. “The target has only just arrived in Paris.”

“I don’t know why they’re panicking. I just obey orders. It’s strange; the eye I’ve had out has just started to hurt. I think it’s what they call a phantom pain.”

“If I were you, I’d take a few phantom painkillers,” Timothy said.

“Very funny,” Roger said. “According to our source at the Ritz, Dodi and Diana will be leaving the Ritz in a short time and driving to Dodi’s apartment. Follow them, but do not execute the plan even if they travel through the Alma tunnel or one of the other five designated sites.”

“Why?” Timothy asked. “We have everything planned.”

“We need to get rid of the backup car before we hit the target. I need to get in touch with Paul first to make sure he’ll be able to dispose of the backup car. Philippe Dourneau will be driving the target and Dodi. The bodyguards, Trevor Rees-Jones and Kez Wingfield, will be following in the Range Rover driven by Jean Francis Muza. We need to make sure that we can dispose of the backup car before implementing any plan.”

“Roger, Roger,” Timothy said. It was his little joke to show that all was well.

“Let me know if anything happens that could affect our plan,” Roger said.

“I will.”

Timothy put the phone back into his pocket and lit a cigarette. Two of the paparazzi were arguing about football. One of them turned to look at Timothy. “Who do you think is the greatest footballer who has ever lived?” he asked. “My friend thinks it’s Pele, but I think it’s Maradona.”

“Pele is great,” Timothy said. “Maradona is even better, but George is best.”

The two paparazzi roared with laughter.

“That’s very clever,” the same man said. “But I don’t think George Best is the best.”

“They’re coming out,” the other man said.

Dodi and Princess Diana walked out of the Ritz hotel, and the cameras began to flash. Princess Diana looked unhappy, and Dodi looked angry. They climbed into a Mercedes and drove off. The two bodyguards followed them in a Range Rover. Timothy flicked his cigarette away and followed the two vehicles along the Rue Combon and then onto the Champs-Élysées. They were travelling within the speed limit. The paparazzi were everywhere. They were in cars and on motorbikes.

The darkened windows of the Mercedes prevented photographs of the couple from being taken when they were forced to stop at traffic lights. Timothy kept a few paparazzi between him and the target. Something must have happened to force them to implement plan B in five days.

The Mercedes pulled up outside Dodi's apartment, and Dodi and Princess Diana climbed out. They were mobbed by the paparazzi, who were desperate to get photographs. It was chaotic. Timothy had never seen anything like it. Dodi and Princess Diana were being jostled from every direction.

The couple eventually forced their way through the paparazzi, with the help of the bodyguards, and entered the apartment. Timothy sat astride his motorbike and lit a cigarette. This cat-and-mouse game could go on for days. It suited him. The longer it went on, the greater the chance there was that the mission would be aborted. From what he could gather from the news, Dodi and Princess Diana were happy and had fallen in love. It was a shame that the men in grey suits could not leave them to enjoy their lives.

His phone rang. "Yes?"

"Where are you?" Roger asked.

"Outside Dodi's apartment."

"What's happening?" Roger asked.

"Nothing. Dodi and Diana are in the apartment. The paparazzi are everywhere. They're being very aggressive and could interfere with the operation."

"I know," Roger said. "Which is why planning is all-important. It's the backup car that's causing us problems. The last thing we want is a shoot-out."

"Will the target be coming out of Dodi's apartment tonight?" Timothy asked.

"Yes, but they're not going to Chez Benoit for a meal as was planned. Dodi has cancelled their reservation. They're upset by the actions of the paparazzi. They'll be going back to the Ritz. Just follow them."

"Okay," Timothy said.

Timothy was not surprised that Roger knew exactly when and where Dodi and Princess Diana were going. It was easy enough to bug phones, apartments and even people.

At nine-thirty, the couple appeared and climbed into the Mercedes. Timothy followed the two vehicles back to the Ritz Hotel. They drove at a normal speed and stopped at traffic lights. Timothy felt sorry for them. They were rich and famous, but they were not free. And what price can you put on freedom? Timothy would love to be rich but would hate to be famous.

The Mercedes pulled up outside the Ritz Hotel. Princess Diana and Dodi climbed out and ran towards the hotel. The paparazzi were everywhere. Dodi looked angry and shouted at some of the paparazzi. Timothy pulled up and sat astride his motorbike. Some of the dozens of paparazzi gathered outside the Ritz Hotel would be MI6 officials, and some would be the men in grey suits.

Timothy saw the paparazzo he had spoken to earlier. "Is it true that Diana and Dodi are about to announce their engagement?" Timothy asked.

"Yes," the man said. "She's pregnant, so they can't wait much longer."

Timothy sat astride his motorbike and waited. If she were pregnant, it could be the reason why they were in such a hurry to kill her. It was unlikely that her pregnancy was an accident. It was probably planned. It could be her way of forcing Dodi to marry her. Women could be very devious at the best of times.

One of his rules in life was to never believe a woman when she says she is on the pill and to always wear a condom. It was a rule that had saved him from fathering many unwanted babies. It was different now that he wanted a child. He would now give anything to father a child, but only if Victoria was the mother. He began to worry about her and hoped she would be worrying about him.

Henri Paul arrived and walked into the hotel at about ten p.m. Timothy's phone rang at eleven-thirty. "Yes?"

"Be ready to move," Roger said. "They're getting ready to leave and will be travelling to Dodi's apartment. We've had a stroke of luck. They'll not be using the Mercedes and the Land Rover that are parked outside the front of the Ritz. They'll be leaving from the rear of the Ritz to fool the paparazzi. They're not having a backup car. Get to the back of the hotel and be ready to execute plan A. It's go, go, go."

"I'm on my way," Timothy said.

He drove to the rear of the hotel and sat astride his motorbike. A small number of paparazzi were milling about and waiting. He could not believe that the target was not having a backup car. It was foolhardy, to say the least.

He lit a cigarette and frowned. If the target was going to Dodi's apartment, they would travel along the Champs-Élysées, so how were they going to execute plan A? The target was probably intending to go somewhere else after she had been to Dodi's apartment.

A short time later, his phone rang. "Yes?"

"They've ordered an extra limo," Roger said. "It looks as if Henri Paul will be driving. Trevor will be their only bodyguard. He'll be travelling in the limo with them. It could not be more perfect."

Timothy was amazed. "Have they gone raving mad? The paparazzi will be all over them."

"It's all thanks to the overzealous paparazzi," Roger said. "Princess Diana's upset by how she's been treated, and Dodi's in a filthy mood. They're determined to lose the paparazzi."

"They won't be able to lose the paparazzi," Timothy said. "There are at least a dozen paparazzi at the back of the hotel."

"I'll have to go," Roger said. "I'll get back to you."

Timothy put his phone into his pocket and took a drag on his cigarette. Why would they be getting rid of the backup car? It did not make sense. And leaving by the rear of the hotel would only fool some of the paparazzi. And even if they drove fast and lost the paparazzi, the paparazzi would be waiting for them when they got to Dodi's apartment. If he were Dodi, he would stay at the Ritz Hotel.

Timothy's phone rang. He took it out of his pocket. "Yes?"

"Is it all quiet where you are?" Roger asked.

"Yes."

"Can you see any police?" Roger asked.

Timothy looked about. "No. Only paparazzi."

"We've had a fantastic stroke of luck," Roger said. "The limo they intend to use does not have darkened windows, which I assume is the reason why they'll be travelling through the Alma tunnel."

"Why?" Timothy asked. "What has darkened windows got to do with travelling through the Alma tunnel?"

"If they travel along the Champs-Élysées, they'll have to stop at the traffic lights, and the paparazzi will be all over them, taking photographs. If they travel along the Cours la Reine by the river Seine, they'll be able to put their foot down and lose the paparazzi."

"They won't lose them," Timothy said. "Some of them have powerful motorbikes."

"There are speed cameras all along the Cours la Reine," Roger said. "If the paparazzi are caught speeding, they'll lose their licence. A speeding ticket won't bother Dodi. Hopefully, by the time the target reaches the Alma tunnel, you and Peter will be the only motorbikes keeping up with them. I need to have a word with John. I'll get back to you."

Timothy put his phone back into his pocket. It did not make sense. Dodi's bodyguards were acting like amateurs. If he were guarding Princess Diana and Dodi, he would insist on a backup car. And he would advise Dodi to get an apartment with a garage. They would then be able to drive straight into the garage before getting out of the car, and would not be jostled by the paparazzi. And to have a limo without darkened windows was asking for trouble.

His phone rang. He took it out of his pocket. "Yes?"

"Has the limo arrived yet?" Roger asked.

"No."

"Everything's set up," Roger said. "Can you see Peter and Matthew?"

Timothy looked about. "No."

"They can see you," Roger said. "Matthew will be in contact with John so that he'll know when to make his move."

"You seem to know everything that's happening at the Ritz," Timothy said. "Who is the source?"

"Fuck knows, but they seem to know everything that's going on. I get the impression that there's more than one source."

"Will the target be travelling through the Alma tunnel tonight?" Timothy asked.

"Yes."

"Why?" Timothy asked. "Where are they going?"

"I don't know. They might just be taking a long way around to Dodi's apartment or going to some other destination. Only contact me if something goes wrong."

"Roger, Roger," Timothy said. He put his phone back into his pocket and sat waiting. It was about to get very interesting.

At twelve-twenty, a Mercedes S280 pulled up at the rear of the hotel, and the driver climbed out. It did not have darkened windows. Henri Paul walked out of the side entrance of the hotel and climbed into the Mercedes. Timothy took a drag on his cigarette. If the target died tonight, it would be because the limo did not have darkened windows, and they were forced to travel through the Alma tunnel. Although they might not be going to Dodi's apartment. They could be going to another destination. They could be going to a restaurant or to a friend's house to escape from the paparazzi.

Trevor Rees-Jones, Dodi, and Princess Diana walked out of the hotel's side entrance and climbed into the Mercedes. Flashing cameras sent shadows dancing about in the darkness.

The Mercedes drove off down the one-way Rue Cambon, and Timothy followed close behind. About a dozen paparazzi were also following on motorbikes and in cars. The Mercedes turned right onto rue de Pivoli. The paparazzi from the front of the hotel were now joining the chase. The Mercedes was travelling a little faster than before, but was still within the speed limit.

Timothy drove past the Mercedes and turned into the Place de la Concorde. He was now about thirty feet in front of the Mercedes. The nearest paparazzi were about fifty yards behind the Mercedes. Timothy drove to the entrance to the Champs-Élysées and stopped his motorbike a short distance from Matthew and Peter on the other motorbike. They held up their cameras as if intending to take photographs.

There was no way Timothy could sabotage the operation. They were obviously being watched by MI6 agents and the men in grey suits, and if Timothy was seen disobeying orders, he would be killed.

Instead of turning onto the Champs-Élysées, the Mercedes drove straight on towards the River Seine. Timothy, Matthew and Peter followed the limo on their motorbikes. It seemed as if the information Roger had been given was correct. The target was not going directly to Dodi's apartment. Everything was now going to plan. If the Mercedes turned into Cours la Reine, their fate would be sealed.

The Mercedes turned onto the Cours la Reine, a dual carriageway, and Henri Paul put his foot down. Timothy, Peter and Matthew followed the Mercedes on their powerful motorbikes. The Mercedes was now doing about seventy miles per hour and was leaving the paparazzi behind. The paparazzi were obviously aware of the speed cameras and were frightened of receiving a speeding ticket. They were keeping to the thirty-one miles per hour speed limit. If the Mercedes crashed at the speed it was now travelling at, the occupants would almost certainly be killed.

As they neared the Alma tunnel, Timothy saw the Fiat Uno travelling towards the tunnel at about thirty miles per hour. Matthew and Peter overtook the Mercedes at high speed and then slowed down so that they would be travelling at the same speed as the Mercedes when they entered the Alma tunnel. The motorbike driven by Matthew was now about thirty feet in front of the Mercedes. Timothy checked his mirrors. There was no sign of the paparazzi.

Matthew's motorbike and the Mercedes swerved to the left to avoid the Fiat Uno that had braked and slowed down to about twenty miles per hour. The braking of the Fiat Uno was too severe, and the Mercedes clipped the left-hand side of the Fiat Uno's bumper. As both Matthew's motorbike and the

Mercedes went over the bump in the road, the strobe light flashed and lit up the tunnel.

The Mercedes veered to the left and hit the pillars. The modified stinger had obviously worked. The noise of the crash was like an explosion. The Mercedes spun around and stopped, facing in the opposite direction. The front of the car now resembled a mangled lump of metal. The horn of the crashed Mercedes was blaring constantly as Matthew's motorbike and the Fiat Uno drove out of the tunnel.

Timothy stopped next to the crashed Mercedes. Henri Paul looked dead, and Trevor Rees-Jones and Dodi were severely injured and would probably die. Princess Diana was lying in the footwell in the rear of the Mercedes. She moved, and so was still alive. She looked to be semi-conscious.

Paparazzi began to arrive, and members of the public were now running towards the crashed Mercedes. When the paparazzi began photographing the target, Timothy drove out of the tunnel.

The target would probably die. She had not been wearing a seat belt and so would have sustained severe internal injuries. The Mercedes had hit the pillars at about seventy miles per hour. She could also have a brain injury.

He took a deep breath. His job was done. It was over. The strobe light and the stinger had worked perfectly. Just before the Mercedes had crashed, the engine had revved up, as if Henri Paul had accidentally knocked the vehicle into neutral and hit the accelerator instead of the brake. The bright light was the last thing that Henri Paul saw. The only good thing that would come out of this, was that it would teach other people to always wear seat belts.

Timothy drove slowly to the other garage. The operation had been successful. Princess Diana was dying and would be dead long before she reached the hospital. He could now go home. Usually, after the successful completion of an operation, he felt elated, but not this time. His heart had not been in this job. He felt sad. It was one operation he would like to forget. It had been an ignominious and undignified end to the life of a remarkable woman who had stood up to the Queen and Prince Charles. The loose cannon had ultimately paid the price.

When he arrived at the garage, the other team members were waiting for him.

"Has the target been eliminated, Tim?" Roger asked.

Timothy took out his cigarettes. "The Mercedes hit the pillars at about seventy mph. I had a quick look at the four occupants. Henri looked dead; Trevor and Dodi looked near to death, and Diana looked as good as dead."

"So, you used the heart attack drug?" Roger asked.

"No. The paparazzi arrived a short time after the Mercedes crashed, and I was unable to use the drug."

Roger looked annoyed. "Fucking hell. Was she badly injured?"

"Not to look at," Timothy said. "But she'll probably die from internal injuries."

"Probably is not good enough," Roger said as he pressed numbers into his mobile phone.

"What a fuck-up," John said. "You should have used the drug, Tim."

"I couldn't. Not with the paparazzi taking photographs."

Roger spent a short time on the phone and then took a deep breath. "It's out of our hands now. All we can do is wait to see if the target dies."

Timothy was worried that they would blame him if the target lived. "I did all I could. I could not administer the drug with the paparazzi taking photographs. She was not wearing her seat belt and should die from internal injuries."

Roger shook his head. "I hope to God she does. Did anything else go wrong?"

"No," John said. "It went as planned. No one will think that it was anything other than an accident."

"Not everything went to plan," Timothy said. "The Mercedes clipped the back of the Fiat."

"Fucking hell," Roger said. "It'll now place the Fiat at the scene and will leave evidence. Did anything else go wrong?"

"Yes," Timothy said. "I couldn't find the stinger. It must be underneath the crashed Mercedes."

Roger put his head in his hands. "What a total cock-up."

"It's all right," Peter said. "There's no need to worry. I didn't drop the stinger."

Roger looked up and stared at Peter. "Why? Why the fucking hell didn't you drop the stinger?"

"It wasn't my fault. I used the strobe light and was about to drop the stinger when Matthew swerved violently. I almost fell off the fucking bike."

Roger turned to Peter. "Why did you swerve?"

"I had no choice. I had to avoid what looked like half a house brick lying on the road. If we'd hit it, we could have come off the bike."

"Where's the strobe light?" Roger asked. "I hope to God you didn't drop it. If you have, we are totally fucked."

"It's here," Peter said, and he pulled it out of his jacket. "As it turned out, I didn't need to drop the stinger. The strobe light did the job."

Roger took out his mobile phone. “I’d better tell them about the cock-ups. They’ll need to make sure that the Fiat Uno is never discovered.” Roger began talking on his mobile phone.

Timothy lit a cigarette and inhaled deeply. He was beginning to worry. Even though Peter did not drop the stinger and John braked too severely, if the target lived, they would blame him for not administering the heart attack drug.

Matthew leaned nearer to Timothy. “I nearly dropped the fucking strobe light when Peter swerved to avoid that brick,” Matthew whispered. “And it’s all John’s fault. He’s a fucking maniac at times. There was no need for him to slow down so much. It was because he slowed down too quickly that the Merc hit the Fiat. It could have all gone wrong.”

“It’ll all be forgotten if the target dies,” Timothy said.

“I’ve got some bad news,” Roger said. “The target’s still alive.”

John looked shocked. He looked at Timothy. “I thought you said that she would die?”

Timothy was surprised. “I thought she would.” He looked at his watch. “I thought she would be dead by now. What is her condition?”

“I’m not sure,” Roger said. “Dodi’s dead, and so is Henri, but Trevor and the target are still alive.”

“I don’t believe it,” Timothy said. “The Mercedes was travelling at about seventy when it hit the pillar, and according to the experts, a person cannot survive such a crash, at least not without sustaining severe internal injuries. And I was sure that Trevor would only last for a few minutes. His face was smashed in.”

“What a fucking disaster,” Roger said. “Two people survived the crash, and one of them is the fucking target.” He looked very angry. “Give me the ring, Tim. I don’t want you injecting yourself and having a fucking heart attack.”

Timothy took the ring that contained the heart attack drug off his finger and handed it to Roger. “What happens now, Major?”

“We wait to see if the backup plan works.”

Peter frowned. “What backup plan?”

“I don’t know the details. It’s all on a need-to-know basis. According to H, the backup plan is to make sure that the target is given the heart attack drug if she survives the crash. They obviously realised that Tim might not be able to administer the drug. By now, she should have been given the drug.”

“I told you the plan was too simple,” John said. “They build them Mercedes like tanks. They have safety features as well as airbags.”

“Is the target in hospital?” John asked.

Roger shook his head. “She’s still in the ambulance. They’re delaying the journey to hospital to make sure she dies. The ambulance has just started to travel to the hospital.”

Timothy looked at his watch. “It’s over an hour since the crash. Surely, they’re not still on their way to the hospital. It’s only a ten-minute journey. The drug should have worked by now. It normally takes just a few seconds, minutes at the most, to work.

“It depends on the dose,” Peter said. “But even a low dose should have worked by now.”

Timothy felt confused. “I don’t know how they’ve managed to keep her out of hospital for so long. The only chance a person has, after such an accident, is to get to hospital as soon as possible to stop any internal bleeding.”

Roger’s phone rang.

While Roger talked on his mobile phone, Timothy sat smoking. If Princess Diana did not die, he would be blamed. They might think that he had not administered the heart attack drug deliberately. His thoughts turned to Victoria. The crash would soon be on the news, and she would know that he had been involved in the attempt on Princess Diana’s life. She could be waiting for him to return or looking for someone else. He prayed that she had not finished with him.

“It’s bad news,” Roger said. “The heart attack drug has not worked. The target was given the drug, but they think the dosage was too small. Apparently, the target did suffer a heart attack, although not a fatal one. She is receiving CPR.”

“If she's receiving CPR, it will prevent the heart attack drug from killing her,” Timothy said. “The heart attack drug only stops the heart from working. The CPR will keep her alive.”

“We’ll just have to wait and see what happens and hope to God she dies,” Roger said. “From what they said, she’s in a bad way and is not expected to live.”

“Is she now in the hospital?” Peter asked.

“No,” Roger said. “She’s just arriving at the hospital.”

Timothy was shocked. He looked at his watch. It was just after two o’clock. “It is now one hour and forty-six minutes since the crash. What the fuck are they playing at? The hospital is only a short distance from the Alma Tunnel. People are going to want to know why it has taken so long to get Princess Diana to the hospital.”

“If she lives, do we go back to finish the job?” John asked.

“I don’t know,” Roger said. “I suppose so.”

"What about our cash?" Peter asked. "If she lives, do we still get our cash?"

"Not until the target's dead," Roger said. "If she lives, we'll probably have to go back and implement plan B."

They drove to the ferry. Peter was driving. As they boarded the ferry, Roger had a call on his mobile phone. They all stopped walking and stared at him.

Roger smiled. "Thanks for letting me know." He put his phone into his pocket. "The target was pronounced dead at four o'clock, and she did suffer a massive heart attack. She also had a torn pulmonary vein."

"Thank God for that," John said.

Timothy felt relieved. "I told you she would die. Even without the drug, she would have died from the internal injury. It just took a little longer than I expected."

"H is as pleased as punch," Roger said. "Let's get aboard the ferry. I need to put my feet up."

"What I need is a drink," John said.

Except for Roger, they all had several cans of lager and then tried to sleep. It had been a long day and an even longer night, and they were all exhausted. It was a rough crossing, and they were all woken up by the swaying of the ferry. Except for Roger, they were all violently sick.

Roger laughed until tears ran from his good eye. "That'll teach you to get drunk."

Timothy felt ill and was glad to get onto dry land. As soon as he was given his mobile phone, he called Victoria. The number was unobtainable. He tried several times. She had probably moved and did not want him to contact her. His depression deepened and began to fight with his tablets. If he did not have Victoria, he did not have a future.

Chapter Thirteen

Victoria woke up. She had fallen asleep on the settee in her lounge. She switched on the television. The newsreader was announcing that Princess Diana had been involved in an accident but had survived. Victoria was shocked, even though she had expected something like this to happen. She was also upset. She did not want Princess Diana to die. She began to worry. If Princess Diana did not die, Timothy would not be coming home, or he might come home and have to go back again at a later date to finish the job.

She poured herself a large glass of sherry and sat down in front of the television. How can this be happening? She was one of the few people who knew that Princess Diana's accident was not an accident.

A news flash appeared on the television. '*We are receiving more information about the car crash involving Princess Diana. She is alive but seriously ill. We do not as yet know the extent of her injuries. Dodi Al Fayed and the driver are dead. Princess Diana's bodyguard, Trevor Rees-Jones, is also seriously injured.*'

Victoria took a long drink of sherry. Pictures of a smashed-up Mercedes came on the television. It did not seem possible that anyone could have survived such a crash. She lifted her empty glass. What was she doing? Drinking on an empty stomach was not a good idea. She walked into the kitchen, put two pieces of bread into the toaster and switched on the kettle. She could see the television from the kitchen. The newsreader was now talking about other items of news.

It all seemed unreal. Timothy could be lying low, and he might not be home for several days. She stared at the kettle. If Princess Diana died, Victoria would have to spend the rest of her life knowing that Timothy had killed her. He might be a professional killer, but it made no difference to how she felt about him. It was becoming more obvious that she not only loved him but also needed him. She felt more alone now than at any time in her life.

Another news flash appeared on the television. "*We have just been informed that Princess Diana has died. Princess Diana died at four am from massive internal injuries.*"

The strength left Victoria's legs, and she sat down on a kitchen chair. It was over. They had succeeded in killing Princess Diana. She was overflowing with all manner of emotions and burst into tears.

*

Timothy and the team drove back to the Midlands in the back of the Transit Van with Peter driving. Timothy felt physically and mentally drained. His depression was the reason he had lost Victoria. If he had not been depressed, he would not have taken tablets and so would not have talked in his sleep. Victoria would now be unaware that he was an assassin and would be waiting for him to come home, and because it was his last operation, he would have been able to plan a future with the woman he loved.

"This was my last op," Timothy said. "I don't care what happens; I won't be going on another op."

"There's no need to worry," Roger said. "It was our last op."

"We'll have to meet up each year and have a Christmas drink," Matthew said. "I'd hate to think we'll never see each other again."

"It sounds like a good idea to me," John said. "We could meet up on the boat. I miss army life, but I'm getting too old for all this excitement. I'll soon be sixty. I suppose it is time to call it a day. What will you do with yourself, Tim?"

"I don't know. I don't think I'll go into security work. I'll probably end up in a boring nine-to-five job."

"I think it's a good idea to keep in touch," Roger said. "I hate the thought of retirement. If I were not ill, I would continue in some capacity. Old age is a bastard. I might be old, but I don't feel it."

"I don't think we should only meet up once a year," Matthew said. "We could all become members of that golf club of yours, Tim, and play a round of golf every few months."

"Sounds like a good idea to me," John said. "I enjoy a round of golf."

They chatted as they travelled back to the Midlands, but Timothy's mind was elsewhere. If Victoria did not want to continue with their relationship, he would have to accept it. He would sell his house and move. A life by the seaside would be a good way to spend his old age. He still wanted children, but only with Victoria as their mother. It would be impossible to find another woman like Victoria. He loved her, and it was going to be extremely difficult to live without her.

He was dropped off outside Victoria's house. He said goodbye to the team and walked through the gate. There was a for-sale sign in the front garden. He was shocked. She was selling up. She might already have moved. His car was still parked in the drive, but there was no sign of her car. He climbed into his car and smoked a cigarette. Would it be worth talking to her to try to persuade her to change her mind, or would it be a waste of time? He still loved her. His feelings were very powerful, but if she did not love him, there was nothing he could do. All he could do was say goodbye and wish her luck.

He climbed out of the car and knocked on the door. There was no answer. He knocked on the door again with greater force to make sure she was not in. She could already be starting a new life somewhere without him. There was no answer.

He walked down the path, climbed into his car and drove off. If Victoria wanted nothing to do with him, and that was the way it looked, what was he going to do, and where was he going to live? His mind refused to work as if it were clinging to the hope that Victoria still loved him. Before he did anything, he would have to see her. He had to know how she felt.

His subconscious mind guided him to the hotel where he used to stay. It was now the nearest thing he had to a home. He checked in, sat down on the bed, and tried to decide what to do. His life felt empty. The larder was also empty, so he would have to do a bit of shopping for the essentials: coffee, tea, milk and beer. He had no intention of cooking and would eat out at a local cafe. He lit a cigarette and sat looking out of the window.

If only Victoria would listen to reason and be more understanding. He was proud of his service in the army and the SAS, as well as of what he had accomplished as an assassin. They had killed people who were a danger to the stability of this country. The choice of the target was not his to make. If he had been in charge, he would not have ordered the death of Princess Diana. He would have stopped her from having Muslim children in some other way. He would have had Dodi killed or drugged her with something to cause a miscarriage.

As much as he regretted being a part of the team that had killed Princess Diana, he had to admit that there was only one way to stop a woman who was hell-bent on destroying not only the credibility of Prince Charles but also the monarchy, and that was to kill her. If she had married Dodi and had his children, it would have made it impossible for either of her two children, William or Harry, to become king. This country had a choice between Princess Diana and the monarchy. It was a choice that had already been made.

Before he went shopping, he decided to phone Victoria again. The number was still unobtainable, and the house phone just rang out. She probably hated him for what he had done. Loneliness pushed in among his thoughts. He needed a drink. There was a public house across the road.

Twenty minutes later, he was sitting at a corner table in the public house on his third pint of lager. She could not have loved him. If she had loved him, she would still want to be with him. Instead of going shopping, he got drunk.

The news on the television behind the bar was about the death of Princess Diana. The French police were blaming the paparazzi.

Chapter Fourteen

Victoria missed Timothy more than she had thought possible. She wanted to tell him that she loved him and was carrying his child. She would have to live with a killer because she could not live without him. It was Monday morning. She had given up her job and was finalising the deal to buy a nursery of her own. All she needed was Timothy's signature. He was probably hiding out in France and waiting for the heat to die down.

She was standing in the lounge of her house and looking out of the window. She was hoping to see Timothy walk up the path. She had spent the whole morning looking out of the window. It was now twelve-thirty. She had an appointment with her bank manager at one o'clock to arrange a bridging loan until she sold her house.

She drove to the bank in a haze of emotions. At times, she felt as if she were being suffocated. She was overjoyed at being pregnant and beginning a new life, but felt depressed by the death of Princess Diana. A part of her would never forgive Timothy for what he had done. When all was said and done, it was wrong to kill another human being. Victoria was also worried about how the knowledge of the assassination, which they would both have to live with, would affect their future relationship.

*

Timothy woke up with a hangover. He was lying in bed in his hotel suite. He switched on the television. The news was mostly about the death of Princess Diana. He made himself a cup of coffee and lit a cigarette. He would speak with Victoria before he left to start a new life, to try and talk some sense into her. He would also have to see his parents. His depression was once again knocking the hell out of his tablets.

He drove to Victoria's house, and even though her car was not there, he knocked on the door. She was not in. He then remembered that it was Monday. She would be at work. He drove to the nursery where she worked and rang the bell. He would ask her to go for a drink with him so that they could have a chat. He had a nasty feeling that he would be wasting his time.

"Yes?" a voice asked through the intercom.

"Can I speak to Victoria?"

"She doesn't work here anymore," the voice said.

"Thanks."

It began to rain as he walked towards his car. He felt disappointed. She had obviously finished with him and was making a new start somewhere. She was probably worried about being killed and might have already left the area. She would be wasting her time if she thought she could hide from MI5 soldiers. If they wanted to kill her, it would not make any difference where she went. They would find her within a few days.

The rain lashed down on his car as he drove to the nursing home to see his mother. The weather now matched his spirits. Visiting his mother was always an ordeal, and he had to force himself to walk into the nursing home. His mother was reading a magazine in the lounge. He kissed her on the cheek and sat down next to her. "Are you all right?" he asked.

"I'm as good as can be expected." She looked over her glasses at him. "Is anything wrong?"

"Why do you think there's something wrong?"

"You haven't had a shave. Are you feeling ill?"

"No. I'm just feeling a bit fed up." He needed to change the subject. "Has Dad been to visit you?"

"Yes. Your father's being very brave. He's more ill than he's making out. He's on painkillers. Are you going to see him? I don't think he's going to live much longer."

"I'm going to see him today. He's had a good life. I hope I get to eighty-five."

"You won't if you keep on smoking," she said. "You have nicotine on your fingers."

"I do intend to give them up. I just don't feel up to it at the moment."

"How's Victoria?" she asked.

"I don't know. She's dumped me."

His mother looked upset. "Why?"

He shrugged. He decided to tell her part of the truth. "She found out that I used to be a soldier. I don't think she likes killing. I think she's a bit of a pacifist."

"So, that's why you're feeling low." She frowned. "No one likes killing, but there must be more to it than that. What reason did she give for dumping you?"

"No specific reason. I think she just went off me."

"There must be a reason," she said. "Ask her what the reason is. Do you still love her?"

"Yes." He already knew why she had dumped him. "I do intend to see her again to see if she wants to give it another try."

"I would," she said. "I was looking forward to having a grandchild."

He stood up. "I'm going now." He kissed her on the cheek.

"Tell your father not to worry if he can't come to see me. I'll understand."

He nodded and left.

Thunder, lightning and torrential rain kept him company as he drove to see his father. He was not in the mood to talk, but he would have to make the effort. It might be the last time he would see his father alive. With both of his parents at death's door, it was a good job he was on antidepressants.

He parked his car, ran up the path and knocked on the door. His father opened the door.

"You've picked a good day to visit me," his father said.

Timothy stepped into the house. "I'm soaked, and I only ran up the path." He followed his father into the kitchen. His father had lost even more weight. Timothy hardly recognised him. The television was on. "How are you feeling, Dad?"

"Bloody awful. They want me to go into hospital. Are you rushing off, or shall I put the kettle on?"

"Put the kettle on. I could do with a cuppa."

His father switched on the kettle. "I've been watching the news. It's all about the death of Princess Diana. They claim it was an accident, although she could have been killed."

Timothy sat down at the kitchen table. "What makes you think she was killed?"

"She was going out with Al-Fayed's son. She should have known better than to go out with an Arab and a Muslim. She was probably hoping to annoy Prince Charles and the Queen. Princess Diana has been making waves for years. If she was killed, no one will ever know. They won't leave any clues like they did with JFK."

They sat drinking tea, chatting and watching the news. The main news was that Henri Paul's blood was three times over the French legal limit. Timothy frowned. They must have switched his blood. Henri Paul was not drunk. Trevor Rees-Jones was a professional, and he would not have let Henri Paul drive if he had been drunk.

"I'm under pressure to go into hospital," his father said. "I've told them that I want to die at home."

"I don't like the idea of you spending your last days in pain," Timothy said. "Do you want me to stay with you?"

"No. I intend to end it when I can't take anymore. I've got a pile of paracetamol tablets." His father sipped his tea. "I had a bad night last night. I intend to visit your mother one more time to say goodbye and then do it. I'll probably do it tomorrow night. I'll get drunk first."

"Isn't there anything they can do?" Timothy asked. "I can afford to pay for the best treatment possible."

His father shook his head. "The cancer has spread all over my body. Trust me to get a cancer that's incurable."

Timothy sipped his tea. He could feel his depression knocking hell out of his tablets. "I wish I could do something."

"You can. Make sure that me and your mother are buried together."

Timothy nodded. "I will."

"When I'm gone, will you visit your mother as often as possible? She enjoys having a visitor."

"I will. I'm moving away, but I'll get back to see her as often as I can."

"How's Victoria?" his father asked. "She paid me a visit a few days ago. She seems like a very nice young lady."

Timothy was surprised. "Why did she visit you?"

"To find out about you. She knows what you do. I don't think she's too pleased."

"She isn't. It's why we split up."

His father looked upset. "It's a pity. She seems like a nice young woman. Is there any way you can patch it up? She would make a good mother."

"I don't know. I intend to give it one more try."

"I would offer some advice, but I've never understood women," his father said. "I had problems with your mother, and we split up several times. We are very different in many ways. Perhaps Victoria will change her mind. I had the feeling that you loved her and wanted to start a family."

"I did love her," Timothy said. "I still love her, and I want to start a family, but I don't think she'll change her mind. She's put her house up for sale and left her job. I think she's already moved on."

"It could be for the best," his father said. "If it's meant to be, it will happen. If it's not meant to be, you'll have to find someone else."

"I don't want anyone else." Timothy stood up and hugged his father. His father's body felt like a bag of bones. This was the last time he would see his father. He began to choke up. "I love you, Dad. I've never told you before, but I think you've always known."

"I know. In the same way that you knew that I've always loved you."

"I'll have to go," Timothy said.

His father followed him to the door. "Have some children before it's too late, and have more than one."

"I'll see what I can do." Timothy took one last look at his father and walked down the path. His father was crying. Timothy began to choke up. Life can be a bastard at times.

The rain had stopped, and the sun was shining, but it did not lift his spirits. He drove away from his father's house, feeling sad and empty. His body felt like cardboard. He had never been close to his parents, but he would miss them. He was dreading their funerals.

*

Victoria sat watching the television in her lounge. Every few minutes, she stood up and looked out of the window. The news channels were saying that Princess Diana's death had been an accident, and they had not said that anybody other than the occupants of the car had been injured, so Timothy should be all right. He was probably still in France, which was why he had not phoned.

The phone rang. She snatched it up. "Yes?"

"It's me," Emma said. "Would you like to go shopping in Solihull with me and Mother this weekend?"

"No." Victoria took several deep breaths. She had expected to hear Timothy's voice.

"Why not?" Emma asked. "Are you still talking to Mother?"

"Yes. I'm just too busy at the moment. I'm selling my house and starting a new business."

"I'm glad that you're still talking to Mother," Emma said. "I'll call you in a week or so."

"Yes. Bye."

Victoria put the phone down and leaned back in her seat. Her heart was beating as if she had been running. Sooty jumped onto her lap. "I wish Tim would phone."

*

Timothy drove to his house. Jane had moved out and had left a note on the hall table. I wish you well, was all it said. He had once loved this house, but it was now full of unpleasant memories. He packed a few personal possessions and his clothes into four suitcases. He would leave everything else to the removal men. He returned to his hotel, collected his things and settled his bill. After filling up his car with diesel, he drove onto the M42. He had decided to try and forget about Victoria and make a new start somewhere on the south coast. It was the warmest part of Great Britain. He would give Weymouth the once-over.

As he drove along, all he could think about was Victoria and what could have been. It would have been better if he had never met her. At least he would not be suffering as if someone were cutting up his body from the inside. He had fallen in love with her and would never love another woman; nevertheless, he would have to find another girlfriend. He did not want to spend the rest of his life on his own. However wonderful his new girlfriend turned out to be, she would never be able to replace Victoria.

*

Victoria could not sleep and sat in front of the television. If only Timothy would give her a call to say he was all right. She was tempted to call him, but was worried they would trace the call. She had no choice but to wait. She tried to lose herself in a romantic film to take her mind off her worries.

*

On Wednesday, Victoria decided to visit Timothy's father to see if he had heard from Timothy. It was unlikely that Timothy would visit his father before seeing her, but it gave her something to do. She knocked on George's door several times. There was no reply. As she walked back to her car, the next-door neighbour came out of her house and walked down the path.

"Do you know when George will be back?" she asked the woman.

"George passed away yesterday," the woman said. "It was such a shock."

"Oh, no," Victoria said. She was saddened by the news. "I didn't know. I was looking for his son, Timothy. Have you seen him?"

"No. He hasn't shown up yet."

Victoria returned to her house and sat down next to the phone with a glass of lager. If Timothy did not return in the next few days, he would miss his father's funeral. From what she could remember, Timothy had not been close to his father.

*

Timothy liked Weymouth and booked into a hotel a short distance from the sea. While he was making a cup of coffee in the kitchen, his phone rang. He took it out of his pocket. "Yes."

"I hate using the phone, but I had to call you," his mother said. "Your father's died."

"Oh. I've been expecting it. Who's sorting out the funeral arrangements?"

"Your father's solicitor. The funeral's been arranged for ten o'clock on Friday at St Mary's church in Solihull. I'll see you at the funeral. Bye."

"Bye."

He put the phone back into his pocket and then took it out again and stared at it. As much as he wanted to make a fresh start, he needed to have one last talk with Victoria. He had to make one last effort. He phoned her mobile. The number was still unobtainable. He phoned her home number on the off chance that she might be there. If she had sold the house, the new occupants might have a forwarding address.

"Hello?" Victoria said.

He was shocked to hear her voice. He had assumed that she had moved. "Hello. It's me."

"Is that you, Tim?"

"Yes. I wonder if we could have a chat?"

"Yes. Where are you?"

"I'm in Weymouth. I'm coming back to the Midlands on Thursday for my father's funeral. Could we meet up?"

"Yes. Are you all right?"

"Yes. Where are you living?"

"I'm still living in the same place. When will you be here?"

"About two o'clock on Friday."

"Okay," she said. "I'll see you at two on Friday."

"Yes. Bye."

He put his phone back into his pocket and lit a cigarette. Victoria had sounded distant, as if she did not want to see him, but she had agreed to speak to him, so there was some hope they could get back together. He missed her more than he could put into words. All he could do was tell her that he loved her and that he needed her.

*

Victoria was very worried. Something had happened. Timothy was not the same person. He could have been injured. He had talked as if they hardly knew each other. Perhaps it had something to do with not being able to talk properly on the phone. At least he had phoned. She might be able to get a good night's sleep now that she knew he was not dead. He would probably explain what had happened when they met on Friday.

*

Timothy left Weymouth early on Thursday so that he would have time to visit his mother. If he intended to see his mother once a week, it would be better if he stayed in the Midlands, at least until she went to join his father. He walked into the nursing home and found his mother sitting in her wheelchair, watching television. He kissed her on the cheek. "How are you bearing up?"

"I'm fine. How are you?"

He sat down. "I'm all right. Will they be able to get your wheelchair into the funeral car on Friday?"

"Yes. It's all been arranged. Will you sell the house and the contents for me? You can keep the money. I won't be needing it. Unless you intend to live in the house?"

"No. It has too many memories."

"Have you seen Victoria?" she asked.

No, but I've arranged to see her on Friday after the funeral. I'm hoping we can patch things up. I was going to tell her all my good points, but I couldn't think of any."

His mother smiled. "Then tell a few lies. I told your father a few lies to get him to marry me. I told him I was a virgin."

He was surprised. "I thought you were. You were only eighteen when you married Dad."

"I was a bit of a hussy before I married your father. I had three boyfriends, and I slept with all of them, although I was a good girl when I was married. I was a loyal and faithful wife, even though I was propositioned dozens of times. Your Uncle Harry was besotted with me, and I had to fight him off several times."

He sat and listened to his mother. Every now and then, he nodded or smiled. He was only half-listening. If he did not make it up with Victoria, he was dreading the future. It had taken him a lifetime to find her, and there was no way he would be able to replace her.

"You look tired," his mother said. "You're not listening to a word I say."

"I was, although I am tired. Driving wears me out." He stood up. "I think I'll get drunk and have an early night." He kissed his mother on the cheek. "I'll see you tomorrow."

"Yes, and don't be late."

Even though he got drunk that evening, he found it difficult to get to sleep in his father's house. It was two o'clock before his eyelids became heavy.

*

The funeral of his father was very depressing. There were only five people at the service: the vicar, his mother and two of his father's neighbours. He pushed his mother to the grave in the wheelchair and watched the coffin being lowered into the ground. It was pointless trying to make sense of life and death. If he tried, it always left him feeling confused. After the vicar had said a few words, he pushed his mother back to the hired funeral car.

"It'll be my turn next," his mother said.

He squeezed her hand. "You'll probably outlive me."

The drive back to his mother's nursing home seemed to take forever. The staff had put on a little spread of sandwiches and drinks, so he was obliged to stay for a while. His mother seemed to be coping well with the death of his father. He had a can of lager and a sandwich. Twenty minutes later, he excused himself, said goodbye to his mother and left. He was not in the mood for small talk and was worried about his meeting with Victoria.

*

Victoria had dressed up as if she were going to a wedding. She wanted to look her best. Timothy had sounded cold and could have gone off her or found someone else. His reason for seeing her might be to say that it was over between them. She felt confused. How could he have gone off her in such a short time? He had been crazy about her when he left for France. But if he still loved her, why had he sounded so cold and indifferent?

She was standing by the window in her lounge. It was fifteen minutes past two. What did he want to talk about? They might have to leave the house if he intends to discuss what he has been doing.

His car pulled up outside, and he climbed out. He looked tired and unhappy and had not shaved. She ran to the door and opened it. He was standing at the gate, looking at her as if he had never seen her before. This was wrong. She should be throwing her arms around him.

Timothy was mesmerised for a few seconds. She looked so beautiful. "Shall we go for a walk so that we can talk?" he said.

"Yes." She now knew that something was very wrong. She closed the door and walked down the path. "Shall we go into the park?"

He nodded.

They walked across the road and into the park. He could sense that something was wrong. She was dolled up but did not seem pleased to see him. She was probably on her way to see some bloke.

"You did it then," she said.

He nodded. He did not know how to tell her that he loved her more than he thought it was possible to love someone, and that he wanted to try and sort out their differences.

She stopped walking. "What's wrong? You seem different. Has something happened?"

"No. I'm just tired. I didn't sleep much last night."

"What do you want to talk about?" she asked. Her heart was thumping wildly in her chest.

He spread his hands. "I was just hoping that we could talk things through."

She frowned. "Talk what through? What do you mean?"

"I'm not… I would like to say that I've got dozens of good points." He had prepared what he was going to say, but was making a right mess of it. "I don't want to upset you. If only we could just talk."

"What are you talking about?" she asked. If he was going to dump her, why did he not just say it and get it over with? "Will you talk in English? What do you want to talk about?"

"Us," he said. "We could talk things through."

"If you don't tell me what this is about, I'll scream," she said.

He stared at her. "It's about us. I know you cannot accept what I am and what I do, what I did. I've packed it all in now. I was just hoping to change your mind."

She put her hands on her hips. "I have accepted what you are and what you've done. I don't like it, but I'll have to live with it. Did you think it was over between us?"

"Yes."

"Are you trying to say that you want to finish with me?" she asked.

"Of course not. I thought you wanted to finish with me."

She was so relieved that her legs almost gave way. "Why? What in God's name made you think that I wanted to finish with you?"

Relief began to pour into his body. By the sound of things, she did not want to finish with him. "You were upset when I left. When I came back, you'd packed in your job and put your house up for sale. I thought you were leaving to make a fresh start. I phoned your mobile and couldn't get through."

"I'm selling my house so that I can buy a nursery, which is why I left my job. And I couldn't answer my mobile because it had been stolen. I've been worried sick about you. I've spent several days waiting by the phone. When you phoned and asked if you could speak to me, I thought that you could not talk over the phone or were brain-damaged."

"So, you still love me?" he asked.

"Of course I do, you fool."

He pulled her into his arms. "I thought I had lost you."

She held him tight. "You're a complete idiot. I thought you no longer loved me."

"I will always love you." He kissed her on the lips. He was overcome with emotion. "I've missed you so much. Are you buying a nursery?"

"Yes. We are buying a nursery. Let's go back to my house. I need a drink." She punched him on the side. "Don't ever do that again. If I disappear, come and find me. I might be in trouble. I'll never leave you without telling you first."

He held her hand as they walked back to the house. "I feel a bit of a fool," he said.

"That's because you are a fool."

They had a drink and then made love on the settee in the lounge. She had never been so happy. She told him about the nursery she hoped to buy and about her plans. She then remembered that he had lost his father. "I shouldn't be this happy, what with your father dying."

"I'm also happy," he said. "My father would not want us to be depressed on his account. If he's watching us now, he'll be pleased that we're together. He always wanted grandchildren."

She held her stomach. She had forgotten all about her pregnancy. "I've got some good news. I'm pregnant. You'll soon be a daddy."

He sat up and stared at her. "Are you serious?"

"Of course. Women don't joke about such things."

He was suddenly overwhelmed by a feeling of joy. He leapt to his feet and punched the air. His fist hit the light shade, and he fell over the coffee table.

She began to laugh. He was lying on his back with his legs over the coffee table and with the light shade on his foot. "You couldn't do that again even if you tried."

He took the light shade off his foot, stood up and hugged her. "I don't intend to try. Are you sure you're pregnant?"

"Yes. I've done three pregnancy tests."

"I can't wait to be a father." He kissed her on the lips. "You'll make a wonderful mother."

"I hope so." She rested her head on his chest. "I want you to promise me that you'll always tell me the truth in the future. I need to know all about you. I can't stand being lied to."

"I promise," he said. "And you do know all about me. I can't tell you about my army life, but I've told you everything else. Well, at least the important things. I bet there are things about you that you've not told me?"

"There isn't," she said. "I've told you everything about me." As she spoke, she realised that there were two things she had not told him. "Well, almost everything."

He frowned. "What haven't you told me?"

She sat down. "My stepfather made me do things to him when I was a little girl, and I was date-raped."

He looked down at her. "Did your stepfather have sex with you?"

"No. I just touched his penis, and when I said I didn't want to do it again, he didn't make me."

He sat down. “Who date-raped you, and when?”

“Three men. It was just before I met you. They date-raped me and my friend Katy. They used condoms, so I didn’t catch anything.”

“Did they drug you?” he asked.

“Yes. I didn’t remember a thing at first, and then the memory of what happened came back in fits and starts. It now seems as if it were a dream.”

“Were they sent to prison?” He could feel anger welling up inside him.

“No. I told the police what happened, but Katy didn’t want to go to court. She didn’t want what happened splashed across the newspapers, and so she told the police that nothing had happened. And because Richard, the bastard, had a judge for a mother, who gave him an alibi, the police did not charge them.”

Her phone rang. She picked it up. “Hello?”

“It’s Steven. How are you feeling?”

“Much better, thanks.”

“Is Timothy still working away?” Steven asked. “

No. He’s home now.”

“Good,” Steven said. “The reason I phoned was to ask if you and Timothy would like to go for a meal with me and Rose this evening?”

“I’ll ask him.” She looked at Timothy. “Would you like to go for a meal with Steve and Rose?” She was nodding her head as she spoke.

“Yes,” he said. He was thinking about the men who had raped his woman, and who would one day suffer the consequences.

“Yes,” Victoria said into the phone.

“Great,” Steven said. “We’ll meet you at the Barley Mow at eight.”

“Okay,” she said. “See you at eight.” She put the phone down and looked at her watch. It was ten to seven. “I didn’t know it was that late. I need a shower and to sort out something to wear.” She rushed upstairs.

He took out his mobile phone and phoned Roger.

“Hello,” Roger said.

“It’s me.”

“Hello, Tim. What can I do for you?”

“I need to know the addresses of three men who date-raped Victoria a few months ago. One is named Richard, and his mother’s a judge. Victoria reported the rape to the police, but they were not charged.”

“Leave it to me,” Roger said. “How’s retirement suiting you?”

“Very well. I’ve always wanted to sit by the fire in my slippers.”

Roger laughed. “I’ll phone you when I have the information.”

“Thanks.”

Timothy slipped his phone into his pocket. Richard, his two mates, and his mother needed to be taught a lesson they would never forget.

Chapter Fifteen

Timothy had never been happier, so he decided to reduce the number of antidepressant tablets he was taking. Victoria was a joy to live with. They had put both of their houses and his father's house on the market and had bought the nursery. There was a self-contained flat above the nursery that would be a perfect place to bring up a child. In a few years, when the nursery had been refurbished, they intended to buy a house. They were both looking forward to the birth of their child. They had decided to get married in November.

They were sitting in the lounge of her house, listening to Roger Whittaker singing, River Lady. She was reading a magazine, and he was watching her. She was beautiful.

She put the magazine down. "I think it's about time I met your mother. You don't go to see her often enough."

"I know. I had intended to see her once a week."

"We can go today," she said.

"Okay. I would like her to see my bride-to-be. Are you intending to see your mother again?"

"I don't know. I probably will, but I won't be seeing her once a week."

During the journey to see Timothy's mother at the nursing home, Victoria began to feel nervous. For some reason, she expected his mother to be bossy and cantankerous. She could not have been more wrong. Within a few minutes of meeting her, they were talking as if they had known each other for years.

"We've set a date for our wedding, Mrs Freeman," Victoria said.

"Call me Norma. When?"

"November the fifteenth," Victoria said. "As soon as we know the sex of our baby, I'll get Tim to decorate the nursery. That is the nursery in the flat, not the big nursery. I'm bursting with excitement."

Timothy sat listening to them chat. The hundred thousand he had earned had come in handy. They would need to spend at least thirty thousand on the nursery. What he wanted now was a holiday. They had decided to spend a week in Greece. He had tried to forget about his last operation, and they rarely talked about it. The world now blamed Henri Paul for the accident and accused him of being drunk when he drove the limo.

He looked at his watch. "We'll have to go, Mum. We've been here two hours."

"I hope you'll come and see me again, Victoria," his mother said. "I've enjoyed myself."

"We'll come every week," Victoria promised.

While they were driving home, his phone rang. Victoria was driving, and so he was able to answer it. "Yes?"

"We need to talk," Roger said. "I'll see you at the boat in thirty minutes."

"I hope this is not another op," Timothy said. "I'm not doing any more ops."

"It's not another op," Roger said. "It's very serious. Get to the boat as quickly as you can."

"Okay," Timothy said.

Victoria was alarmed. "Who was that? Don't even think of going on any more ops. You promised me it was over."

"It is. It's nothing to do with an op. They just want to speak to me."

"What about?" she asked.

"I don't know." He did not want to alarm her, and so he did not tell her that something serious had happened. What could be very serious? Roger was not the sort to get into a flap about anything unless it was a matter of life and death. Timothy began to worry.

As soon as he got home, he climbed into his car and drove to the boat as fast as he could. Perhaps the press had discovered something about Princess Diana's death that proved it was not an accident. For the life of him, he could not think what could have happened that Roger would regard as very serious.

When he drove into the car park near the boat, he was surprised to see that the cars of John, Peter, Matthew and Major were there. He ran to the boat. The four of them were waiting for him. "What's going on?" Timothy asked.

"The Major was waiting for you to get here first before telling us," John said.

"It's a long story, but I'll make it as short as possible," Roger said. "I think that men from MI5 are about to kill us."

"Fucking hell," John said. "The bastards."

"Why do you think MI5 wants us dead?" Peter asked. "They know they can trust us."

"I don't know. I suppose they're trying to reduce the number of people who know what happened to Princess Diana. I took out insurance when we took on the last op so that we would not be bumped off. I left a letter with a solicitor, instructing them to release the letter to the press in the event of my death. If they kill us, the press will be told everything. I told H that I had taken out the insurance. Did anyone else take out insurance?"

They all shook their heads.

"I intended to," Timothy said. "Why are you worried if you took out insurance?"

"I no longer have that insurance. The solicitor's office was broken into, and the letter was stolen. The only way they could have known about the letter at the solicitors was if they had been following me before the op. I think we were all followed day and night from the moment they told us about the op."

Matthew frowned. "It doesn't mean that we'll be killed. It's just MI5 being careful."

"I thought that at first, but I wanted to make sure," Roger said. "I worked out how they would kill us if they decided to. They'll no doubt be using the other assassination team that was supposed to have been in the south of France when we were in Paris. If I were in their place, I would, first of all, kill Paul. He also knew about the Princess Diana op."

"I would expect them to hit us all at the same time," Timothy said. He was not convinced that they were about to die. Roger was worrying over nothing. It was probably because he was ill.

"They only have a four-man team," Roger said. "They cannot hit all of us at the same time. They would feel safe to hit Paul because we have nothing to do with him, and so we would be unaware that he had been hit. I would be next. They would then hit the four of you. I don't believe this team would be told why they were hitting us. And with us out of the way, only H and a few people at MI5 and MI6 and the palace protectors would know that Princess Diana's death was not an accident."

"I know you're a brilliant strategist, Major, but this time, I think you're overreacting," Matthew said. "All we need to do is take out insurance."

"It's too late for that," Roger said. "We're all being followed, and they'll know what we do and where we go."

"So, they know that we're here?" Timothy asked.

Roger nodded.

Peter handed around cans of lager. "If Paul gets hit, I'll then begin to worry. Up until then, I intend to carry on as normal. I don't think they'll be stupid enough to hit us."

Roger looked at the can and handed it back to Peter. "If I drink that, I'll be sick. Paul has already been hit."

Timothy was shocked. "How do you know Paul has been hit?"

"Let me explain what's been happening. As soon as I knew about the assignment to eliminate Princess Diana, I had a nasty suspicion that after we had hit the target, we would be hit. The letter I left at the solicitors was a test to see if I was being followed. As soon as it disappeared, I knew that we would eventually be hit."

"The disappearance of the letter does not mean that we're going to be hit," John said. "They're just being careful. And how do you know that Paul's been hit? He lives in Scotland."

"I've not finished telling you what's happened," Roger said. "Joseph, a friend of mine who works for me, went to Scotland and has been watching Paul and sticking to him like glue. Joseph's an ex-SAS man. He's seventy-three, but he still knows his stuff. He phoned me yesterday evening and told me that two men had knocked on Paul's door. When Paul opened the door, they shot him in the head, bundled his body into the boot of their car and drove off. Paul no longer exists."

"The fucking bastards," John said.

Timothy began to worry. "They might not have been MI5 men. According to your theory, Major, you should now be dead."

"I would be if I had not given some milk to the cat. At the moment, I'm living in a block of flats, and gunshots would be heard if they tried to shoot me, so they tried to poison me. I always give the cat the cream off the top of the milk when I have a cup of coffee. It was a close thing. I was just about to drink my coffee when the cat had a fit and died. This happened this morning. I left my flat through the garage at the back and was not seen. By now, they'll know that I'm not dead, and they'll be coming after us. I suggest we stick together, or we won't stand a chance. When they hit us, I expect some of us to die, but because we're expecting them, some of us might survive. Our only hope is to kill all four men in the other assassination team."

Timothy was now very worried. "What about our families?"

"They should be safe. They know we're professionals and that our families are unaware of what we do."

"What are we going to do?" John asked. "We're unarmed."

"We're going to fight the bastards." Roger threw a bunch of keys to John. "Get the bags out of my Land Rover. Peter, you go with him."

John and Peter climbed off the boat.

"When do you expect them to hit us?" Timothy asked. He was worrying about Victoria.

"Tonight or tomorrow," Roger said. "By now, they'll know that we're on this boat. I want the boat moved further along the river, and I want a lookout posted on the bank within the hour."

John and Peter returned with four bags and placed them on the table. "It's just like old times," John said. "It's a case of who dares wins."

"This is different," Roger said. "This time, we are the target." He opened the bag and handed out handguns, ammunition and hand grenades. "We're up against professionals, and we need to be extra vigilant. It's a case of who dares the most wins."

John looked angry. "They'll regret trying to hit us."

Roger looked at Peter. "If we keep in contact by mobile phone, will they be able to know what we're saying?"

"No. Not unless you or the phones are bugged, and because you're on John's boat, and no alarm is going off, you can rest assured that you and your mobiles are not bugged."

"Let's get the boat moved," Roger said. "There are too many people around the pub for my liking. Move the boat to a quiet stretch of the river. I intend to set a little trap for our friends. If we kill all of the other assassination team, we might be able to make a deal with MI5."

Timothy checked his gun and put several clips of ammunition and three hand grenades into his coat pocket. He was beginning to feel angry. After a lifetime's work for this country, this was his reward.

They moored the boat further along the river. It was now dark. "What's the plan, Major?" John asked.

"Because of the terrain, they'll be on foot. It's unlikely that they'll use a boat. I suspect that all four men will keep to one side of the river. Our only hope is to be ready for them. We don't have vests, but we do have night sights. I want you, John, and Matthew to wait on the bank. Stay close to the ground in case they have night sights, and watch both banks."

Roger gave John and Matthew night sights, and they climbed out of the boat. Several shots rang out, and Timothy, Roger and Peter dived onto the deck for cover.

"They're on the other bank," Timothy whispered.

It was now deadly quiet.

"Push that bag over to me and kill that fucking light," Roger whispered. "How the fuck did they get here so quick?"

Timothy pushed the bag towards Roger and switched off the light. "We have to get off the boat, Major. They're bound to use grenades, and we're sitting ducks."

"Don't move," Roger said. "They might have night sights."

There was a whoosh sound followed by an explosion on the far bank.

"Are you using a grenade launcher, Major?" Timothy asked.

"Yes. It'll give the bastards something to think about."

Four more explosions rocked the far bank.

"I think that should have got them," Roger said. "I wonder if John and Matthew were hit? I've a nasty feeling they were. You two will have to investigate."

"I can't move," Peter said. "I've been hit in the chest."

"Fuck it," Roger said. "Is it bad?"

"Yes, very," Peter said. His voice was very faint. "The bastards have killed me."

"John. Matthew," Timothy shouted. "Are you all right?"

There was no reply.

Timothy stood up, jumped from the boat onto the bank and dived behind a mound of earth. He had not been shot at. If the men who were trying to kill them were still on the far bank, they would have at least tried to shoot him. His instincts told him that the men were either dead, seriously injured or had retreated out of range of the grenade launcher. Five grenades, well-spaced out, can do a great deal of damage.

"John. Matthew," Timothy shouted. "Where are you?"

There was no reply. They had obviously been hit.

"They're either dead or seriously injured," Roger shouted. "See if you can find their bodies."

It was now pitch black, and Timothy had to feel around for the two bodies. He found them and felt for a pulse. There was no pulse. "They're both dead."

"Get back on the boat," Roger said. "If the bastards aren't dead, they'll have moved out of range by now. We need to get out of here before the cops arrive."

Timothy climbed back onto the boat and, while keeping his head down, sailed the short distance to the pub. "How's Peter?" he asked.

"He's dead. We must have been hit by at least three men. If they're not dead, they could be anywhere."

"What are we going to do?" Timothy asked.

"Go on the run. I'll then make the bastards regret their actions."

"I need to warn Victoria," Timothy said. "And if we go into hiding, I'll be taking Victoria with us."

"Not a good idea. They could be waiting for us at your house. Phone her and tell her to go and stay with her mother or her sister."

"I'll do it now." Timothy phoned Victoria.

"Yes?" Victoria asked.

"It's Tim. Pack a bag and go and stay with your sister or your mother, and stay there until I get in touch with you."

"Why?" she asked. "What's wrong?"

"Just do as I say. Leave now."

"Okay. I'll phone Steve. I don't want to go to my mother's or my sister's."

"Phone me when you've moved," Timothy said. He ended the call and put his phone in his pocket. "Someone must have heard the explosions."

"I know, which is why we need to get as far away as possible, as quickly as possible."

They moored the boat and walked to the car park. There were dozens of people walking about and sitting at tables.

"We should be safe in among the crowds, but keep your hand on your gun just in case," Roger said.

"I always do."

"Follow me in your car," Roger said.

They climbed into their cars and drove out of the car park. In his rear-view mirror, Timothy saw a police car drive into the public house car park. They had only just got out in time. They drove for a few miles and pulled over to the side of the road. They had not been followed. Roger left his car and climbed into Timothy's car.

"They'll know what cars we're driving by now," Roger said. "They'll also know that we're alive. They'll have seen us get into our cars."

Timothy drove off. "What do we do?"

"I'm just trying to think what they will do. They'll probably stake out your house. If I were you, I'd get to your house first and wait for them to arrive. I intend to pay H a visit first thing tomorrow. Thanks to Joseph, who had his own detective agency for fifteen years, I know where H lives. I also know where several top MI5 and MI6 officers live."

Timothy began to worry. "It's too dangerous to visit H. They could kill you."

Roger nodded. "I know, but it's a chance I'll eventually have to take. But before I visit H, I'll tell him about my insurance. I would also take out insurance if I were you. I would leave information with a solicitor."

"I will, first thing tomorrow."

*

Victoria packed some clothes into a suitcase. She was a bundle of nerves. She had been unable to contact Steven. She phoned Timothy. "Are you all right?" she asked.

"Yes? Are you at Steven's?"

"No. I've not been able to contact him. I'm still at my house. I don't know where to go."

"I thought you had left by now," Timothy said. He sounded angry. "Go into Birmingham and book into a hotel. And get out now. Your life could be in danger. Phone me when you get there."

"Yes, okay." She was annoyed that he would not tell her what was going on. She was also frightened. She tried once again to phone Steven but could not contact him. She did not want to go into a hotel. She picked up her suitcase, walked towards the bedroom door and stopped. The loose tread on the stairs had squeaked. Someone was walking up the stairs.

She began to panic. It could be someone coming to kill her. She put her suitcase down and looked for somewhere to hide. The bed went down to the floor, and the wardrobes were full. There was nowhere she could hide. She could hide behind the curtains, but they did not touch the ground, and her feet would show. She climbed silently into the washing basket and pulled the lid over her head. Even though she was small, it was a very tight squeeze. She then realised that there was a hole in the basket next to her face. It was now too late to move or turn out the light. The bedroom door was opening.

A man holding a gun walked into the bedroom. He looked into the wardrobes, walked over to the window and took a mobile phone out of his pocket. "I'm at the house," he said. "Yes. It's empty. The lights are on, so someone left in a hurry."

She had never been so frightened in her life. She was very near to the man, and if he looked at the basket, he would see her face.

"What were they doing with a grenade launcher?" he said. "We should have been told they were military men." He walked over to the light switch and switched off the light. "Don't worry. They're as good as dead."

Victoria realised what was happening. This man was waiting for Timothy to come home so that he could kill him. She had her mobile phone in her hand. She would have to warn Timothy, but if she spoke on her phone, the man would hear her. She would have to wait until he left the room. She then realised that Timothy might phone her, and the man would hear the ringtone. She quickly turned off her mobile phone. She would call Timothy if the man left the room.

*

Timothy dropped Roger off in the centre of Solihull and drove to Victoria's house as fast as he could. He hoped to get into position before the assassins arrived. He had a handgun, several grenades and a rifle with telescopic sights. He was hoping that by now, Victoria had booked into a hotel and was safe. As he drove, he phoned her. The number was unobtainable. Her phone battery was probably dead.

*

Victoria prayed that Timothy would not come home while the man was here. The man lit a cigarette and sat on the dressing table by the window. Every now and then, he farted. The room was filled with a vile smell. Why were they trying to kill Timothy? And who were they?

*

Timothy parked a short distance from Victoria's house and looked for a place where he could observe the house without being seen or disturbed. It was dark, but the streets were well-lit. The only decent vantage point was from the top of a flat garage roof on the far side of the road to Victoria's house. He picked up the bag containing the guns, climbed out of the car, and looked about.

The other assassination team had not arrived; otherwise, he would be dead. They would be able to see him clearly and would not need night sights to kill him. He reasoned that they had expected to kill him while he had been on the boat with the others and so would not be waiting for him at Victoria's house.

There was no one about. He walked to the garage, climbed onto the roof and lay down next to the bag containing the guns. Overhanging branches made it an ideal place to observe Victoria's house without being seen. He took the rifle out of the bag and looked through the telescopic sights. There was a street lamp right outside Victoria's house. Even though he was over a hundred metres from the house, by looking through the telescopic sights, he could see it clearly. From this position, he would be able to see anyone entering or leaving the house or observing it.

*

Victoria hardly dared to breathe. The man was looking out of the window. His phone rang. He took it out of his pocket. "Yes. I'm still here. Where are you? There's no sign of either of them. There's nothing else we can do." There was then a long period of silence as he listened to the person who had phoned him. "Yes," he eventually said. "Yes. Phone me when you're in position." He put the phone into his pocket and turned around. She could see him clearly in the light from the landing. He was handsome and was about thirty-five. He did not look like a killer. But neither did Timothy. The man began to pace up and down.

*

Timothy was tired, and he was finding it difficult to stay awake. He heard a noise and turned his head to one side to listen. Someone was walking up to the garage. He turned his attention back to observing Victoria's house. It was probably the owner of the garage. Even if whoever it was went into the garage, they would not see him. He was well hidden.

"I'm almost in position," a man said.

Timothy lifted his head and listened. The man was speaking on a mobile phone.

"I got here as quickly as I could," the man said. "Have you spoken to H? What did he say?"

Timothy's eyes opened wide. The man was talking about H. The man was obviously one of the other assassination team. He was probably intending to climb onto the garage and use it as an observation point. Timothy put down the rifle and picked up his handgun.

"We should have been told," the man said. "No wonder they had grenade launchers. Did you find out why they are to be eliminated? That's a load of bollocks. Slim's in the house. I'll phone him."

Timothy aimed the handgun at the point where he expected the man to climb onto the roof.

"I'm almost in position, Slim," the man said. "Ed and Colin are dead. We were set up. I've just found out that the bastards are ex-SAS. Yes. We need to be very careful. I know. Are you still in the house? Good. If you see anything, let me know."

Timothy was thankful for the information that there was a man in Victoria's house and that at least two members of the team were dead. Timothy needed to kill both men.

A hand appeared and gripped the side of the roof. A rifle with telescopic sights was pushed onto the roof. When the man's head appeared, Timothy shot him between the eyes. The back of the man's head flew off, and he fell to the ground.

*

Victoria heard what sounded like a gunshot. The man ran to the window and looked through the net curtains. The man had just been talking on the phone to another man. From what was said, the other man was watching the house. The other man must have fired a gun. She prayed that he had not shot Timothy.

"I hope he got the bastard," the man said to himself. He took out his phone. "Answer your phone, you fucking idiot."

*

Timothy looked through the telescopic sights at Victoria's house. The mobile phone of the man he had just shot began to ring. It was not very loud, and he decided to leave it where it was. It would not be heard from the road. The man in the house had probably heard the gunshot. If he came out of the house, he was dead.

Timothy focused the telescopic sights on a car parked outside Victoria's house. It looked like Victoria's car. He checked the registration number. It was in a shadow, and he could not make it out. He looked at the car. It had a dent in the door. It was Victoria's car. Why was her car parked outside her house?

*

Victoria had to fight the desire to cough. The tickle in her throat was painful. The man ran from the room and then ran back in with his phone in his hand. "I've tried to call him," he said. "He doesn't answer. How the hell would I know? Yes. It was definitely a gunshot. I want them here ASAP."

*

Timothy took out his phone and phoned Victoria. "Fuck it." The number was still unobtainable. Her phone battery must still be dead. By now, she should be at the hotel, but why had she left her car? The car could have broken down, in which case she would have taken a taxi.

He frowned and scratched his chin. She had never let the battery run down on her phone before, so she must have switched it off, but why? Why would she turn her phone off? She would know that he would phone her. It then dawned on him. She was still in the house. She was hiding in the house and had turned her phone off so that Slim would not hear it ring if he phoned her.

He looked through the telescopic sights at Victoria's house. The bedroom net curtains moved. It was probably Slim, but it could be Victoria, so he could not risk taking a shot. What should he do? Normally, he would wait for the man to come out. It took him just a few seconds to realise that he would have to go into the house and rescue Victoria. She might already be dead. The only way she could be alive was if she was hiding somewhere in the house. He would have to hurry. If Slim found her, she would be shot.

He put the rifle and the handgun back into his bag and climbed off the roof. The dead man was lying in a bush. Timothy dragged him behind the garage and ran to his car. If Slim had heard the shot, he would have called for backup. They would now be on their way and could arrive at any time. He climbed into his car and drove towards Victoria's house. He was in full view of Slim, but he had to take the risk.

*

The man, who was looking out of the bedroom window, picked up his phone. "What car does the target drive?" he asked. There was a short pause.

"It's him. It's him. He's parking the car by the side of the house." The man ran from the room.

Victoria began to panic. The man could be talking about Timothy. If he was, it meant that Timothy was about to enter the house. She would have to warn him, but how? She could not risk turning on her phone.

The man ran back into the bedroom. "He's got out of his car." The man was now whispering into his phone. "I think he's about to enter the house. What is your ETA? Then make it five minutes. I'll stay in the front bedroom. Yes. He's on his own."

Victoria had to do something. Other men would soon be arriving. Timothy was on his own and would not stand a chance. Why had Timothy come to the house? It was probably because he had not been able to phone her. She then remembered her car. Timothy had seen her car parked outside and realised that she was still inside the house. He was entering the house to rescue her.

*

Timothy let himself in the back door. It was not locked. If Victoria had left, she would have locked up. He held his gun out in front of him and walked across the kitchen. The lights were on. Slim could have left the house while he was climbing down from the garage roof, or he could be hiding somewhere in the house.

Timothy was in a very dangerous position, and he stopped in the hall to take stock of the situation. Slim was probably in one of the bedrooms. If Victoria was hiding in the house, she would either be under the stairs or in a wardrobe. There was nowhere else she could hide. He checked the lounge. It was empty. He opened the cupboard under the stairs. It was empty. He began to walk upstairs.

What he was doing was not only dangerous, it was suicidal. He was not wearing a bulletproof vest. Slim was bound to kill him. His one hope was that he would also be able to kill Slim. They would both probably die, but it had to be done. The woman he loved, who was carrying his child, would die if he did nothing. It was a risk he had to take. If Victoria died, he would not want to live. He had a nasty gut feeling that Slim had already killed her.

*

Victoria was watching the man who was standing behind the slightly opened bedroom door. He had his gun in his hand. How could she warn Timothy? If she did nothing, the man would shoot him. Perhaps Timothy had not entered the house and would leave before the other men arrived.

*

Timothy trod on the squeaky tread on the staircase and pulled a face. Slim would now know that he was here.

*

The man aimed his gun at the door. Victoria began to panic. The man had obviously heard the squeak of the loose tread on the staircase and would now know that Timothy was halfway up the stairs. She had to do something. She could not let Timothy be killed.

*

Timothy took a deep breath and continued to walk up the stairs. This was probably his last day on Earth. He reached the landing.

*

Victoria was terrified, but she was determined to do something. She could not let the man she loved die. "He's behind our bedroom door," she screamed. The man spun around. She closed her eyes. The man fired his gun three times.

*

Timothy put four shots into the bedroom door. He then ran into the room. The man was lying on the floor. Timothy shot him twice in the head and looked about. There was no sign of Victoria. He had heard the man shoot her, so where was her body? It must be behind the bed. He began to choke up, and his eyes filled with tears. She had given her life to save him. "Victoria. Why did you do it?"

Victoria opened her eyes. The man was lying on the floor, and Timothy was in the room. Timothy did not look injured. She stood up. "I had to warn you," she said. The strength left her legs, and she sank back into the laundry basket.

He wiped the tears from his eyes, ran to her and lifted her out of the basket. He could not believe that she was alive. He hugged her. "I thought you were dead. I heard him shoot you."

"He must have missed," she said. It was wonderful to be hugged. "I thought you'd been shot."

He looked about the room. "He did not miss. They don't miss. What the hell did he shoot at?" He walked over to the curtain and pulled it to one side. There were three bullet holes in the wall. "He must have thought you were hiding behind the curtains."

Her hands flew to her mouth. "I almost hid behind the curtains."

"Thank God you didn't."

She suddenly remembered the other men. "Some of his friends are on their way here. They'll be here in a few minutes."

He put another ammunition clip into his gun, picked up the dead man's gun, and grabbed her hand. "Let's go."

"What about my suitcase?" she asked.

"Forget it. We have to get away before the other men arrive."

They ran down the stairs, and he opened the front door a few inches to make sure that the other men had not arrived. There was no sign of them. He opened the door. As they ran out of the house, a car drove onto the drive and screeched to a halt. The car was about six feet from them. Four men climbed out. The car's headlights were blinding Timothy, but he could just make out that the men were all armed with handguns.

"Get down on the ground," Timothy shouted. He aimed his handguns at the men and opened fire. Two were down before they could return fire. He felt a bullet hit his arm as he ran to his right. He hit another man in the head. He felt another bullet hit his left hand and was forced to drop one of his guns. He shot the last man, who was now crouched down to reduce his body size. The bullet hit the man in the chest.

Victoria was in a state of shock. She was lying on the ground and had watched Timothy shoot four men. It was frightening but also unreal, as if it were a scene from a movie. She stood up and watched him shoot each man in the head. She felt numb with shock.

"Get into my car," he said.

They ran to his car, climbed in, and he drove off.

She looked back. "You killed all of them."

"Yes. I was very lucky. I could never do that again."

"I don't know how you managed to shoot them. They were hiding behind the car doors, and the car's headlights were on you."

He drove onto the main road and looked in the rearview mirror. They were not being followed, and he began to relax. "I could only see their silhouettes. If there had not been a street light outside your house, I would not have been able to see them, and I would now be dead."

"I used to moan about that street light being there. It shines into my bedroom at night. I'm now glad it's there."

"I've been hit," he said. "There's a first aid box in the glove compartment. I need you to bandage my wounds."

She was shocked. "What wounds? Have you been shot twice?"

"Yes." He pulled up on the side of the road and took off his coat. The wounds were beginning to hurt. He had a bullet hole in his hand and a flesh wound on the arm. "Hurry up and stop the bleeding. We need to get as far away as possible. We cannot afford to be stopped by the police."

She bandaged his wounds as quickly as she could, and they drove off down the road. She could hear police sirens in the distance. “Are you in pain?”

“Yes, but I’ll live. We need to hole up somewhere.”

“Who were those men, and why were they trying to kill you?” she asked.

“We’ll talk about it later.”

As he drove towards Birmingham, he began to fill up with a burning anger. The people he had worked for and risked his life for were now trying to kill him. The bastards. They should be thanking him for what he had done for them. If he lived, he would make them regret what they had done.

He turned into the car park of the first hotel he saw and stopped his car. “We’ll book in here when it opens in the morning.” He turned off the engine and lights. “I’m absolutely knackered. I’ll have to get some sleep.”

“Didn’t you get any sleep last night?” she asked.

“No. It’s been one hell of a night.” He adjusted the seat as far back as it would go and closed his eyes.

“You should go to hospital to get your wounds stitched,” she said.

He did not reply and began to snore.

She closed her eyes. They were in danger, but if Timothy could not protect them, no one could. Even though she felt protected by Timothy, she was still filled with fear. Timothy was a professional, but so were the men who were trying to kill him. She opened her eyes. She was too frightened to sleep.

*

She woke up. She was sitting in the car and must have fallen asleep. It was ten o’clock, and the hotel was open. She shook him gently. “Wake up.”

He opened his eyes and looked about. “What’s wrong?”

“Nothing. The hotel’s open now. You’ll sleep better in a bed.”

They climbed out of the car and checked into the hotel. He was as stiff as a plank of wood, and his wounds were very painful. He would have to get some painkillers. Their room overlooked the main road, and they stood looking out of the window. “I’m sorry,” he said. “I didn’t want this to happen.”

She put her arms around his waist. “It’s not your fault. I’m just relieved that we’re both alive. I still can’t believe that you killed five men.”

“I killed six men.”

“When did you kill the other man?”

Tiredness flooded over him. “I was lying on a garage roof across the road from your house. When a man climbed onto the roof, I shot him. He was a sniper and was hoping to kill me.”

“What are we going to do?” she asked.

"I don't know yet." He walked to the bed and lay down. "I need time to think, but first, I need to sleep."

She sat down and watched him. He was very brave. He had risked his life to save her and had killed six men. Who were those men, and why were they trying to kill him? She had so many questions to ask.

Chapter Sixteen

Timothy woke up and stretched. His wounds felt as if they were on fire. Victoria was lying on the bed next to him. As soon as he moved to get off the bed, she woke up.

"Where are you going?" she asked.

"To the loo."

While he was in the toilet, she climbed off the bed and looked out of the window. They were probably safe in this hotel. She saw herself in the mirror. She had slept fully clothed and looked a mess. She also looked frightened.

He walked back into the bedroom and phoned Roger. "What's our next move, Major?"

"I was just about to phone you. It's not safe to talk on the phone. They might be able to work out where we are from the phone calls. They might even have the phones bugged. I've got some safe mobiles. We need to meet."

"Where and when?" Timothy asked.

"Meet me at the place where the horse kicked over the table, and make sure you're not followed. Where are you?"

"In Birmingham, at a hotel with Victoria."

"Book out of the hotel now," Roger said. "Bring Victoria with you. I'll give her a safe mobile to use. She'll then have to stay somewhere safe. I'll expect to see you in about an hour."

"Make that two hours," Timothy said. "I have a few things to do. He put his phone into his pocket and flexed his left hand. It was very painful to move.

Victoria had been listening to what Timothy had said. "Who were you speaking to?"

"To Major. His name's Roger. He's the leader of our team. We have to leave now and check out of the hotel. Roger has a safe mobile phone for you to use. You'll then have to stop at Steven's. You should be safe there."

"Where will you be going?" she asked.

"To sort things out." He lit a cigarette. He was worried about Victoria. They could threaten to kill her to put pressure on him. "I've changed my mind. I want you to go on holiday. Get some cash out of the bank and go somewhere nice in this country. If you have to use your bank card, use a cash machine and then move to another area. Do not visit your mother, sister, or any of your friends."

"I would like to stay with you," she said.

"That's impossible. I intend to kill the men who are trying to kill me. It'll be much too dangerous for you."

"When will I see you again?" she asked.

"I don't know." He pulled her into his arms and hugged her. "When you get the phone from Roger, only use it to phone me. Do not phone anyone else."

"I won't."

He kissed her on the lips and placed his hand on her stomach. "You mean everything to me. We need to look after our baby. I want to sort things out so we can live a normal life."

"Be very careful," she said. "I love you."

"I love both of you," he said. "Before we go, we need to do a spot of writing. You can write, and I'll dictate. Better still, we'll book out of the hotel and do the writing in a library."

"What library?"

"The nearest library. We'll ask someone in the hotel where it is."

They checked out of the hotel and drove to the library. It was only a short distance down the road. When they were seated at a table, he dictated to her, and she wrote down a detailed account of how Princess Diana had been assassinated and the names of those involved. She was fascinated. "Would you have injected her with poison if the paparazzi had not been there?"

He nodded. "Let's get it photocopied."

They made four copies in the library and addressed them to four different newspaper editors. He then put each of the four copies into four larger envelopes.

"Are you going to post them?" she asked.

"No. They're our insurance. Put them in your bag. I want you to leave a copy at four different solicitors on your travels."

"What do I tell the solicitor?" she asked.

"I'll show you. We can leave one copy with a solicitor in Birmingham. But first, we need to eat."

They parked the car on a side road and had a meal in a McDonald's restaurant. She watched him eat. He looked calm and composed. She had not realised how brave he was. He had been fighting and killing people all his life. "Who are the men who are trying to kill you? And why are they trying to kill you?"

"They're MI5 soldiers. I think they want to kill us to reduce the number of people who know that Princess Diana was assassinated. They attacked us yesterday and killed three of our team. There's only me and Roger left."

She was shocked. "Oh, my God." She shook her head. "It must have been terrifying. Do you ever get scared when you're fighting people?"

"No. It was just a job." He looked at her. "I never used to get scared. It's different now. For the first time in my life, I'm frightened about what might happen."

"Why?"

"Because I now have something to lose."

She reached across the table and squeezed his good hand.

After their meal, they walked to the nearest solicitor's and were shown into Mr Tring's office. "How can I help you?" Mr Tring asked. He was in his forties and had his long hair tied up in a ponytail.

"I would like to leave an envelope with you for safekeeping," Timothy said. "It's a form of insurance. Inside the envelope, there's an addressed envelope. I would like you to put the addressed envelope in the post if something happens to me."

"How will I know that something has happened to you?" Mr Tring asked.

"I'll call you every three months," Timothy said. "If I leave it for four months, put the letter in the post. I'll use a password when I phone. The password is Rat."

The solicitor smiled. "We can do that for you. It'll cost you one hundred pounds a year to be paid in advance."

Timothy gave him a hundred pounds, and they left the solicitor's office.

"If we leave a letter at four solicitors, it's going to cost us four hundred pounds," she said.

"It'll be worth it if it keeps us alive."

They left the car and took a taxi to the Crooked Leg public house. Roger was waiting for them. "This is Victoria," Timothy said. "Victoria, meet Roger."

She shook hands with Roger. "I'm pleased to meet you, Roger." He looked the opposite of what she had expected. He looked more like a respectable businessman than an assassin. "Have you hurt your eye?"

"I've had it out. I've got cancer. Sit down and have a drink."

"Victoria won't be stopping," Timothy said. "She's going on a long holiday. Did you bring the phones?"

"Yes. We cannot be too careful from now on. We're up against very intelligent men." He handed a phone to Victoria and a phone to Timothy. "You don't have to top them up. The payments will be made for you. They're registered in false names. How are you bearing up, Victoria? It must be very difficult for you."

"It is. Will you be able to sort things out so that we can live normally again?"

"I think so. It'll take time, though."

"How long?" she asked. She prayed he would say weeks and not months.

"I don't know. I would not plan to see Timothy for at least two weeks, and don't phone him unless it's very important. He'll phone you." He smiled. "Enjoy your holiday."

She hugged and kissed Timothy. "Do you want to know where I'm going?"

"No. Tell me when I phone you. Don't stay in the same place for more than a week. I'll phone you every evening."

She left them and took a taxi to the railway station. She decided to go to Blackpool. It was as good a place as any. She felt all mixed up. What was happening did not seem real. If she told Steven what was happening to her, he would not believe her. Since meeting Timothy, her peaceful life had changed dramatically, and she was now a fugitive on the run. She did not mind what she had to do, as long as it was eventually sorted out so they could live without fearing for their lives.

She placed her hand on her stomach. Her life now contained everything she had dreamed of. She had her man and would soon have a child, but did she have a future? Only time will tell.

*

"Victoria seems like a very nice young lady," Roger said.

"She is. I need a drink. Do you want one?"

"Yes. I'll have a fruit juice."

Timothy bought a pint of lager and a fruit juice and sat down at the table. He took a long drink of lager and wiped his mouth with the back of his hand. "I needed that."

"I also need a stiff drink, but I have to make do with a bleeding fruit juice."

"Imagine there's vodka in it," Timothy said."

"I would if it would work, but fruit juice doesn't have a kick. Did you meet up with them? I gather by your bandaged hand that something happened."

"Yes. I was shot twice. One of the team was waiting for me in Victoria's house."

"I expected as much," Roger said. "Where's the other bullet wound?"

"It's a flesh wound on the arm."

"What happened?" Roger asked.

Timothy took a long drink of lager and emptied the glass. "Another member of the team turned up. He tried to get onto the garage roof where I was, and I blew his head off. I killed him easy enough, but the man in the house, a man named Slim, now realised that I was there."

"How did you kill him?" Roger asked.

"It was a bit tricky. Victoria was still in the house."

Roger looked shocked. "Fucking hell. I thought she'd gone to her mother's."

"She was hiding in a linen basket in the bedroom where Slim was. I had no choice but to go into the house to rescue her."

Roger frowned with one eye. "How the fuck did you manage to kill him? I would have expected him to have killed you."

"Victoria risked her life to warn me that a man was waiting behind the bedroom door."

"How did she warn you?" Roger asked. "Did she phone you?"

"No. I was about to enter the bedroom when she shouted, he's behind the bedroom door, and I shot him through the door."

"That doesn't make sense," Roger said. "If she was in the bedroom with Slim, and she shouted, he would have shot her."

"Slim thought Victoria was hiding behind the curtains, and he put three bullets into the curtain. I owe Victoria my life."

"She's a very lucky young lady," Roger said. "And a very brave one. You did well. We now have just two men to kill."

"Before I killed Slim, I heard the first man I killed talking on the phone. You killed the other two men in the team with the grenade launcher when they attacked the boat."

Roger looked pleased. "Fantastic. That's one team out of the way. There's only the team leader left. I wonder if there's another team that H can use? We might not be out of the woods yet."

"There is another team of four," Timothy said. "I met up with them."

Roger looked concerned. "There is? You did? What happened?"

"As I left the house with Victoria, the team of four arrived, and we had a little shootout. It was when I got shot."

Roger stared at him for a few seconds. "What happened?"

"I killed all four of them."

Roger looked amazed." "Bleeding hell. That'll teach the bastards. It'll make our lives a lot easier, although they can soon put another team together. I have a feeling that they'll now make every effort to eliminate us. I'm glad now that I was prepared. I never completely trusted H."

"The sniper I overheard talking on the phone said that they hadn't been told that we were ex-SAS, which means that they had not been told that we were the team who assassinated Princess Diana."

"I suspected as much," Roger said. "If they set up another team, they'll be professionals, and they will be told that we are also professionals." He leaned back in his seat and smiled. "I always knew you were A1. How did you manage to kill all four of them?"

"They arrived in one vehicle and climbed out at the same time. They were amateurs."

"They didn't realise who they were up against," Roger said. "If we meet up with any more of H's men, they'll all be top professionals and fully briefed. What concerns me is that I've been unable to contact H, and if we're to make a deal, we must contact him."

Timothy began to feel angry. "I want to kill H. I want to kill as many of them as I can."

"You might have to if we can't make a deal." Roger looked at his watch. "We'll have to leave. I've hired a Porsche. Not in my name, of course. I'll be driving. Now that I'm not drinking, I don't have to worry about being over the limit."

"Where are we going?" Timothy asked.

"To London, to meet Joseph. You'll like Joe. He's a bundle of laughs."

They drove to London listening to a cassette of Dean Martin.

*

Victoria looked out of the window of the train as it sped along. Her future now depended on what Timothy and Roger could do. She opened a packet of chocolate biscuits. It was not going to be easy. How can you persuade someone not to kill you? Timothy and Roger will probably have to risk their lives. She bit off a piece of a chocolate biscuit. More men would probably die before it was resolved.

She had every faith in Timothy. He had shot the sniper as he climbed onto the garage and had then risked his life to rescue her. She took another bite of the chocolate biscuit. He shot the man through the bedroom door and then shot four more men. It was difficult to believe what had happened, even though she had seen it with her own eyes.

When the four men jumped out of the car, she almost died of shock. Her legs had turned to jelly, and if she had not thrown herself to the ground, she would have collapsed. She had watched Timothy blazing away with his guns. He hit two of the men in the head. He was as cool and calm as if it had been a game. He then ran to his right and shot the other two men.

She put the rest of the chocolate biscuit into her mouth. She always ate chocolate biscuits when she was worried. She would be eating huge amounts of them over the next few weeks. She felt depressed, worried and lonely. It would be nice to be able to talk to someone. She hated being on her own. She smiled and placed her hand on her stomach. "I wish you were old enough to talk to," she whispered.

*

Timothy woke up and stretched. He hated sleeping in a car. They were in London. "I needed that sleep. I've been having it a bit rough lately."

Roger smiled. "I know what you mean. We're meeting up with Joe in a little pub. We'll not be returning to our homes and families until it's sorted. I didn't tell Victoria, but we might not make it. Our chances at the moment are less than even. They'll now be out for our blood, and they hold most of the cards."

"You'll think of something, Major," Timothy said. "You always do." He had known Roger for years, and there was no one better than him at analysing situations and coming up with a solution.

"I shall give it my best shot," Roger said.

"What do you know about H?" Timothy asked.

"All there is to know. About five years ago, I employed Joe to follow H and check up on him and all the contacts he made. His real name is Jonathan Hide. He's married and has two children and three grandchildren. He visits a gay brothel once a week. I want you to talk to him and tell him to contact me, or you'll kill him."

"He'll probably have a bodyguard," Timothy said.

"He does. He's had a bodyguard for the last two days. The bodyguard shadows him everywhere. I want you to kill the bodyguard. It'll prove to Jonathan that we mean business."

"I need ammunition," Timothy said. "Can you get what we need?"

"I can get almost anything. At least Joe can."

They pulled into a public house car park in Wood Green and climbed out of the car. The public house was called the Broken Leg. They had travelled from the Crooked Leg to the Broken Leg.

Joseph Peters walked towards them. "You're late," he said. He held out his hand to Timothy. "I'm Joe. I've heard all about you. Let's go inside and have a drink."

Timothy shook Joseph's hand. "I've heard all about you as well."

They followed Joseph into the public house. Joseph was tall and thin, totally bald and wore glasses. His wrinkled face was his most prominent feature. He walked with a slight limp and looked at least eighty. They bought drinks and sat at a table.

"Timothy's already eliminated six of them," Roger said. "I told you he was good."

Joseph looked amazed, and he punched the air with his wrinkled, bony hand. "Fucking hell. It's just like old times. I hope my heart holds out. I've got the materials you asked for, Major, in my car. What's our next move?"

"Is H still going to work, Joe?"

"Yes. Same place, same time."

"I want you to show Tim where Jonathan lives and works and the route he takes to and from work," Roger said. "I also want you to show him where Sarah and Richard live." He placed three photographs on the table and pointed to them. "This is Jonathan; this is Richard, and this is Sarah."

Timothy looked at the photographs. Sarah was good-looking, slim, and about forty-five. Richard was average-looking, well-built, and about sixty. Jonathan was about fifty, ugly, fat, and bald.

"I know who Sarah and Richard are," Roger said. "I know where they live, where they work, and all about their families and friends. What I don't know is why they keep in contact with Jonathan. I don't think they are part of MI5 or MI6."

"They might be Jonathan's friends," Timothy suggested.

Roger shook his head. "No. They're definitely not Jonathan's friends. They're upper class, and Jonathan's middle class. I have a feeling they might be the palace protectors. I'm hoping that Jonathan will enlighten me."

"I've put together a file on MI5 and MI6 officials," Joseph said. "We now know all of the top people." He pointed to the photographs. "I took them. I was in a car at least fifty yards away at the time. There's nothing I can't do."

"Joe's the best," Roger said. "Which is why I'm leaving him everything in my will. I don't want the wife to get a penny. I'll have to leave her the house, but everything else goes to you, Joe."

Joseph frowned and stared at Roger. "Are you serious?"

"Yes," Roger said. "The wife will contest the will if I leave my cash to you, so I intend to give you the money before I die. When I begin to get ill, which will be within the year, I intend to give you a cash bonus of one and a half million pounds."

Joseph looked shocked. "Fucking hell. What about your kids?"

"Your kids need it more than mine," Roger said.

Joseph leant back in his seat. "How did you know I had kids? No one knows about my family."

"I do," Roger said. "It's my job to know these things."

"How many kids do you have, Joe?" Timothy asked. He was warming to Joseph and was already convinced he could trust him completely.

"Five," Joseph said. He took a drink of his lager. "I have eight grandchildren and four great-grandchildren, and they could do with some cash. One of my grandchildren has Down syndrome." He reached across the table and shook Roger's hand. "Thanks. You've always been a gentleman."

"Not according to the wife," Roger said.

"Where did you get all that money from, Major?" Timothy asked. "Are you a bank robber?"

Roger smiled. "I went into the property market in nineteen seventy. I bought my family house and a row of derelict houses in Oxford with the money left to me by my father. I had the derelict houses done up and sold them after the boom of nineteen seventy-three. I bought them for about thirty thousand pounds each, spent about twenty thousand pounds on each house and sold each house for over two hundred and fifty thousand pounds. It set me up for life. My family home is now worth nearly two million pounds."

They talked about their lives, sampled the public house cuisine (it was the worst food Timothy had ever tasted) and left the public house at ten-thirty. Timothy was almost falling asleep standing up. "Where will we be living?"

"We'll be living separately," Roger said. "I'll drop you off at your hotel. Make sure your phone is always turned on and charged up. Did you get Tim a motorbike, Joe?"

"Yes. He can collect it tomorrow. I know exactly what to do. I'll brief Tim tomorrow. I'll pick you up at your hotel at about ten, Tim."

Timothy nodded.

Roger gave Timothy a lift to a seedy-looking hotel, and he checked in using the false ID that Roger had given him. Roger was a top professional, and if he could not find a way to defeat H and his cronies, no one could.

*

Victoria was sitting at her hotel bedroom window, watching people walk along the seafront. She had spent the day walking on the beach. Loneliness hung over her like a dark cloud. She had no idea how Roger and Timothy were going to persuade the men who were trying to kill them to leave them alone. It was bound to involve violence. All she wanted was to live normally, run her nursery and look forward to a future with Timothy and their children. It was not too much to ask.

It was dark, and the illuminations were on. A tram rumbled along. It was after eleven o'clock, but the promenade was as packed now as it had been during the afternoon. The people seemed to be enjoying themselves. It was about time she had a bit of happiness. She took a bite of a chocolate biscuit. She did not believe in God, but tonight, she intended to pray for the first time in case a creator did exist. She was going to ask him to look after Timothy and bring him safely back to her.

Her phone rang. She picked it up. "Yes?"

"It's me," Timothy said. "Are you enjoying your holiday?"

"No, I'm not. I hate being on my own. Where are you?"

"I'm in a hotel in London. Where are you?"

"I'm in Blackpool. I used to like Blackpool. I now hate it, and I don't want to ever come here again. I feel lonely even when I'm surrounded by people. Do you know how long you'll be away?"

"No. We'll be trying to negotiate some sort of compromise. Did you leave an envelope with a solicitor?"

"Yes. Would it be possible for me to see you every few days or even once a week?"

"No. I might be followed. Memorise the name and address of the solicitors. Don't write it down. I'll have to go. I have a full day ahead of me tomorrow."

"Just be careful," she said.

"I will."

*

Timothy ended the call, put his phone on charge, took off his coat, trousers and shoes and climbed into bed. The lager was having its effect, and he was falling asleep as his head hit the pillow.

Chapter Seventeen

Timothy opened his eyes and looked at his watch. It was just after nine. He looked about and blew out his cheeks. The place was a dump. The wallpaper was hanging off in a dozen places, and there were more damp patches than he could count. Thankfully, the sheets and the duvet were clean. His hotel suite consisted of a small bedroom containing a bed, a chest of drawers, and a wardrobe, and a bathroom.

He checked his gun (it was loaded and ready for action) and climbed out of bed. Despite his injuries, which still hurt to the touch, he was also ready for action. Until now, killing had been just a job that had to be done. It was now very different. This time, it was personal. He had been betrayed by men he trusted. They were treating him as if he were the enemy. Instead of giving him a medal for all his hard work, they were trying to kill him. He was now filled with a need to kill as many of them as he could.

At five minutes to ten, he picked up his phone and walked to the front of the hotel. Joseph was waiting for him in an old van.

"Get in," Joseph said. "We've got lots to do."

He climbed into the van, and they drove off. "I need a few things, Joe. I need a change of clothes, a toothbrush and a shaver."

"We can get them on the way. I'll show you where Sarah lives first. She lives in a big house in Mayfair. Richard lives in Chelsea, and Jonathan lives in Totteridge."

After seeing where Sarah, Richard and Jonathan lived and doing a bit of shopping, they drove the route that Jonathan took to and from work.

"Does the bodyguard travel in Jonathan's car?" Timothy asked.

"No. He travels behind in a black Ford. How are you going to kill the bodyguard and then talk to Jonathan before he gets home?"

"Pull over here," Timothy said. They were on the A 1000. "This looks like an ideal spot. I'll be able to kill the bodyguard and catch up with Jonathan before he gets home. I'd like you to watch my back."

"It'll be my pleasure. I'll be a short distance behind you. Are you going to do it today?"

"Yes, why not. Shall we go and get the motorbike?"

They drove off.

"This might be an old van, but it's a good runner," Joseph said.

"It's a bit like you, Joe," Timothy said.

Joseph smiled. "I think it's in better shape than me."

They drove to a large lock-up garage in Southgate.

"I have everything you need," Joseph said. He opened the garage doors, and they walked inside. "Do you want a spare handgun?"

"Yes." Timothy took the handgun and examined the motorbike. "Can this be traced?"

"No. It's been bought using a false ID."

Joseph handed him a bulletproof vest and a crash helmet. "The vest is designed to stop most bullets from a handgun. I'll be in constant contact with you by radio. Keep the earpiece in your ear at all times. If the police follow you, I'll direct you where to go to lose them. Any questions?"

"No."

Timothy felt uneasy and was less confident than he usually was. He was used to being part of a team, and the only backup he had was an old man in his seventies. "Do I bring the bike back here?"

"No. You might be caught on a camera. I'll need to change the colour of the bike and the registration first. We'll stop off somewhere after you've seen Jonathan." He looked at his watch. "It's time to move out."

Timothy climbed onto the motorbike and started it up. It sounded very powerful.

"Don't bother to check where I am," Joseph said. "I'll keep you in sight. I hope everything goes all right."

"So do I," Timothy said.

Timothy drove the powerful motorbike to Finchley and stopped on the side of the road. He sat astride the motorbike. Joseph was talking almost non-stop into his earpiece.

"Jonathan drives a blue Vauxhall Vectra," Joseph said. "I'll tell you as soon as I see it. Can you hear me clearly?"

"Yes. I'll follow the black Ford to the traffic lights, and as soon as we know that there are no other agents involved, I'll shoot him through the window. I'll try and shoot him when he stops at the lights."

"This is just like old times," Joseph said. "I hope my angina doesn't play up. He's here. Jonathan's passing me now. Can you see him?"

"Yes, and I can see the black Ford. It's four cars behind the Vauxhall."

Timothy pulled out a short distance behind the Ford. "Can you see any other agents, Joe?"

"No. It's all clear."

The Vauxhall stopped at the traffic lights, and four cars behind, the Ford also stopped. Timothy pulled alongside the Ford and shot the driver in the head through the front offside window. Timothy looked through the shattered window. The driver was slumped in his seat with a hole in the side of his head. The lights changed, and the Vauxhall sped off. Timothy roared after the Vauxhall and pulled alongside.

Jonathan kept glancing at Timothy. He looked terrified. Timothy gestured with his gun for Jonathan to pull over. When he was ignored, Timothy shot out the back windows. The Vauxhall skidded to a halt.

"Don't kill me," Jonathan cried. "For god's sake, don't kill me,"

Timothy pulled up next to the offside front window and aimed his gun at Jonathan. "Bang, bang," Timothy said. "Speak to Roger, or the bangs will be real. You can go home now."

The Vauxhall sped off, and Timothy turned off the main road. "Any sign of any backup, Joe?"

"No. I think we're home and dry. Continue down here and take the first right. I think we best get out of London."

Timothy began to relax. It had not been as difficult as he had expected.

"A car and two motorbikes are coming up behind us at high speed," Joseph said. "Your best bet is to turn off this road and hide in a side road. I don't think you'll be able to outrun them. Take the next left."

Timothy turned onto a side road, pulled in between two parked cars and crouched down on the motorbike. A short time later, a car and two motorbikes sped past the road junction at high speed.

"They didn't see you," Joseph said. "Continue down the road. I think we can lose them."

As Joseph's van pulled into the side road, Timothy roared off. "Take the next right," Joseph said.

Timothy was surprised that Jonathan was important enough to have an army of minders. He then realised they were not guarding Jonathan; they were after him. They had obviously expected him to contact Jonathan. It had been a very close shave.

Timothy followed Joseph's instructions until they were in Church End.

"Stop here," Joseph said.

Timothy stopped, and Joseph pulled up behind him in the van. They were next to a wall and not being overlooked.

"Well done, Joe. You saved my bacon."

"All in a day's work," Joseph said. "In the back of the van, you'll find a different coloured jacket and helmet."

Timothy swapped the red jacket and red helmet for blue ones and watched Joseph change the motorbike's number plates and cover the red parts of the motorbike in blue stickers. The motorbike was now blue. "Very clever, Joe. Where do you get the number plates from?"

"I make them." He grinned. "I'm thoroughly enjoying myself." He looked about. "Let's go back to the garage. There's no need to rush."

Timothy drove back to the lock-up garage, with Joseph following about a hundred yards behind. They were not followed.

As soon as the motorbike had been locked up in the garage, Timothy phoned Roger. "We're at the garage," Timothy said.

"How did it go?" Roger asked. "Were there any problems?"

"Nothing we couldn't handle," Joseph shouted over Timothy's shoulder.

"They were waiting for us," Timothy said. "Jonathan had five minders. The ones we knew about were in the Ford: two on motorbikes and two in a high-powered car. I killed the one minder in the Ford and was leaving the scene when the other minders appeared. I don't think I would have been able to outrun them, and I would have been killed if it had not been for Joe. He spotted them, and I was able to hide."

"I thought they might have some backup," Roger said, "which is why I told Joe to keep his eyes peeled. Did you manage to speak to Jonathan?"

"Yes. I told him to speak to you; otherwise, he would die."

"How did he take it?" Roger asked.

"He's shit scared, but I'm not sure he'll talk to you. He might go into hiding."

"I'm going to give him a call from a public phone box," Roger said. "I don't think he'll go into hiding. It'll mean he won't be able to see his children and grandchildren. I'll meet you at the Broken Leg in about two hours."

Timothy and Joseph had a meal at a back-street café and then drove in the van to the Broken Leg public house. Roger was waiting for them.

"I'll get the drinks," Roger said. "It's my treat."

They sat down at a table with their drinks.

"Did you speak to Jonathan, Major?" Timothy asked.

"Yes. He answered the phone on the second ring. We're going to meet tomorrow at ten in the morning and talk."

"Can you trust him?" Joseph asked. "You could be walking into a trap."

"I have no choice. If we're going to sort things out, we need to talk. I don't think I'll be killed. I told Jonathan about Sarah and Richard, and I named several top MI5 and MI6 personnel. He was amazed. I also told him that if anything happened to me, he would die, and so would fifteen of his colleagues. I think he's ready to make a deal. When I speak to him, I'll leave my phone on, so that you can listen in."

Timothy began to feel angry. "If you're killed, I'll kill the fucking lot of them. Where are the files you have on them? I'm totally pissed off. They should be thanking us, not trying to kill us."

"The information's on a disc," Roger said. "Joe has several copies stashed away." He handed Timothy a small envelope. "That's your copy."

"If anything happens to me," Joseph said, "there's a copy of the disc taped to the underside of a drawer in the lockup garage. There's also one hidden in the van."

Roger smiled. "I think we have the edge on them."

Timothy was not so sure. He had a feeling that the odds were not on their side, at least not yet.

*

It had rained non-stop all day, and Victoria had spent the best part of the day sitting in cafes and restaurants. She had been chatted up several times. The time dragged. The day seemed like a week. It was eight-fifteen in the evening. She was sitting in a shelter by the beach. The rain had eased a little and was now just spitting. She felt lonely and depressed, and her mind was filled with worry. As brave as Timothy was, he could still be killed.

A car pulled up near her. It was full of young men. They climbed out and walked towards her. "Hello, darling," one of them said.

Victoria stood up. She felt frightened. She would not be able to run away from them, and the few people who had braved the awful conditions might not come to her aid. "My boyfriend will be here in a minute," she said.

"I don't think so," the same young man said. "How would you like to be fucked?"

"And how would you like to be totally fucked," a deep male voice said. The owner of the voice, a huge policeman, walked from behind the shelter.

The five men ran to the car, climbed in and drove off.

Victoria's fear was replaced by relief and then anger. "Thanks for helping me. Thugs like that make me sick."

"It's my job to help people. I don't think they'll bother you again." He looked down at her. "It's getting dark, and it might be a good idea for you to go home. It's not wise for a woman to be out on her own after dark."

"I was about to go to my hotel," she said.

"As soon as I've finished my fag, I'll walk with you." He took the cigarette from behind his back and took a drag.

She smiled. "I didn't think police officers were allowed to smoke on duty?"

"They're not. I don't care anymore. I retire at the end of the week. I've been a police officer for twenty-five years. I've personally watched this country go to the dogs. There's no respect anymore. There are more killings and violence now than when I started on the beat."

"Why is that?" she asked. It was nice to talk to someone; it might help to take her mind off her worries.

"We're too soft; that's why." He took a drag and flicked his cigarette nub over the wall onto the beach. "Which way is your hotel?"

She pointed. "It's about five hundred yards away."

She put up her umbrella, and they began to walk towards her hotel. "I remember an old lady saying that when she was young, people were not mugged."

"She was right. We're not firm enough with the youngsters. They should be taught at a young age to behave. It would help if we brought back approved schools."

It was nice to talk, and for a while, she forgot about her worries, but it was only a brief respite. By the time she was sitting in her hotel room, they had all returned and were lined up in her head. Was Timothy still alive? Was he hurt? Had he been successful in his negotiations with the men who were trying to kill him? When would she see him?

She had spent the whole day wondering what Timothy would be doing and worrying about him. She had been so upset that she had not been able to eat her evening meal. She had no idea how she would survive weeks of not knowing what was happening.

She made herself a cup of coffee and sat with the phone at her side, looking out the window. The rain was lashing down, but a few people were still walking along the seafront despite the bad weather.

At ten-thirty, her phone rang. She picked it up." Yes?"

"It's me," Timothy said. "How are you?"

"Worried sick. It's so good to hear your voice. Are you all right?"

"Yes. I'm fine."

"What's happening?" she asked.

"They've agreed to talk to us. Roger's going to see Jonathan tomorrow. We might be able to make a deal."

"Thank God for that," she said. "Will you know if you have made a deal by the time you phone me tomorrow night?"

"Yes. How have you spent the day?"

"It's rained all day. I couldn't even go for a walk along the beach. I tried, but as soon as I opened my umbrella, the wind blew it inside out. I walked from one café to the next. What did you do?"

"I went to see Jonathan to persuade him to talk to Roger."

"Was it dangerous?" she asked.

"Yes."

She began to worry. "Don't tell me the details until it's all over. You haven't been hurt, have you?"

"No, but my wounds are playing up. I miss you. I can't wait to get my hands on your body."

"And I can't wait to feel your hands on my body. If Roger makes a deal with them, will you be able to come home?"

"Yes."

"I can hear talking," she said. "Where are you?"

"I'm in a pub. Roger and Joe have just left. I'm a little drunk."

"I suppose you want to go to your hotel?" she asked.

"Yes. I'm knackered."

"Take special care," she said. "I love you."

"I love you as well. I'll phone you tomorrow."

Chapter Eighteen

Timothy was sitting on his bed in his hotel suite. It was eight o'clock in the morning. He phoned Joseph. "Do you have a computer, Joe?"

"Yes, in the office. Why?"

"I'd like to see what's on the disc."

"I'll come and pick you up," Joseph said. "I'll be there in thirty minutes."

Joseph took Timothy to a small, dusty office that had not been cleaned for years. Books and files lay everywhere. A computer sat on a desk in the corner.

"What a dump," Timothy said.

"Yes, but the rent's cheap."

Timothy spent two hours memorising as much of the information on the disc as he could. There was a file on thirty-two people. Some of the files were several pages long. It was very detailed, even down to the names of their pets and where they went on holiday. "How did you get all this information, Joe?"

"It took five years. He touched his nose. "It's amazing what you can get out of a dustbin."

"With this information, I'll have no trouble eliminating them," Timothy said. "Major's even listed them in order of importance."

"What will you do if they kill Major?" Joseph asked.

"I'll kill every person listed on the disc."

"It'll not be easy," Joseph said.

"I know." Timothy lit a cigarette. "But what else could I do? I wouldn't be able to go home, and with Major dead, we'll not be able to negotiate. If they kill Major, I'll never be able to live a normal life. What will you do if they kill Major?"

"Help you, of course. We'd make a good team."

Timothy's phone rang. He took it out of his pocket. "Yes?"

"It's me," Roger said.

"Good morning, Major."

"I'm at the meeting place," Roger said. "I'm sitting on a bench by the Cutty Sark. I've just spotted Jonathan walking towards me. You'll be able to hear what he says. You can also speak to me. I'm wearing an earpiece, so Jonathan will not be able to hear what you say. Where are you?"

"We're in Joseph's office.

"I'll speak to you when Jonathan's gone," Roger said.

It went silent for a while.

"You're five minutes late, Jonathan," Roger said.

"It's a wonder I'm here at all, Jonathan said. "I've been speaking to Sarah. She's in a vile mood."

"How are your minders?" Roger asked.

"After what happened, I've dispensed with bodyguards. Timothy's very good at what he does. My bodyguards were supposed to be top professionals. How did he do it? I assume it was Timothy? He was wearing a helmet, and I couldn't see his face properly."

"I don't talk about things like that," Roger said. "Were you followed here?"

"I don't think so. Before I came here, I bought a complete wardrobe of clothes. Everything I'm wearing now is brand new, and I'm not wearing my watch. I've also left my phone in my car. I don't want anyone to know I'm meeting you or know what we talk about."

"And what are we going to talk about?" Roger asked.

Timothy lit a cigarette. It was about to get interesting.

"I was against killing you and your team," Jonathan said. "I was overruled. I know that if we don't come to some agreement, I'll be killed. I don't want to die. I'm prepared to do anything; just don't kill me."

"Who overruled you?" Roger asked. "Who wants us dead?"

"It's not MI5 or MI6. It's the men in grey suits. We call them the palace protectors."

"Who are they?" Roger asked.

"I only know two of them. Sarah and Richard. I've just had a blinding row with Sarah. I said that if we continued trying to kill you and Tim, some of us would die. She's determined to have you killed. She's going into hiding as we speak."

Joseph grabbed his coat. "I'm on my way. I'll see you later."

"Joe's gone to follow Sarah," Timothy said.

"I don't know if I can trust you, Jonathan," Roger said. "You should have warned me about what Sarah was doing. I lost some good men."

"I was being followed night and day, and my phone was bugged," Jonathan said. "There was nothing I could do. You've got to believe me."

"The team we killed, Slim and his mates, were they the other assassination team?" Roger asked.

"Yes. They're all dead. They didn't know about the assassination of Princess Diana. The men who will come after you and Tim also won't know about Princess Diana. Only a few people in MI5 and MI6, as well as a few palace protectors, know what happened. I'll do anything you want; just don't kill me. Is Timothy watching us now?"

"I believe you're telling me the truth," Roger said. "If I find out that you've lied to me, you'll die."

"I'm not lying to you," Jonathan insisted.

"I need time to decide what to do," Roger said. "I'll phone you when we need to meet again. In the meantime, see if you can find out more about the palace protectors."

"I can't. We don't have the authority to investigate them. No one knows who they are. We believe that there are only a dozen or so. Sarah's paid one million pounds a year. What I do know is that Sarah's very close to the royal family."

"And she refuses to negotiate?" Roger asked.

"Yes, totally. She said that you and Tim would be dead in a week. She has powerful friends and gives orders to the heads of MI5 and MI6. She's feared by everyone. She's known as Sarah Hoover and has powers to match."

"We'll have to deal with her," Roger said.

"It'll make my day if you do," Jonathan said. "By now, she'll be in hiding. She'll probably be in Buckingham Palace."

"I'm going now," Roger said. "I'll phone you."

There was a period of silence.

"Sarah needs to die," Timothy said. "Has Jonathan gone?"

"Yes. I'll meet you at your hotel. I'll drive past the hotel, and you can see if I'm being followed. I'll be in a black cab. I'll be there in about forty minutes."

Timothy took a taxi to his hotel and waited by the window for Roger to drive past. He lit a cigarette. By now, Sarah would be in hiding. He was hoping that Joseph had been able to follow her. He needed to kill her if he wanted to be free and live a normal life with Victoria. Roger drove past in a black cab and turned left. He was not being followed. None of the cars following the taxi turned left. He phoned Roger, and they agreed to meet at the Broken Leg. Timothy could do with a drink.

*

Victoria bought herself a thick romance novel and began to read it in a shelter on the seafront. It might get her mind off her worries. An hour later, she put the book in the bin. She could not concentrate. Her mind was too full of worries. She began to walk along the beach, a few feet from the breaking waves. It was a cold, windy day, and the beach was crowded with holidaymakers wearing coats and hats.

From the age of about twelve, she had dreamed of meeting a wonderful man, falling in love and having his child. Her dream had come true, but there was no sign of a happy ever after. The man she loved had a death sentence hanging over his head. She had a nasty feeling that she would be bringing up her baby on her own. Timothy had managed to kill six men, but he could not be expected to kill all of the men who were after him. One day, Timothy could die.

It was sobering to think that the men that Timothy had killed were someone's son, boyfriend or husband. They might have even been fathers. People would be mourning them. Life was a mystery at times. For the life of her, she could not understand why men had to kill. It would break her heart if she had to bury Timothy.

She stopped walking and stared out to sea. If Timothy were killed, they would probably get rid of his body. She would not even have a grave to mourn over.

*

Timothy sat down in the Broken Leg public house with Roger. "I heard what was said," Timothy said. "Do you believe him?"

"Yes, for what it's worth." Roger sipped his orange juice. "You'll have to kill a few of them to try and change their minds."

"It's Sarah we need to kill," Timothy said. "I'm hoping Joe was able to follow Sarah, who by now will be in hiding. If I know where she lives, she's as good as dead. Do you know of any other palace protectors?"

"No, but I know the families and relatives of Sarah and Richard, and I know some of their friends. We'll have to hit their families and friends. We have nothing to lose."

Roger's phone rang. He took it out of his pocket. "Yes. Good. I hope it's good news, Joe."

Timothy tried to listen. "Does Joe know where Sarah's holed out?"

Roger nodded. "Tim's on his way." Roger put the phone into his pocket. "Joe was able to follow Sarah. A car with tinted windows drove out of Sarah's garage, and Joe followed it to a house in Potters Bar. He's been observing the house with binoculars and has just spotted Sarah in the back garden. Take the motorbike." He handed Timothy a key. "Joe will meet you at the corner of Right Street and Lode Lane."

Timothy took the key. "I'm on my way."

It was three-thirty when Timothy met up with Joseph.

"I've been observing the house," Joseph said. "They have two men sitting in a car at the front of the house, but no one at the back. Follow me on the bike. I've found a place to park out of the sight of prying eyes."

They drove for a short distance and parked the van and the motorbike on a side road.

Joseph took an A to Z of London out of his pocket. "I'll wait here. If anything goes wrong, phone me, and if I see anything, I'll phone you." He opened the A to Z and pointed to where they were. "I'll follow you when we leave, and we'll take this route. Put your earpiece in, and I'll direct you."

"I'm assuming you've got the sniper's friend?" Timothy asked.

"I certainly have. It's loaded and ready to go." He took the rifle, which was wrapped in a coat, out of his van and handed it to Timothy. He pointed. "Follow that path to the fence, and you'll have a clear view of the back of the house from the top of that tree. I'll wait here. I intend to hide in the back of the van and keep watch."

Timothy walked up the path and stopped next to the tall oak tree that Joseph had pointed to. He could see the roof of the house, but he would have to climb the tree to be able to see the house and garden. The house was over two hundred yards away. He looked up at the tree. There were no small branches that he could reach to hold onto. It was going to be very difficult to climb, especially while carrying a rifle. He was just about to phone Joseph to ask him how he had managed to climb the tree when he saw that several large screwdrivers had been driven into the trunk.

He put his phone back into his pocket, climbed up the tree and sat on a thick branch. The branches and leaves hid him from the view of anyone travelling along the road where Joseph was, but he had a clear view of the house and most of the back garden. He looked through the telescopic sights of the high-powered rifle. He could see several windows and an open French window that led onto a patio. There was no sign of anyone.

Timothy phoned Joseph. "I'm in position, Joe. The French windows are open. It's a cold day. Why would they be wide open?"

"Fuck knows," Joseph said. "Earlier today, I saw Sarah and a woman I've never seen before walk out of the house and around the garden. The other woman could also be one of the palace protectors."

"I'll eliminate both of them if I see them," Timothy said.

Timothy slipped his phone into his pocket. He could be here for hours. He lit a cigarette, pulled his coat around his shoulders and waited. It occurred to him why Sarah and her female friend had walked around the garden. They were probably worried that the house was bugged, and they wanted to talk without being overheard.

*

Victoria took a tram ride along the seafront. It was autumn, and the holiday season was coming to an end. An old woman sat down next to her.

"Have you fallen out with your boyfriend?" the woman asked.

Victoria turned to look at her. "Why do you think I've fallen out with my boyfriend?"

"Because you're on your own in Blackpool. You don't see many young ladies on their own on a tram."

"My boyfriend's working away from home, so I thought I'd take a holiday."

"It's not the time of year for a holiday," the old woman said. "What does your boyfriend do?"

"He blows up buildings."

"He ought to blow up Prince Charles and Camilla," the old woman said. "They made Princess Diana ill." She opened a newspaper. "Look at this." It was a photograph of the car in which Princess Diana had died. "What a way to die. If you ask me, she was murdered."

"Victoria was shocked. "Why do you think she was murdered?"

"She spoke out against Prince Charles and the Queen. I think they had her bumped off. The poor girl. God knows what will happen when her sons find out what happened to their mother. I hope Prince Charles never becomes King."

"I thought it was just a car accident?" Victoria said.

"It's been made to look like an accident," the old woman said. She stood up. "It's my stop. Bye."

"Bye," Victoria said. She looked out of the window. Even without any evidence, some people were already thinking that Princess Diana had been murdered.

*

Timothy had been in the tree for several hours, and it was getting dark. A young boy closed the French windows and drew the curtains. The curtains of the bedroom windows were also drawn, and lights were switched on.

When it was too dark to see, Timothy climbed down the tree and phoned Joseph. "I'm coming back to the van, Joe. I can't see a bloody thing."

"Okay," Joseph said. "We'll call it a day."

Timothy climbed onto his motorbike and followed Joseph in the van. They met Roger at the Broken Leg public house.

"How did it go?" Roger asked.

"I didn't see the target," Timothy said. "I'll return in the morning and try again."

"I'll watch Richard's house tomorrow," Joseph said. "It might be worth following a member of his family. They might lead us to his safe house."

"This could go on for months," Roger said. "I think we need to hit a target and stir them up." He took out a notebook. "But who do we hit?"

"If we hit one, it'll send them all into hiding," Timothy said. "Especially those at the top. At the moment, they'll be totally absorbed in finding us. Give it a couple of days. I might get lucky. I'll get there early in the morning, and if Sarah feels safe, she might come out into the garden."

Roger nodded. "A few days won't hurt."

They had a meal at the pub, and Timothy drank until he was merry. He could not afford to get drunk. He needed his wits about him at all times. At nine-thirty, he drove back to his hotel on the motorbike. He needed to have an early night.

*

At ten o'clock, Victoria's phone rang. She picked it up. "Yes?"

"It's only me," Timothy said. "Are you all right?"

It was wonderful to hear his voice. "Yes. What's happening?"

"Nothing. It's a waiting game at the moment. Where are you?"

"I'm in my hotel room. Where are you?"

"I'm in bed. I have an early start in the morning."

"Don't tell me what you'll be doing," she said. "I don't want to know. This waiting is driving me mad, and I'm sick of Blackpool. I think I'll move on tomorrow. I think I'll go to York. I've always wanted to see the city of York."

"I'm sorry for all the trouble I've caused you," he said. "I never expected this to happen. I joined the army and then the SAS to help keep this country safe. I was very patriotic when I was young. After the way I've been treated, I don't give a damn anymore. It wouldn't bother me if they did get rid of the Queen."

"It's not your fault," she said. "You were just obeying orders. The papers are full of Diana's death. They're blaming the driver. They say he was drunk. Did you see the driver?"

"Yes. I watched him walk to the Mercedes. He wasn't drunk."

"I suppose I'd better let you get to sleep," she said. "I'll probably be awake all night."

"Goodnight, sweetheart," he said. "I'll phone you tomorrow."

"Yes. Goodnight, Tim. Stay alive for me and the baby. We need you."
"I will."

Chapter Nineteen

It was beginning to get light when Timothy climbed into the oak tree that overlooked Sarah's safe house. He had hidden his motorbike in some bushes. He was half asleep. His phone rang. "Yes?"

"It's Joe. Are you still in bed?"

"No. I'm in a fucking tree, and it's freezing cold."

Joseph laughed. "I'm lying on a shed with water dripping on me from the leaves of the trees. It's not the life a man of my age should have. I should be sitting in a rocking chair in a nursing home with my slippers on."

"I don't see you in a nursing home, Joe," Timothy said.

"You're bleeding right there," Joseph said. "I want to die with my boots on. I'm not really complaining. I'm having the time of my life. If I see Richard or Sarah, I'll phone you. Have a nice day."

"I'll try to."

A door on the side of the house opened, and four Alsatians ran out into the garden. They were followed by the little boy Timothy had seen yesterday. The large garden of another house separated Timothy from the Alsatians so they would not detect his presence. The dogs chased a squirrel up a tree. Timothy began watching the house through the rifle's telescopic sights. He was probably wasting his time. Sarah could be miles away by now.

A short time later, the dogs followed the boy into the house, and it began to rain. At first, he was dry; the leaves protected him, but after a while, large drops of water began to drip on him. He could feel the water running down his neck. Tomorrow, he intended to wear a waterproof coat that had a hood. The rain stopped, and the sun came out, but the drips of water continued to fall on him. They made pat, pat sounds as they landed on his coat.

He lit a cigarette and looked at his watch. It was twelve-thirty. The French windows opened, and three people walked into the garden. He rubbed out his cigarette and put the nub into his pocket. He did not want to leave anything at the scene that might carry his DNA. He looked through the rifle's telescopic sights. It was Sarah. She was with a woman he had not seen before and a man who had his back to him. They walked down the steps and onto the lawn. The man turned around. It was Richard.

Timothy took aim at the man's chest and gently squeezed the trigger. The gun fired, and the man fell to the ground. The two women stood looking about. He shot Sarah in the chest and the other woman in the back as she ran towards the house. He then shot each of them in the head as they lay on the ground. He did not have to collect the spent cartridges; they were not ejected from a sniper's rifle.

He climbed down the tree, ran to his motorbike and drove off. It would take the men at the front of the house at least four minutes after they had been told what had happened to get to the tree where he had been sitting, and by then, he would be miles away. If he were followed, he knew of several places where he could lose a car.

When he was on the outskirts of Hatfield, he stopped the motorbike and phoned Joseph.

"Yes?" Joseph said.

"Both targets are down, Joe," Timothy said. "I'll meet you at the Broken Leg in about two hours. Give Roger the good news."

"Both targets?" Joseph asked.

"Yes."

"Fucking hell," Joseph said. "Well done. I'll see you in two hours. Leave the bike and the rifle in the garage."

"I will," Timothy said.

Timothy drove onto the A414 and drove back to London on the A10. He felt elated. With Sarah out of the way, they might be able to come to some agreement with MI5. He would not be able to relax until he had left the rifle in the garage. If he were stopped by the police, the rifle could tie him to the deaths of three people, and so he would have to shoot his way out. It would upset him to have to kill a policeman, who would only be doing his job, but he would still do it without hesitating.

When he had left the motorbike and the rifle at the garage and was on his way to the Broken Leg public house in a taxi, he began to relax. By now, the palace protectors and MI5 would know about the three deaths. It should put the fear of God into them. And if they did not agree to a deal, he would continue killing them until they did. They could not all go into hiding. MI5 and MI6 would not be able to function if all their staff were in safe houses. He now felt that he had the edge.

Roger and Joseph were waiting for him in the lounge of the Broken Leg public house.

"I've already spoken to Jonathan," Roger said. "All hell's broken out. They've asked Jonathan to contact us to broker a deal. I'm meeting him tomorrow at ten in the morning."

Timothy was amazed. "I only disposed of the targets just over two hours ago. They must be very worried."

"They are," Roger said.

"They're worried that you'll pop off a few more of them," Joseph said. "I'll get the drinks in." He stood up and walked to the bar.

"I'm going to ask for a million pounds," Roger said. "I think you could do with a grubstake."

"I think I've earned it," Timothy said. "Unlike you, I don't have money to burn." He lit a cigarette. "If they agree to call off the dogs, what's to stop them from killing us at a future date?"

"Nothing, if that's what they intend to do. I'll inform them that we've taken out insurance, and if we die, the world will know how Princess Diana was assassinated. I'm also hoping to bluff them. I'll tell them that I have men working for me and that they'll kill Jonathan and some high-ranking MI5 and MI6 people if we're killed. I'm also going to give them a list of some of the names I have in my notebook. I know nearly everyone connected with MI5 and MI6. I'm hoping it'll be enough to convince them that it's to their advantage to let us live out our lives in peace."

"I'm willing to take a chance," Timothy said. "I want my life back. I don't want to spend the rest of my life on the run. And if I am killed, I won't know anything about it."

Roger nodded.

Joseph put the drinks on the table and sat down. "I've not enjoyed myself so much for years. It's been just like old times. If they agree to call off the dogs, does it mean I can retire?"

"No," Roger said. "I can always find something for you to do. You can retire when I die."

Timothy felt safe enough to get tipsy. After sleeping with Victoria, he found it difficult to get to sleep on his own. He missed her more than he would admit to anyone. It had been a tiring day, and by nine forty-five, he could hardly keep his eyes open.

Roger smiled. "I'd get some sleep if I were you, Tim. You look knackered."

"I am." He stood up. "I'm off. I'll see you tomorrow."

At ten-thirty, he climbed into bed and phoned Victoria.

*

Victoria was holding her phone when it rang. "Yes?"

"It's me," Timothy said.

"Hello, Tim. I've been waiting for you to phone."

"Hello, sweetheart," he said. "Are you having a good time?"

"No. You sound drunk."

"I am. I've had a tiring day. Are you all right?"

"No. I want to go home."

"We might be able to go home," he said. "They've agreed to talk. Roger's seeing them tomorrow. Where are you? Are you in York?"

"No. I'm still in Blackpool. Why do they want to talk now and not yesterday?"

"They've realised that they're not invincible. I managed to persuade them to talk to us."

"Don't tell me how," she said. Timothy had probably shot one of them, and she did not feel up to knowing the details.

"I'll know what's happening by about noon tomorrow," he said.

"I'm going to travel back to Birmingham first thing in the morning," she said. "If it doesn't work out, I'll travel to York. I can't wait to see you. I feel I haven't seen you for years."

"We'll make up for it," he said. "I'm falling asleep. I'll phone you tomorrow."

"Yes. Goodnight, Tim."

*

As soon as Timothy woke up in the morning, he phoned Roger.

"It's eight o'clock, Roger. I didn't want you to oversleep."

"I've been up since six o'clock," Roger said. "It's a force of habit. I'll do the same as I did the last time so that you can listen in when I speak to Jonathan. The newspapers are beginning to talk about the possible assassination of Princess Diana. By the look of things, MI5 are having a job keeping a lid on it. I don't think they'll want to risk any more information leaking out and getting to the press. And even if they didn't realise it before, they now know that we're professionals. I'll phone you back later."

Timothy had breakfast with Joseph in the seedy café. The food was diabolical, and he pulled a face. "The only foods in this café that taste like it should, Joe, are the beans and the bacon. The eggs are like rubber; the sausages are little more than bags of fat, and the tea tastes like nothing on earth."

Joseph smiled. "I like the people here, and I've got used to the place, but the food is a bit rough. If you notice, I always have cornflakes and a cup of coffee."

Timothy pushed the plate away from him. "I think I'll have cornflakes next time."

After Joseph had eaten his cornflakes, they drove to the Broken Leg public house and sat at a corner table. To fill the hole in his stomach, Timothy bought two bags of nuts and three packets of crisps. He intended to wash them down with a pint of lager. He was beginning to like the Broken Leg public house. It had a friendly atmosphere. They sat drinking and waiting.

*

Victoria packed her few possessions and checked out of the hotel. She was intending to go to Birmingham until she remembered the two envelopes. She took a detour and caught a train to Manchester. She would leave an envelope at a solicitor's office in Manchester and one in Stoke-on-Trent.

If Timothy and Roger came to some sort of agreement with the men who were trying to kill them, she could begin to live again. They had their houses to sell and a nursery to refurbish. And there was the baby to prepare for. She was determined to be optimistic.

*

Timothy's phone rang. "Yes?"

"It's me," Roger said. "I'm on the bench. Jonathan's walking towards me."

"What's happening?" Joseph asked Timothy.

"Major has met up with Jonathan," Timothy said.

"Hello, Jonathan," Roger said. "Sit down."

"How the fuck did you do it?" Jonathan asked. "And how did you know where they were?"

"We're professionals," Roger said. "I thought you knew that."

"They're convinced that you have several men working with you," Jonathan said, "and they're willing to guarantee your complete safety for silence."

"It's what we've been asking for," Roger said. "We also want two million pounds."

"Two million pounds," Jonathan said. "That's a bit steep. We have to live within a strict budget. Why do you want two million pounds? You already have more money than you could spend."

"We have put expensive contracts out on you and your colleagues," Roger said. "We don't trust you. If you kill us, you and many of your colleagues will die."

"We could manage five hundred thousand," Jonathan said.

"A million, and that's as low as I am prepared to go," Roger said.

"Okay," Jonathan said. "You have us over a barrel."

Timothy punched the air. "They've agreed to leave us alone."

"Great," Joseph said.

"The palace protectors are shitting themselves," Jonathan said. "They'll only speak to us over the phone. And the heat is on. The operation to assassinate Princess Diana was not as successful as we had at first thought. The bump with the Fiat Uno was bad enough."

"What else went wrong?" Roger asked.

"Loads of things," Jonathan said. "We thought we had everything covered. We even arranged for the road to be swept and disinfected a few hours after the crash. There was a cockup with the switching of Henri Paul's blood to prove that he was drunk. They found high levels of carbon monoxide in the switched blood that would have prevented Henri Paul from driving the car. God knows how they're going to explain it. They also cocked up when switching Princess Diana's blood."

"Why did they switch Princess Diana's blood?" Roger asked.

"She was pregnant, and they were worried that her pregnancy would show up in the blood," Jonathan said. "The switched blood contained zero alcohol, but at her post-mortem, they remarked on the strong smell of alcohol coming from her stomach when they cut it open. They also partly embalmed her so they would not be able to detect the pregnancy. There's also a video being shown on all the news channels, showing that Henri Paul was not drunk on the night of the accident."

"Trevor would not have let Henri Paul drive if he had been drunk," Roger said. "What else went wrong?"

"It's what could go wrong," Jonathan said. "You could tell your story. What we want to know is what happens if you die of natural causes."

"Nothing if I die," Roger said. "I'll only last another twelve months at the most. But the world will know exactly what happened to Princess Diana if Timothy or a member of his family dies."

"What if Timothy dies in an accident?" Jonathan said.

"Then you're fucked," Roger said. "You'll have to hope that he lives until he's eighty. When can we have the cash?"

"In a few days," Jonathan said.

"Just out of interest," Roger said, "who administered the heart attack drug?"

"I'm not sure. I think it was when they gave her the injection to calm her down," Jonathan said.

"Why would they want to calm her down?" Roger asked. "Was she conscious?"

"Oh, yes," Jonathan said. "For some reason, she thought that they were trying to kill her, and she ripped out the drip they had to put into her arm. She shouted at them and accused them of being murderers and told them to leave her alone."

"Why would she think they were trying to kill her?" Roger asked.

"She told several people before her death that Prince Charles would try to kill her in a car crash and make it look like an accident so that he could marry Camilla," Jonathan said.

"Bleeding hell," Roger said. "Even if she suspected that she would be killed, how would she know that she would be killed in a car crash?"

"We don't know," Jonathan said. "It was just a lucky guess. After she was injected with the heart attack drug, they had to wait for over an hour so that the drug could not be detected in her blood, which is why she did not arrive at the hospital until one hour and thirty-six minutes after the crash."

"They'll find it difficult to explain why it took the ambulance over forty minutes to get Princess Diana to the hospital, a journey that should have taken six or seven minutes," Roger said.

"I know. "I'm sorry for what happened. It was not of our doing. I wish you well and give our regards to Timothy and the other members of your team."

"I will," Roger said.

Joseph, who had been listening with his head close to Timothy's ear, slapped Timothy on the back. "We did it. We did it."

"It looks like it," Timothy said. He took a long drink of lager. He felt as if a large weight had been lifted from his shoulders.

"Jonathan's walking away," Roger said. "I'm going for a meal. I'll see you at the pub in about three hours."

"Okay, Major," Timothy said.

Timothy was overjoyed. They had pulled it off and should be able to live normal lives again. He lit a cigarette and phoned Victoria. "I've got some good news," he said.

"I hope you're going to tell me that we can go home and that we'll not be killed?" she said.

"Yes, I am. I'll fill in the details when I see you. Where are you?"

"I'm on the train on the way to Stoke-on-Trent. I've left an envelope with a solicitor in Manchester, and I'm going to leave the last one in Stoke-on-Trent. I won't be in Birmingham until this evening."

"I won't be back for a couple of days, but you can go home," he said. "Don't tell anyone what has happened, and never talk about Princess Diana. If anyone asks, say that you've been away with me to the Lake District."

"When will I see you?" she asked.

"I don't know. I'll phone you later this afternoon. Bye."

"Bye," she said.

Timothy put his phone back in his pocket and finished his drink. "I feel like getting drunk," he said.

"They can still kill you," Joseph said. "I don't trust them."

"I have no choice," Timothy said. "I don't want to spend the rest of my life looking over my shoulder."

Later that afternoon, Roger joined them in the Broken Leg public house, and they sat down in the lounge at a corner table. "It's time to go home," Roger said. "I think they've got the message."

"I don't trust them," Joseph said. "What happens if you both get killed?"

"Then it's up to you, Joe, to make sure that the press have the disc," Roger said. "You could kill some of the bastards if you feel up to it."

"I'm not up to it," Joseph said. "My eyesight's not what it used to be, and my hands shake too much to hold a rifle. And with my dodgy ticker, I have to be very careful. I do have some ideas. I could poison some of them. I have the poison."

"Don't take any risks," Roger said. "But if we're killed, go after Jonathan first."

"I'll do what I can," Joseph said.

"What do we do now?" Timothy asked.

"Stay hidden until we get the cash," Roger said.

"Will it be all right if I spend a couple of days with Victoria in Birmingham?" Timothy asked.

"Yes. You can take the motorbike. We need to get rid of it. Cover it in petrol and burn it in Birmingham. I'll call you if anything happens."

"The motorbike's in the garage," Joseph said. He handed Timothy the key to the garage. "Lock up the garage and shove the key under the door. I've got another key."

Timothy shook hands with them and took a taxi to the garage. It was over as far as he was concerned. There was nothing more he could do. He would have to trust the bastards if he wanted his life back.

Chapter Twenty

Victoria was travelling on the train from Stoke-on-Trent to Birmingham when her phone rang. Her heart began to thump wildly in her chest. She was worried that something had gone wrong and the news would be bad. She picked up her phone. "Yes?"

"It's me," Timothy said. "Are you all right?"

"Yes. What's happening? Have they agreed not to kill you?"

"Yes. Where are you?"

"Thank God for that. I'm on the train heading for Birmingham. Have they definitely agreed not to kill you?"

"Yes, and I think they mean it."

"I hope so," she said. "Where are you?"

"I'm in Birmingham. I've just set fire to a motorbike, and I'm on my way to New Street Station. How would you like to spend the night with me?"

"Are you serious?" she asked.

"Yes. I'll meet you off the train."

"It'll be wonderful to see you again," she said. "How are your wounds?"

"They're beginning to itch, which is a good sign. I can't wait to see you."

"I'll get there as soon as I can," she said.

*

Two hours later, they met up in Birmingham and checked into a hotel. As soon as they were in their room, he pulled her into his arms and kissed her on the lips. The need for her body overwhelmed him. They threw off their clothes and made love on the carpet. It was extra special.

For a while, after they had made love, she lay in his arms. She needed him more than she had needed anyone. "I don't want to be parted from you again."

He kissed her on the lips. "There's no need to worry. Everything's going to work out just fine."

She was bursting with happiness. They had a meal and a drink in their room and made love in the shower. "Can we go home?" she asked when they were sitting in bed watching television.

"You can. "I want to get the money first."

"What money?"

"We've asked for compensation."

She sat up. "How much compensation?"

"A million pounds."

She was shocked. "How much will you get?"

"All of it, I think. Roger's rich, and he's leaving his cash to Joe when he dies, so I think I'll be getting all of it. I need to stay in hiding until I get the cash in case they change their mind."

She leaned against the pillow. "A million pounds. I can't believe it. We'll be set up for life." She picked up two cans of lager and handed him one. "It's time to celebrate, and it's about time you told me what happened. Who is Joe?"

He opened his can and took a drink. "When we get home, they might bug the house, so after tonight, we must never talk about what happened. I don't want them to know that you knew about the assassination of Princess Diana. I've stopped taking the antidepressants, so I should stop talking in my sleep."

"Why can't we talk about it?" she asked. "What difference does it make?"

"They might renege on our agreement and kill me and Roger," he said. "If they think that you know about Princess Diana, they'll also kill you."

She began to worry. "If they know that I saw you kill those four men, it's obvious that I must know something."

"Yes, but they don't know that you also know about Princess Diana," he said. "I suppose we'll have to talk about what happened. Act as if I've told you that I owed money to the men who were after me and that they were gangsters, and now that I've killed them, we don't have to worry."

"I am worried," she said. "I thought it was all over, and we were safe to live normal lives?"

"We are, I hope," he said. "Do you want to know what happened?"

She nodded and took a long drink of lager.

"The person who wanted us dead was a palace protector and not someone who works for MI5 or MI6. For the last five years, with the help of Joe, Roger has built up a dossier on MI5 and MI6 people, so we know who they are and where they live. I went to see one of them. I killed his bodyguard and frightened him. He then agreed to speak to us."

"Who was this man?" she asked.

"I don't think I should tell you their names. He told us that MI5 and MI6 did not want to kill us but that the head of the palace protectors disagreed with them and wanted us dead. She went into hiding, but we found her."

"She." Victoria was shocked. "Is the head of the palace protectors a woman?"

"Yes. I killed her and two other palace protectors, and they agreed to talk to us. Roger told them that he had a dossier on dozens of MI5 and MI6 people and that they would die if they killed us. He implied that we had men working for us. We also told them that if we died, the world would know how Princess Diana died."

"Do you have men working for you?" she asked.

"Only Joe and he's an old man."

"What can we do?" she asked.

"We've done all we can. I don't think they'll risk killing us. If they do, everyone will know that Princess Diana was assassinated, and that's the last thing they want. I think we've done enough. I hope so. When we get the money, I intend to try to live normally."

"It's not going to be easy," she said.

"I know. The good thing is, if they're going to kill me, they'll do it within a few days. If I survive for a month, I think I'll be all right."

She did not know what to say. They were in an impossible situation, and there was nothing they could do about it. "I'm going to be optimistic. I don't think they'll want the world to know that Princess Diana was assassinated."

"Let's hope you're right." He placed his hand on her stomach. "We've got the first of many children on the way, and we are going to have a busy few years ahead of us."

*

Two days later, he had a call from Roger saying that he had a million pounds in a big bag. Timothy returned to London, and Victoria went back to her house. Timothy banked the money in four different banks and caught the train back to Birmingham. He was being philosophical about what might happen. He had done all he could. If he could change anything about his past, he would not have become an assassin. It was not just a dangerous job; it was also a thankless one.

Chapter Twenty-One

Victoria was sitting in the lounge of their new house in Knowle. It was a fantastic house. It had five bedrooms, a large lounge, a study, a huge kitchen and a double garage. Sooty walked in through the open patio doors and jumped onto her lap. "How do you like the garden, Sooty?"

The garden was huge and was more like a small park. It was what she liked most about her new house. They had already spent most of the million pounds on this house, new cars, a holiday in Greece, and to pay off the mortgages on her old house, Timothy's house and his father's house, which they were now renting out. They would be good investments for their children.

She placed her hand on her distended stomach. She relaxed more with each day that passed, and now believed that they would not be killed and did have a future. Timothy had gone to London to meet Roger. He would not be back until late. She missed him. She did not feel safe without him. Timothy was a brave man and a good man, despite what he had done. She was proud of him and loved him as much as it was possible to love someone. She smiled. Her dreams had finally come true.

*

Timothy met Roger outside Westminster Abbey on a cold, windy day. They shook hands. Roger had lost weight, and the sparkle had gone out of his good eye.

"I'm glad you could make it," Roger said. I wanted to see you one last time."

"You don't look too good," Timothy said.

"I don't feel too good. The cancer has spread all over my body. I'm on morphine. The pain's horrendous. I've left the morphine off today so that I can talk to you. Morphine makes you feel as if you're blind drunk."

There was not much Timothy could say. "I recently buried my father. He had cancer."

"It's a bastard," Roger said. "But life goes on. How is the wife?"

"She's doing fine. We sold the nursery and bought a house. We don't need to work anymore. We make more than enough to live on from our investments."

"You deserve it," Roger said. "You more than earned it." He smiled. "I read in the paper that three men in Birmingham had their legs and arms broken and were castrated. It's not safe to go out anymore."

Timothy smiled. “The bastards won’t date-rape anyone again. The judge who gave them an alibi had a serious accident and is now in a coma.”

“She deserved it,” Roger said. “Did you know that Princess Diana wrote a letter before she died, saying that she was convinced Prince Charles was going to kill her so that he could marry someone else?”

Timothy was amazed. “No. We knew that she suspected that Prince Charles was going to have her killed, but I didn’t realise she had written it down. Was the note in her own handwriting?”

“Yes.” Roger gave Timothy a piece of paper. “This is a copy of the letter.”

Timothy read the letter.

'I am sitting here at my desk today in October, longing for someone to hug me and encourage me to keep strong and hold my head high. This particular phase in my life is the most dangerous - my husband is planning 'an accident' in my car, brake failure and serious head injury in order to make the path clear for him to marry Tiggy. Camilla is nothing but a decoy, so we are all being used by the man in every sense of the word.'

Timothy was shocked. “Bleeding hell. She not only predicted that she would be assassinated, she also predicted exactly how it would be done.”

“It’s an amazing letter,” Roger said. “She probably wrote the letter as insurance to prevent Charles from killing her.”

“Is this letter public knowledge?” Timothy asked.

“Not yet. God knows what will happen when it does become public knowledge.”

“I’m totally shocked,” Timothy said. “When this becomes public knowledge, people will realise that she was assassinated.”

“I agree, but it’s not something I’ll be worrying about. I need some morphine, and so I’ll have to be going. It’s been a pleasure working with you, Tim.”

“Likewise, Major.”

Timothy watched Roger disappear into the crowds and walked to his car. He felt sorry for Princess Diana. She had been a good person and a brave person. Even though she expected to be killed, she still did what she felt was right. People believe that Henry Paul was responsible for her death. When the letter she had written becomes public knowledge, they will know that she expected to be assassinated in a car accident. Will the public believe that she was assassinated? Only time will tell.

EPILOGUE

The author of Die Lady Die believes that a film about the assassination of Princess Diana should be made based on the novel Die Lady Di, and here are the reasons why.

If Princess Diana's death was a premeditated murder, then there must have been a reason to kill her. There must have been a motive. There was a very strong motive. She intended to marry a Muslim and have his children. There is no way that Muslims would ever be accepted as a part of the British Royal Family, so the palace protectors had a choice: either to assassinate Princess Diana or let the Royal Family be destroyed. They decide to save the royal family.

Megan Markle, the Duchess of Sussex, is a woman of mixed blood. She is part black, and some of her ancestors can be traced back to Africa. She is now a part of the British Royal Family, and this has upset some people. Most people now accept her because she does not look black and is a Christian. The people of this country would not have accepted her if she had been a Muslim and had been wearing a hijab (a head covering).

The photographs taken of Princess Diana kissing and hugging Dodi Al-Fayed show that they were in love. Many people believe they were about to get engaged. Mohmed Al-Fayed said that Princess Diana and Dodi had told him they were getting engaged. We do know that Dodi had bought a very expensive engagement ring while he was dating Diana. If she had married Dodi and had his children, a girl and a boy, it would have all but destroyed the Royal Family. If you disagree with this, then just imagine a modern-day royal photograph. It would include today's royal family as well as Princess Diana, Dodi Al-Fayed, and their two children. Princess Diana's daughter would now be about twenty-eight and would be wearing a head covering: a hijab.

Many people believe that Princess Diana hated the Queen, the Duke of Edinburgh, Prince Charles and Camilla. Princess Diana's hatred was reciprocated by them, and they deliberately turned her life into a nightmare. Princess Diana was a very intelligent woman. She was well aware of how powerful the British Royal Family are, and she feared for her life and expected to be assassinated.

The Mishcon Note refers to a note reportedly made by Mishcon during a meeting he had with Princess Diana on 30th October 1995. During the meeting, which also included Diana's personal secretary, Patrick Jephson, Diana reportedly said that she had heard from a source that efforts would be made to get rid of her by April 1996. She told Victor Mishcon that a car accident would be staged where she would end up dead or be seriously injured.

Ten months before she died, Princess Diana still believed that she would be killed in a staged car crash. She wrote that she would be killed in a vehicle, and the killers would try to make it look like an accident. She wrote that her death was to make way for Tiggy so that she could marry Prince Charles. This is what she wrote: *I am sitting here at my desk today in October, longing for someone to hug me and encourage me to keep strong and hold my head high. This particular phase in my life is the most dangerous - my husband is planning an accident in my car, brake failure and serious head injury in order to make the path clear for him to marry Tiggy. Camilla is nothing but a decoy, so we are all being used by the man in every sense of the word.* She gave the note to Paul Burrell. Tiggy is Alexandra Legge-Bourke. She was the nanny to Prince William and Prince Harry from 1993 to 1999.

Some people think that Princess Diana was ill, deranged or paranoid to think that she would be assassinated. Let us examine the facts, and you can decide for yourself if she was assassinated.

The Di Lady Die novel about the assassination of Princess Diana states that:

1) Princess Diana's assassination was premeditated and planned, and a white Fiat Uno was used in the Alma tunnel to position the limousine that Princess Diana was travelling in so that it was close to the concrete pillars in the tunnel.

2) That two men on a motorbike posing as paparazzi overtook the limousine and used a strobe light that looked like a camera to blind the driver of the limousine for a few seconds so that the limousine would crash into the pillars in the Alma tunnel.

3) That Princess Diana was injected with a drug to cause her to have a fatal heart attack

4) That because the heart attack drug could be detected in the body for up to an hour after it was injected, Princess Diana's trip to the hospital was delayed.

We will now examine the facts to prove that what was written in the Di Lady Die novel did actually happen.

1) A witness to the crash, Sabine Dauzonne, saw a white Fiat Uno driving out of the tunnel. There was evidence found at the scene of the crash of traces of white paint and of a broken taillight, and we now know that the limousine carrying Princess Diana was hit by a white Fiat Uno seconds before the crash in the Alma tunnel. Dauzonne said that the Fiat Uno she saw had scratches on the rear panel and a damaged taillight. James Anderson, a paparazzo, drove a white Fiat Uno, and when it was photographed after the crash, there was rust all around the car, except on the rear panel that would have been hit by the limousine. It had been replaced or painted. The French did not test the paint on the car to see if it was the car involved in the crash. In 2000, Anderson was murdered. He was shot in the head and burned in his locked car.

2) A witness to the crash, Francois Levistre, says he heard a huge noise in the tunnel. Just before he heard the huge noise, he saw a car and a motorbike enter the tunnel and saw the motorbike cut in front of the car. There was a white flash, and the car crashed and reared up like a horse. Tests were carried out to find out what could have caused the bright flash of light that Mr Levistre saw. They took Mr Levistre into the Alma tunnel and flashed camera lights, but he said they were not bright enough. When they flashed an antipersonnel light, a strobe light, he said that it was the same brightness as the light he saw on the night of the car crash.

3) Princess Diana, even though she was very fit and healthy, suffered a massive heart attack after the crash. Fire Sergeant Xavier Gourmelon heard her say, Oh my God, what's happened? The French medics said at the inquest into Princess Diana's death that they tried to put a drip in her arm, but she was agitated and pulled it out. The French medics said they had to hold her down and inject her with a sedative to calm her down, and then put a drip in her arm. While this was being done, she was shouting and talking in English. It is clear from the note she wrote and gave to Paul Burrell that she believed she would be killed in a car crash. When she realised that she had been in a serious car crash, did she suspect that this was the car crash that was meant to kill her? It was a very serious car crash. The limousine was smashed up, and the people with her in the car were seriously injured. Did she think that the French medics who claimed to be helping her were, in fact, trying to kill her, and was

she shouting at them to leave her alone? It was after being injected that she had the massive heart attack and would have died there and then, had she not been given CPR.

4) They claim to have rushed Princess Diana to hospital. This is not true. She should have been rushed to the nearest hospital, a journey that would have taken just a few minutes. It would be obvious to any paramedic or doctor by looking at the smashed-up Mercedes that the vehicle had hit a concrete pillar at over seventy mph, and so Princess Diana, who was not wearing a seat belt, would almost certainly have suffered some internal injuries and would need an operation to save her life. Princess Diana had suffered a serious internal injury and had a ruptured pulmonary vein, but she could have been saved if she had been rushed to hospital. President Reagan was shot in 1981 and suffered a similar injury to Princess Diana, and he was saved because they rushed him to hospital. The accident Princess Diana was in happened at 12-25 am, but she did not get to the hospital until 2-06 am. It took one hour and forty-six minutes to get her to hospital. She was eventually put into an ambulance, but it still took the ambulance, which had an escort of two police cars and two police motorbikes, 41 minutes to travel a 10-minute journey. The ambulance passed two hospitals on its journey to La Pitie-Salpetriere hospital, which was four miles away. They rushed President Reagan to hospital because they wanted to save his life. They delayed Princess Diana getting to hospital because they wanted her to die. They claim that taking such a long time to get seriously injured people who have been involved in a high-speed accident to hospital, is how it should be done. This is nonsense. If a person has had a heart attack or has a badly cut leg, then it is right to stabilise them and then take them to hospital, but when a person has been involved in a high-speed accident, there is obviously a need to stabilise them first, but they must then be rushed to hospital. SAMU ambulances in France are not equipped to perform major surgery. For the ambulance not to go to the nearest hospital and to take forty-one minutes to travel a distance that should have taken ten minutes is a crime. It is so sad. Princess Diana's heart was still beating when she eventually got to the hospital, thanks to the efforts of people giving her CPR, but it stopped 6 minutes later. Many people think that Doctor Jean-Mark Martino, who was in charge of the ambulance, killed Princess Diana as surely as if he had put a gun to her head and blown her brains out.

There is even more evidence to prove that Princess Diana was assassinated and that there was a cover-up. I will list them.

1) At the time of the crash, many of the cameras leading up to the Alma tunnel were not working.

2) 6 hours after the crash, the Alma tunnel was disinfected and reopened.

3) The French authorities conducted a private investigation into the crash and refused to let anyone else examine the evidence. No one was allowed to examine the DNA in the blood samples taken from Henri Paul and Princess Diana to prove that it was their blood. Mohamed Al-Fayed was told that he would be arrested if he tried to investigate the crash.

4) Princess Diana's blood was switched. They switched her blood because they believed she was pregnant with Dodi's child. The switched blood did not contain any alcohol, but at her autopsy, it was remarked that there was a strong smell of alcohol coming from her stomach. It was well known that she had wine with her meals.

5) Princess Diana's body was partly embalmed. They did this to prevent anyone from discovering that she was pregnant. It is illegal to embalm someone in France. It can only be done with the permission of the next of kin, who was Prince Charles.

6) They claimed that Henri Paul was three times over the limit and was drunk when the crash happened. The videos of him at the Ritz Hotel, taken just before the crash, prove beyond a doubt that he was not drunk. There was no alcohol found at his flat to prove that he was an alcoholic.

7) Henri Paul's blood was switched with blood from someone at the hospital that contained a high level of alcohol. This was to prove that he was drunk. There was one huge problem for those who switched the blood; the blood also contained a high level of carbon monoxide. It was between 12 and 21 per cent. The normal is between 2 and 4 per cent. They have admitted that they cannot explain why Henri Paul would have such a high level of carbon monoxide in his blood. If Henri Paul's blood did contain a high level of carbon monoxide, it would mean that he had breathed in the carbon monoxide before he came on duty that night. A sample of his blood was taken about two hours after the crash, and because of the half-life of carbon monoxide, when he was videoed at the Ritz Hotel, his blood would have contained double that of the 12 to 21 per cent (about 24 to 42 per cent) and he would be suffering from headaches, nausea, vomiting, vertigo and confusion and would not have been able to drive the limousine. There is no way that his blood could contain such a high level of carbon monoxide, so it was obviously switched with blood that did contain the high levels. They switched his blood with the blood of a man at the hospital who got drunk and killed himself by attaching a pipe from the exhaust

pipe of his car to the inside of his car. This man would have a high level of alcohol in his blood, but also a high level of carbon monoxide. The people who switched Henri Paul's blood did not expect the blood to be tested for carbon monoxide as well as for alcohol. They normally do not test for carbon monoxide.

It is sad to think that Princess Diana is now regarded by many people as a fool for thinking that she would be assassinated. People covering up the assassination have claimed that she had lost all reason and was unbalanced and paranoid. She was ill but not deranged. The film needs to be made to prove that she was not a fool and was not unbalanced and paranoid, but was right in not only predicting that she would be assassinated, but also predicting how she would be assassinated.

I don't think anyone has ever predicted that they would be killed and described how they would be killed. If the film is made, it will, hopefully, change the way Princess Diana is remembered. She deserves to be remembered not only as a good and caring woman but also as an intelligent woman.

Printed in Dunstable, United Kingdom

68329801R00117